MYTHIC REVEALED

Mythic Revealed

A Fantastical Sci-Fi Drama

JUSTIN K. NUCKLES

Contents

Dedication   viii

Prologue   1

1   3

2   18

3   29

4   39

5   53

6   77

7   86

8   97

vi ~ *Contents*

9   113

10   132

11   142

12   154

13   174

14   194

15   207

16   221

17   231

18   243

19   255

20   262

21   278

22   286

Contents ~ *vii*

23 294

24 303

25 314

Epilogue 328

Acknowledgments 331

About The Author 332

For Deby:
You believed from the very beginning

First Printing, 2022

Prologue

The girl with the bird tattoo skimmed the message she had just received one more time. If these reports were correct, this was what they had been waiting for. A little shiver ran up and down her spine as she considered the implications.

She hurried down the dimly lit passageway, coughing as she passed one of the torches that lit this area of the catacombs. Like the main catacombs of France, the walls of this network of tunnels were adorned with skulls. Unlike the main catacombs, here each skull bore a name and a date, burnt or carved into the forehead, she never could decide which. Also, unlike the main catacombs, here the skulls smoldered with golden light, as if they had once been on fire, and had burned down to nothing but embers. Each suture, crack, and orifice exuded a dim gold light that flared slightly as she passed, creating effectually a shadow of light as she flew down the hallway.

The girl pushed open a heavy wooden door, just in time to watch as the young German man kneeling on the floor screamed, dissipating into a cloud of tiny black particles like smoke that slowly coalesced into a vortex then ascended upwards and disappeared before the Wolf's hands. Caine, the Wolf, raised his eyes, his long, dark hair falling in tight curls all around his face.

"It must be important, for you to have interrupted me in such a fashion," he said, closing his eyes and breathing deeply as his face flushed slightly.

"It is." The girl held out the device, its luminescent screen shining eerily on his face, casting shadows that caused it to look strikingly similar to the skulls outside.

He read silently. "When did they manifest?"

"This is our first indication."

He handed the device back and picked up his long black coat from where he had laid it on a dark wooden table. "The Aberration will not be far behind. I'll be leaving immediately; I have an invitation to extend. Assemble the Faithful for my return. Where are they?"

"The United States. Illinois."

***

Chapter 1

I sat on the porch of my parents' house, the one I'd grown up in, and I stared at my bloody hands. I stared at my hands because I couldn't stomach the thought of looking at what those hands had just done. I glanced down at the revolver on the porch next to me and looked quickly away.

Is this real? Did I really just do that? My mind raced over the events of the last day, grasping for something, anything I might have done differently that might have led to a different outcome.

Already too late. It would have to have been earlier. I'd have needed to act sooner, made some different choice, to avoid what just happened. Once it started down that path, there was no stopping it; my brain ran back to weeks before, when it all began. Weeks before my parents were dead and in the ground; before I'd been forced to put them there.

***

The halls of the University of Southern Illinois Child Development Center always smelled like a mixture of diluted bleach (which I loved), cheap hot dogs (which I didn't love), and that permanent old school building smell (which I was ambivalent on). I poked my head into Ms. Loretta's classroom.

"Ms. Loretta, you need anything?" I'd been promoted to Assistant Director as part of my internship, finishing up my Bachelor's in Psychology with an emphasis in Child Development. Ms. Loretta, an upbeat, perpetually-smiling Black woman in her mid 60's, looked up from where she was helping one of her children finish a painting and said, "No, I'm good, James. Thank you."

I smiled and nodded my head in acknowledgement, then high-fived Kenny, the five-year-old who was fighting my knee to get my attention right at the door. At 6'2", my hand was nearly at my waist before it was low enough for him to hit. I'd been in Kenny's classroom when he was two, and his part-time baby-sitter for the last three years. His parents, an attorney and a dermatologist, had taken a liking to me and paid me well to be their go-to babysitter on weekends and any weeknight they wanted off and I could fit into my calendar. Between the sitting, working in the center, and scholarships, I'd been able to pay for the last three years of college without any student loans so far, a fact for which I was extremely grateful.

I let myself back out into the hall and was walking toward the main office when Ms. Kendra, who was on break, popped her head out of the staff room and said, "Hey, James, aren't you from a town downstate somewhere?"

I nodded. "Yeah, how come?"

She stepped back from the door, holding it open.

"You better come see this, man."

I stepped into the break room and she held up her phone. It was a local news article. The headline read:

> Southern County Declares State of Emergency
> as Mysterious Outbreak Baffles Health Officials

I'd seen dozens of posts from friends back home on social media for the last couple of weeks about a "Man-Flu" going around down there. "Flu symptoms so bad, you actually feel as bad as all men say they do," one female friend had posted.

"Whoa," I said. "That's not good."

"No, it ain't," Kendra said. "Just watch; all the stores are gonna' sell out of toilet paper and hand sanitizer again. Just watch."

***

A week later, the headlines changed.

> Southern Counties Shutting Down as Outbreak
> Fatalities Rise

Then, again.

Mysterious Illness Non-Communicable; Specialists
Investigating Potential Environmental Origin

My parents still lived on our family's farm in one of those counties. I brought up my mom's number on my phone and dialed one night, sitting up in bed in my small dorm room.

"Jamie? Is everything okay?" Mom answered after a couple of rings.

I didn't beat around the bush. "Hey, Mom? You and Dad need to get out of town! Have you been following this outbreak thing down there? They're thinking it might be caused by something environmental to the area at this point. You guys should come stay with me for a few weeks."

"Sweetie, it's nice to know you're thinking about us, but I promise, we're in the safest place we could possibly be. There's too much we have to take care of right now to think about leaving." Mom seemed maddeningly calm.

"No, Mom, I'm telling you, you guys need to get out! Have you been following the news? Have you seen the case maps? It's a perfect circle. There is something going on down there; you need to leave!"

"James, we have things here that we need to take care of. We're not going to pick up and leave." Her tone had taken on that "Don't you dare, young man" quality I remembered as a young teen. There was no arguing with her. I waded in anyway.

"Mom! What on earth could you possibly have to do down there that would be more important than saving your own lives?! Have you even seen the latest statistics? They're up to a twenty percent infection rate! I'm telling you, you need to leave!" I hadn't argued with her this way since Jr. High. I didn't love it.

"James Strader, don't you raise your voice at me. I've told you that we have things to take care of down here that can't wait, that we'll be all right. Your father and I are adults, we've seen a lot of scary things, and you need to accept that when I tell you that we're already doing everything in our power to do, I mean it!"

The conversation didn't extend much past that. I hung up defeated and furious. Why wouldn't they leave?

Not even a week later, the fires started. They swept through several of the towns all around where I'd grown up, destroying hundreds of houses and businesses. I called my parents multiple times a day, checking in, but mostly trying to convince them to evacuate. The conversations went nearly word-for-word the same as the first call when I'd blown up. They assured me they'd be fine, and that they'd keep an eye on things.

The fires would have been devastating on their own. Instead, they were immediately followed by completely out of season storms that produced gale-force winds and dumped rain in a constant deluge for days. I scrolled through the news on my phone in equal parts horror and fascination as houses that had been on the banks of rivers and the shores of lakes for decades washed away or were swallowed by water that far exceeded its banks.

By that time, the rest of the world was watching with me. The fires and the storms followed the same consistent, and therefore baffling, pattern as the illness had. When news graphics showed the impacted areas on a map, there was nearly perfect overlap. Whatever was happening at home was in defiance of nature; there are no coincidences *that* significant.

According to the news, the governor had reportedly started debating officially evacuating and quarantining the entire region, which seemed unnecessary, since, according to other news reports, nearly everyone who was capable of leaving had already done so.

It was only a day after that that everything simply stopped.

They stopped announcing new cases of the illness, the last of the fires were declared contained, the storms blew themselves out, and the rivers and lakes receded. Whatever we had watched unfold in southern Illinois was apparently over.

***

I hadn't heard from my parents in over a week. I figured that phone lines and internet cables were probably all down, but that didn't keep me from worrying and trying their cell phones multiple times a day. That made it all the more shocking when I got a strange call from Mom. It was about a week and a half after everything calmed that she called me from a restricted number in between classes.

"James, we need you to come home. There's a situation here that we need your help with. I can't say any more right now, but we need you to come home as quickly as you possibly can."

"Mom, is everything okay?"

It was like she didn't even hear me, as if she were leaving me a voicemail. She simply ended the call by saying, "I love you, Jamie. Be strong." Then the line clicked, and she was gone. My stomach filled with ice, and my hand shook as I lowered the phone from my ear.

***

Not having a car, I tried to find a ride home, but no one I asked was remotely interested in giving me a ride to the epicenter of the world's most shocking news for the past several weeks. No taxi service, ride share, or even rental car service would accommodate me, either: too much liability. To make matters more challenging, law enforcement and the National Guard had set up roadblock checkpoints to discourage people from going in until more was figured out. It wasn't a hard quarantine, merely a precaution.

After two days of frantically calling service after service and meeting nothing but dead ends and laughs on the other end, I finally realized that the only way

I was going to get home was on my bike. The city around USI had amazing infrastructure for bicycles. One of the best in the country, actually. It was part of the reason I'd chosen to enroll there. Unfortunately, that wasn't going to help me at all on the ride home. Most of the roads between here and home were small two-lane highways with almost no shoulder. Not my favorite, as an amateur cycling enthusiast. I'd been riding my bike daily for years, even done a few long-distance races. It wouldn't be my longest ride. Longest ride ever, no; longest ride without support, yes. I figured if I rode hard, only stopping for food and rest when I absolutely needed to, I could make it home in about 11 or 12 hours.

***

I left at a frosty 4:00 in the morning, three days after I'd gotten the call from Mom. I had emailed my professors that I had a family emergency in the affected region down south, and they all seemed pretty understanding.

I tried to call each of my parents' cell phones one last time before I jumped on my bike. No answer, just like all the other times I'd tried since the fires and floods. How had Mom gotten a call out? I shook my head in confusion and returned my phone to the backpack with several bottles of water, a box of energy and protein bars, some fruit, a change of clothes and a few extra layers, just in case. I just needed enough to get me home. I clicked the strap on my helmet, and wheeled away into the dark, the street lamps the only witnesses to my departure.

People are always surprised that I ride a bike year-round. They seem shocked that I'd ride one even in the winter. Most people don't realize just how much heat you'll produce, pedaling a bicycle hard for even more than a few minutes. The November morning cold wasn't a problem.

Several mind-numbing hours later, I reached the checkpoint. A National Guardsman waved me down and I braked, rolling to a stop just a few feet in front of him.

"Sir, I'm gonna' have to ask you to turn around," he said, smiling politely between his chinstrap and sunglasses. "The area beyond this point is limited to essential personnel and residents only."

"My parents live in the area," I explained, breathing heavily. "I got a call a few days ago from my Mom, saying there was some kind of trouble, and she asked me to come home. I don't have a car, and I couldn't beg, borrow, or steal any other ride, so—" I gestured to my bicycle.

"Some kind of trouble?" The soldier laughed. "Have you watched the news?"

I nodded. "Yeah, that's why I'm coming home; I was worried before. Now, I'm freaking out."

He smiled again, and his eyebrows disappeared into his helmet. "Where ya' comin' from?"

"USI."

He coughed in laughter. "You rode all the way from USI?"

I nodded.

"That's something else." He shook his head. "And did you say that your mom called you a few days ago?"

I nodded again. "Why?"

"The utilities and services are all a mess down there. Phone lines, cell towers, internet services; they're all down. The whole region is basically a communication dead zone. It's been that way for a few weeks: since the storms started. They're saying it's gonna' take at least another few weeks to get any of it even partially restored."

I frowned. "Huh. Well, she called me a few days ago. I don't know how that's even possible, but she did."

"Huh," the soldier echoed. "Stranger things, I guess, right?"

I shrugged.

He turned and lifted the gate that leveled across the road so that I could pass. "Just be careful down there; emergency services aren't functioning at this point. If anything happens, you're essentially on your own."

I nodded and leaned into my pedal to get rolling again. The checkpoint quickly disappeared behind the trees as I pumped down the hill, racing toward home.

***

I arrived at my parents' house after about 11 hours of riding time in the cold, with a few hours' break for food, water, and rest. I rode slowly up the final hill that led to the house, came around that final bend, and the pill-shaped mailbox, the one made from an old, decommissioned World War II bomb with "Strader" painted on the side (my great-grandfather had a strange sense of humor) came slowly into view.

In the past, whenever I had ridden past that old mailbox, I'd always gotten the same feeling: "I'm home; things will be all right now." That feeling was conspicuously absent.

The farm— really just a couple dozen wooded acres with a few chickens, a goat or two, and a sour old pig, Mr. Urnck— was too quiet. It was 3:00 in the afternoon: there were normally a thousand different tasks my parents took care of together this time of day.

That brought up another oddity; with everything that had happened, between the fires and the storms and flooding, I had expected more damage. Apparently, Mom and Dad had been right about something. The farm was virtually untouched.

Mom and Dad weren't necessarily what I'd typically call "preppers." They didn't have anything beyond the typical mistrust of government common to the area, didn't have an arsenal of military look-alike high-capacity weapons and ammunition, and didn't even know terms like "SHTF" or "bug-out," I didn't think. We had several different hunting rifles all growing up, but Dad had said he never felt like we needed anything beyond that. Said if things ever came to that, we'd be taken care of. I never really understood what he meant by that. But they were good country folk who liked to be prepared and look out for the people they loved.

This property had belonged to my family for nearly four generations now, counting me. My great-grandfather (the one who'd built the mailbox) bought it after the war and it had been in my family ever since. Both Mom and Dad were really close to their grandparents and had learned and adopted a lot of their attitudes.

In a world where everything was almost made to throw away, Dad still had and knew how to fix almost every major appliance and power tool he'd ever owned. Whether it was electric, gas-powered, or hand-operated, it seemed like Dad had the skills to fix it. Sometimes he would stay at his machine shop in town for days at a time, working on his endless projects.

Mom was the type of woman who still ground her own wheat to make her own homemade bread and hung her laundry out to dry on a clothesline, year-round. She preferred things that took time, "Process over product," she always said. She was a great lover of people: listening to, talking to, lifting up people. She was a therapist in a small town; not very busy, but very well-loved. She just always seemed to know how to say exactly what someone needed to hear.

We'd always had a large supply of food storage on hand, as well. We'd had a conversation once when Dad had told me that he didn't consider himself a "prepper," merely prepared; said "prepper" had a doomsday quality to it that didn't suit him.

So, where were they? Everything looked fine. Why did I have the distinct feeling that it wasn't?

I peeked into the shop on my way past; there were some things out of place. Dad wasn't inside. I continued on toward the house.

I was on the porch with my hand on the doorknob before I registered the smell. Growing up having animals and spending a lot of time in the woods hunting with Dad, I knew the smell of decay. The smell of death. The house reeked.

Completely panicked, I threw open the door and rushed in. The stench knocked me backward. I threw up the granola bars and apples I'd eaten on my ride home.

I found both of my parents in the house. Dad was lying on the tile floor leading from the entryway into the kitchen, his .357 revolver next to his outstretched left hand, while Mom was in the kitchen almost to the hallway leading back to the bedrooms. Both had serious wounds in their backs, Dad one on his right arm as well, and both of them had obviously been dead for a while. It was all I could do to grab two sheets from the hallway closet and cover them both, then I sank down to the floor and cried. I crawled on my hands and knees out to the porch, sucking in the clear air.

Hours passed before I could do anything aside from lie there. The smell had long since stopped registering.

I walked slowly back to the door and stared numbly in at my father's form on the floor, now draped in the bed sheet, and knowing there was one more, my mother's, exactly like it in the hallway.

I was on my own. The National Guardsman had been explicit; if anything happened down here for the next couple of weeks, we were on our own. I was on my own. There was no one to call about my parents, nothing to do but bury them. I refused to let them sit there like cadavers in a morgue until some unknown time when a coroner could come get them. I'd bury them myself.

***

I didn't finish burying my parents until early morning; I dug all night. It went fast in the beginning; I attacked the dirt at first, drove all of my rage, all of my hatred, through the handle and into the cold ground. It was obvious my parents had been murdered. After I burned through the rage, there was smoldering anger. Each shovel load was an additional thought of revenge. When the anger was gone, then came the sadness. I don't know if you've ever tried to dig (or really do anything) while heaving sobs, but it's near impossible. After that, there was only numbness for a while. That only lasted until the blisters burst, though. Then came the pain.

Like an idiot, I hadn't worn gloves. At first, I kicked myself; if I'd have worn good gloves, I wouldn't even have blisters right now. But then I remembered something Dad had always said that his dad told him about gloves: "the only thing you can do better with gloves on is pee your pants." I laughed in between sobs when I remembered that. I could hear him saying it, the way he'd emphasize the word "pee" in the sentence, instead of "pants" like you would naturally. He hated wearing gloves; he thought they just got in the way. I looked up, expecting and prepared to say something to him about that line, when I saw instead the two draped forms I'd moved outside, and the pain in my hands migrated up my arms and settled deep in my chest. It sat there like a coiled snake: dark, loathsome, and volatile.

I finished without thinking any other clear thoughts. Night was giving way to day, and there were two slight mounds of fresh, dark earth to mark my efforts. I turned and flung the shovel in the direction of the shed as hard as I could. It donged flatly several feet away and lay there. I wouldn't pick it up again. If I tried, I would throw up, and so it sat there, a visual reminder of the one event I'd always remember and never stop trying to forget.

I walked up to the porch and I sat down next to the revolver, where I'd placed it when I'd started digging. I sat on the porch of my parents' house, the one I'd grown up in, and I stared at my bloody hands.

Chapter 2

I was still sitting on the edge of the porch, my hands still filthy and covered in blood from my popped and raw blisters, when I heard a heavy metallic clang, coming from the direction of the shop.

I walked in the open door and the familiar smells of wood dust and the oil Dad used when cutting metal almost made me forget why I was in there. But something was different. Dad's anvil and its stand, which were always in the same spot in the middle of the room, were tipped over, lying on the floor in front of his work bench. There were several other things also out of place and untidy, unlike the clean shop my dad usually kept. And then it hit me; why was the door open? I blinked, coming back to the present. Was there someone in here? I picked up one of Dad's heavy forge hammers. My hand lit up in pain. I'd forgotten my blisters. I bit my lip, but I didn't lower the hammer.

I stood inside the doorway for another moment or two, trying to decide whether I'd imagined the sound, when I heard a new one. The squeak of metal sliding on metal and then a solid thunk.

"Hello?" I shouted into the shop. I then heard a

faint little voice followed by an insistent shooshing. I backed out of the doorway and stood outside the shop. Was that a child? Why was there a child in the shop?

Another moment passed, then I heard the unmistakable sound of a child, a young one, crying followed by more shooshing. There wasn't only one person here. My heart beat a little bit quicker. Who were they? Had they lost their parents to all of the madness in the last several weeks and wandered in here looking for help? That could explain why things were all out of sorts.

If someone was crying, and they were out here alone, then the younger one might be hurt. I stepped into the shop again, still thoroughly puzzled as to where they might be, and my eye was drawn back to the anvil and its stand. Looking closer at the floor, I could see the shape where the stand had been; there was less dust, and the wood slats of the floor weren't as sun-faded there. There was also a hole, a perfect circle drilled into the floor there.

No. There was no way. I'd lived in this house my whole life, played in this shop for days and days on end. There was no way there could be a trap door or a shelter under there. Dad would have told me about it. And yet, as I watched, the hole suddenly went from black to a yellow as a light turned on.

I took a few more steps forward and the light turned off again as the shooshing resumed.

"Hello? I heard some crying, is everything okay down there?"

No answer. The crying resumed, probably from behind a hand, I'd guess from the additional muffle.

"My name is James. Do you need some help?"

There was still no response from the hole in the floor. A thousand thoughts were flying around my head, most of them questions. Who were these kids? How did they get into this cellar in my dad's shop? Why was there a hidden cellar in my dad's shop?

"I'm going to open the trap door, okay? I'm not going to hurt you." I bent over and pushed my finger into the hole. I pulled up, and nothing happened. There was absolutely no movement, no hint of a trap door anywhere, aside from the obvious fact that my finger was in a drilled hole, and I had seen a light down there, however briefly.

I put my ear to the hole, listening. I could hear lots of breathing, and movement, and some loud sniffs. Turning, I put my eye to the hole, and a small finger promptly pushed into it.

"Ow! Son of a --!" My eye watered and throbbed.

"Steven, don't!" I heard from the hole, then the crying started back up again.

"It's okay, I'm okay," I called, holding my eye closed with one hand, wincing through the burn and sting. "This is a trap door, right? Is there a latch or a lock on that side? I can't seem to get it open from here." Silence was my only answer. I was not about to stick my eye or ear to the hole again.

"How about I go outside, and you can open it your-self, all right? That way you can close it again if you don't feel safe." I stepped noisily outside and called loudly, "Okay, I'm outside."

There was no response for another several seconds, then the deep thunk sounded again as a large bar or stop was slid back, and the trap door rose from nearly invisible casings in the seams of the wooden floor planks, a forehead and two scowling eyes coming slowly into view.

"Are you Steven?" I asked, my fingers still holding my burning eye closed.

The eyes widened in surprise, then scowled even deeper. "How do you know my name?" the boy asked.

I gestured at my recovering eye. "I heard your sister —at least I assume she's your sister— say your name after you poked me in the eye."

The eyes widened briefly— was that fear? – before scowling and narrowing again. "Come over here and I'll give you something else to cry about," the boy said. There was a thwack, then the boy yelped.

"Cut it out, Steven." A girl's head pushed up further and into view, lifting the trap door. "Do you know Mr. Strader?" she asked, looking hopeful.

"I do." Dad must have put them here. It was the only explanation for how they could be here. They certainly couldn't have put the anvil in place on top of the door themselves. It was the anvil falling that I'd first heard.

"Where is he?"

My throat got tight. "He's... not here anymore."

"Is he dead?"

It occurred to me how many terrible things these kids must have seen in recent weeks, that she asked so directly outright like that if he was dead.

"He... he is, yeah."

"What about Mrs. Strader? Is she dead, too?"

The lump in my throat had needles, now. All I could do was nod.

"Not again." The girl's words nearly broke my insides; they heaped on the black mound in my chest. She looked down and behind her. "Bethy, let Mary go. We've got to leave again."

There were four children down there? "Wait," I said. "What's your name?"

"My name's Jessica Danton, sir," the girl said.

"Where are you going, Jessica? My name's James, like I said. Why were you in this... cellar? How long have you been here?"

Jessica shrugged. "A few days, I guess. Maybe three or four? Mr. and Mrs. Strader brought us out here and told us not to make any noise or come out until they came and got us, but they never did. We were finally able to get the door open when we heard you coming and hid again. We ate the food in the packs down here. I hope that's okay." Her whole body communicated shame: she looked down, her shoulders slumped, and she made herself as small as possible, like she wanted to disappear altogether.

I nodded. "I'm sure that's just fine. Why did they put you down there? Was there anyone else here when they did?!" my voice rose in volume, and I took an anxious step forward, hoping that maybe they'd seen something, anything that could tell me who had killed my parents.

Jessica was frozen, not moving when she'd heard my voice start to rise. Steven had a slingshot in his hands, pointed at me and pulled tight. I was scaring them.

I took another couple of steps backward, raising my hands to show I wasn't a threat. I'd forgotten that I was still holding the hammer. I dropped it in the grass.

"Sorry, I didn't mean to get excited. I'm confused. And angry. But not at you," I stammered, seeing both their eyes widen. "I was hoping you kids might know something about who killed my parents. Heck, I didn't even know this cellar was here. I grew up in this house, and I never even knew we had a cellar. So, I guess I'm double surprised. Not only do we have a cellar, but it's full of kids!" I laughed, but it was short and too forced to put any of us at ease.

Steven lowered his slingshot and let it go slack, but he still held the pouch and scowled like he wanted to shoot me anyway.

Jessica wasn't looking at me. She'd backed down the hole, and I could hear her saying quiet things to the other two little girls who were still in the cellar. Soon I heard her say Steven's name. He glanced behind him, then lifted himself all the way out of the cellar. Another little head came into view, this one long-haired with quick, shy little eyes. Steven reached down and helped her the rest of the way up and out, where she stood quietly, one hand curled up to her face, covering half her mouth, a brown teddy bear hugged in the crook of her elbow. She looked young, I'd guess between four and six.

"You must be Bethy," I said. The little girl looked down and stepped further behind Steven.

Finally, Jessica stepped up and into view, followed closely by the small face of a girl who couldn't have been any more than three. She was practically a baby.

"Mary?" I asked, looking at Jessica, then nodding at the toddler.

Jessica nodded. "Yes, sir. Don't worry, we're leaving." She started slowly guiding Mary to the door, who, when she saw me, started whimpering again.

"Wait, wait, wait," I said, taking a step inside the doorframe. I immediately wished I hadn't. Steven's hands whipped up, and there was a sharp thwip as my already torn hand lit up in pain.

"Gah! Are you kidding me?!" I shouted. Four things happened all at once when I yelled. Jessica ran to the back of the shed and started scrambling at the window, Bethy went white and stood stiffly in place, Mary collapsed to the ground in a swoon, and Steven— well, Steven ran at me.

Fortunately for me, I was way bigger than Steven, or he would have done some damage from sheer ferocity.

I grabbed onto his wrists with both hands, holding them out from me, but then he started kicking. After one or three painful encounters with my shins,

I finally gave one surge of effort and lifted him off the ground by his wrists for a moment. I shot one leg out and dragged him backward over it, driving his feet out in front of him and guiding him down to the ground on his rear as gently as I could. He sat there, still for a moment, probably more in surprise than anything else. I let him go and stepped back again, cradling my freshly throbbing hands.

"All right, my bad. I'm gonna' stay back here, okay?" I had one coherent thought push up through my brain: trauma. These kids had all experienced or witnessed some serious trauma. Between Jessica's comment about "again," when I told her my parents had died, and her matter-of-fact questioning if they'd died, and all the kids' reactions to what they perceived as my imminent threat, I would have put money on it. Someone had seriously mistreated these kids, long before the events of the last few weeks. I needed to approach this way differently.

"This door locks from the inside. Why don't you close and lock it, okay? I'll be outside here."

Steven leaped up and slammed the door closed, and I heard first the knob lock, then the dead bolt, and finally something heavy scraped over the floor to in front of the door. I sighed sadly and my heart winced as I realized that this was not the first time these kids had barricaded themselves in a room.

"I'm sorry; I shouldn't have moved in on you like that. You probably thought I was trying to hurt you. That's not at all what I meant, okay? I would never hurt you. I do have some questions, but they can wait until you're ready, okay?"

There was no reply for several seconds, and then Jessica's and Steven's eyes lifted up over the window-sill and peered out at me. I held out my hands again, empty palms up, and then I sat down cross-legged in the grass.

The window creaked open an inch, and Jessica asked loudly, "What are your questions?"

I breathed in and out slowly and deeply, trying to calm my own racing thoughts. I had so many, where to even begin?

"So, how did y'all end up on the farm? Did you wander here, or did my parents bring you here?"

"They brought us here."

"They did? Okay. Where from?"

"They came and got us when the Miltons died."

Okay, now we were getting somewhere. "Who were the Miltons? Are those your parents?" I didn't think so, but I had to be sure; after all, I'd heard of some kids distancing themselves from their parents by calling them by their first or last names before.

"No, our dad is a bad man. The Miltons rescued us from him."

So, probably some sort of foster situation. "Got it. So, are you from here in town?" The Miltons must have been friends of my parents in town who had died in all the madness. That could explain why my parents had four young kids, for sure. That's the sort of people my parents were.

"No, we live in Springville."

"Springville?" Springville was an hour away by car, right in the heart of the affected zone; were they placed that far away with the Miltons? "But were the Miltons here in Sockneyville?"

"No. Springville."

All right, now this made no sense. I'd never met, never even heard of the Miltons before. Why would my parents have ended up with their foster children after they passed unexpectedly when they lived an hour away? Surely there had been someone closer who would have stepped in to take the kids? This was making less sense.

"So, why did my parents put you in the cellar? You said you've been down there a few days?"

"She told us to hide, like Mr. Milton did before he died." Jessica called.

Why would they have needed to hide while they were with the Miltons?

"Did she tell you why you had to hide?"

"She told us someone was coming, and that they couldn't know that we were here."

"Did she say who was coming?" my blood was boiling and the black in my chest swelled; the mystery visitor was probably the person who had killed my parents.

"No. Only that it was important for us to stay in the cellar and not make any noise. That was the last thing she said to us."

None of this information was helpful. I wasn't sure

I was going to get anything else that would help me understand more of what had been going on. All that was left was for me to decide, *what now?*

I was pretty sure Child Protective Services was a thing of the past down here, at least for the time being. My parents were dead, the Miltons, whoever they were, were dead, and the Dantons were bad people, based on both Jessica's report, plus what I could guess based on the kids' behavior in general. Where did that leave them?

The answer came slowly, bubbling up through the mess of questions and puzzles: it left them here, with me; they didn't have anywhere else to go. It was squarely on me to load them up in my parents' SUV and turn them safely over to Protective Services. The black knot of pain in my chest tightened. This wasn't what I came home to do.

Chapter 3

As it turned out, the kids each had a bag with some clothes and odds and ends in it. Once I got them out of the shop, I got them each squared away in the leftover bedrooms for the night before we would take off in the morning. I decided I'd take my old room, so after talking it over with Jessica, I put her and Mary in Mom and Dad's old room, and Steven and Bethy, short for Elizabeth, in the guest bedroom.

Thinking back to all the mandatory work trainings and journal articles I'd ever read on the topic of trauma, I tried to give the kids as much control over the current situation as possible. I'd read somewhere that it wasn't good to ask traumatized children a whole lot of questions about their past, so I didn't. I tried to keep things focused on the here and now and stay positive without being fake or over the top.

I went out to the cellar again alone that night. I was curious about this cellar that my parents had never told me about and wanted to explore it a bit more. When I lowered myself down the steep ladder into the cavity, I was surprised at how roomy it was. The cellar was cylindrical, like a giant soup can turned on its side and half-buried in the ground. It was probably made from a piece of big metal duct: the sides were corrugated, and strong. When I pushed on it, the metal didn't flex or give in the slightest. Wooden shelves, probably intended to serve as both tables and beds when paired with the thin mattresses and blankets I saw rolled in one corner, lined the walls.

There were a few small bins of my old toys, some board games, and a whole lot of wrappers and water bottles scattered around, evidence of its stint as a shelter for the four young kids who were now keeping warm in my parents' house. The remains of what were probably several 72-hour emergency kits were piled up on one of the shelves. On the floor in a corner sat a sealed 5-gallon bucket whose use I didn't even have to guess at, based on the number of flies arcing around its top.

Why hadn't my parents told me about this? Why? During tornadoes when I had still lived at home, we had always gone into the large walk-in closet in my parents' bedroom to hunker down. Why hadn't we used this? Why keep something like this a secret from me, unless it was something illegal or immoral, or both? I really couldn't think of any other reason for it, but that thought made me sick. It didn't fit with everything I knew about Mom and Dad at all. But that brought me right back to the original question: why, then?

When had the Underground Railroad been a thing? No, that didn't make sense; this metal was certainly newer than that. Plus, the Railroad was prior to when my great grandfather bought and built up the land for the farm. Underground Railroad was out, then.

So, why? Why? WHY?! I kicked one of the boxes of toys in frustration. Toys went everywhere, hitting the far end of the cellar and dropping to the floor. I sat down on one of the table-bunks, leaned my head back against the cold, curving metal of the side, closed my eyes, and took a few deep breaths. It wasn't the cellar that made me so upset. Sure, it didn't make a lot of sense that they hadn't told me about it, but it was the fact that I still didn't know why they were dead that bothered me so much. If it were someone who had killed them to loot or something, there would have been things missing. As it was, things were out of place, as if someone had looked for something, but nothing was missing.

Did it have something to do with the kids? I couldn't dismiss the fact that the Miltons had died soon after they had rescued the kids, too. Was there a connection there? It seemed like too large a coincidence to dismiss entirely. Maybe it had been the Dantons? I didn't know how they would have found the children at the Miltons', but it didn't seem entirely impossible. If it was the Dantons, where were they now? The darkness in my chest clinched and squirmed.

When I calmed down, I slid off the bunk and started putting toys back in the bin. An old action figure with a cape, had fallen right at the base of the wall. I was about to reach out and put it in the box when the cape fluttered. I watched closely for another several seconds, not sure if I'd imagined it or not. No, it definitely moved subtly back and forth.

I put my hand to the floor as well and felt a small breath of air tickle the small hairs on the back of my hand. This wall, the end of the cylinder, was corrugated metal, the same as the walls and ceiling of the tube, with nothing aside from a line of rivets running up the center of the wall, joining the two pieces that made it up.

Examining the seam closely from floor to ceiling, I found one rivet that had a familiar symbol etched on the head. Bringing up my wrist, I looked at my medical ID wristband. The wristband was a wide band of metal, probably ¼" thick and ¾" wide, that on the inside, against the skin of my wrist, had my name and some medical details: blood type, allergies, things like that, and on the other, the side that showed to the world, was this same symbol. Nothing fancy or even terribly unique, it was a simplistic image of a shield with a sword and an axe crossed behind it. Growing up, I'd always pretended it was our family's coat of arms, or a secret emblem belonging to some secret band of heroes. Typical little boy stuff. As I'd gotten older, I figured it was a poor attempt at making a boring piece of medical info "cool." Seeing it on the head of a rivet in this secret people-hiding cellar? A shiver brushed my arms and goosebumps squeezed the skin tight.

I reached out with a finger and pushed on the rivet. Nothing. I pushed again, harder. Nothing. It didn't move. Okay, so not a button. I pushed, one by one, on the rest of the rivets in the line, just in case. Still nothing. It was too big a coincidence to not mean something, though. I ran my hand up the seam again, pushing periodically to feel for something, anything.

Nothing, until I ran my hand over the rivet two above the etched one. At that point, I heard a quick sliding and tapping, repeated twice. I pulled my hand back, shocked. It was too much. Finding a secret cellar was one thing, but finding evidence of another secret room within that cellar? My parents were boring! I mean, they had certainly been nice enough. They were good people. But the type who had secret rooms within secret rooms? Hardly.

Maybe the rooms didn't originate with my parents, at all. It was true; this was great-grandpa's farm, wasn't it? He fought in Europe during World War II and lived through both the Red Scare and beginnings of the Cold War. I forced myself to breathe out. That was it. That had to be why these rooms were here. It still didn't explain why my parents didn't tell me about the rooms, or why they were involved with the kids in the first place, but it helped clear up a piece, at least.

I had another sudden realization, given the time-frame Jessica had given me. There was a good chance that the kids were with my parents the last time I had spoken with them. Surely, Mom would have mentioned something significant like that? So why hadn't they?

Back to the matter at hand. I pushed again on the

spot two rivets above the etched one, putting both hands on it and pushing. I even put my shoulder on the spot and pushed, straining against the wall. Nothing budged, and there was no sound. Frustration came rushing back. I put my hand back on the etched rivet. Nothing happened. I slid my hand upward, sliding more slowly up the seam. This time, when I heard a slide and a tap, I stopped immediately. I was hardly even touching the metal, my hand barely resting on it; not pressure-activated, then. It had to be something else.

My wristband. My wristband was directly over the embossed rivet, nearly touching it. I pulled my hand away, and the sliding tap sound repeated. More intentionally, I pushed the wristband directly onto the rivet, not even touching any of the metal with my hand. Slide-tap. Pulled back. Slide-tap. I did it quickly a few more times. Some sort of magnetic release, then? A solution, but it only led to another question, which led to others. Why did my wristband unlock a secret room in a secret cellar used to hide people?

When I pushed on the panel while holding my wristband to the rivet, it pushed in slightly, something clicked, and then the whole panel pushed outward several inches. I wrapped my fingers over the door edge and pulled backward.

The entire panel swung back toward the cellar wall, opening onto a room at least as big as this one. This new one had far more in it, though.

I don't know exactly what I expected when I pulled

back that door, but it certainly wasn't what I found. A row of filing cabinets completely lined the left wall, and on the right, there stood a big wooden desk, a monster piece of furniture, with an old wooden rolling desk chair pushed under it. On top of the desk, horribly out of place by comparison, sat a laptop. So much for my parents not being involved in whatever was happening on this side of the door. Above the desk on the wall, the symbol hung in real life, an actual shield with a sword and axe crossed behind it. In one corner of the desk, a large radio system and a microphone on a stand sat covered in dust.

I laughed to myself. This was absurd. My parents were what, spies? What was all this?

I pulled open the top drawer of the cabinet nearest me. It was dusty and full of old file folders. There were tabs with years and then months going back from 1951 in the front to 1948 in the back. I shut the top drawer and squatted down to open the bottom. This one went from 1946 to 1945. I pulled open the December tab of 1945 and pulled out a folder. It had a name on the tab at the top: CROSS, TIM.

Opening the folder, I was disappointed to see that there were only a few pieces of paper inside. One was an index card with only a few lines of text:

Harrison Blakely
1785 N. Cromwell St.
Prescott, AZ
D: April 7, 1981

There was also a newspaper clipping, an article with a headline that read, "Local Boy Wins Regional Science Fair." The article described how a young man, Tim Cross, won the regional science fair for his project, a refining process for coal that allowed it to burn cleaner, hotter, and longer. There was no mention of a Harrison Blakely in the article.

Well, that was cool, but why would this article be in my parents' secret filing cabinets? Not just my parents. This was from 1945. That meant my great-Grandfather Strader. Why had he cared about some regional science fair winner? Maybe the next folder would shed more light. This one was "Schubert, Mary." Inside was the same basic formula: one index card, one news article. This notecard read:

Agnes Klum
228 S. Burleigh Ave.
Ashland, Kentucky
D: September 26, 1983

The newspaper article reported on some poor girl, Mary Schubert, whose mother and father both developed acute amnesias only to have her grand-mother soon after suddenly suffer some sort of stroke that left her in a completely vegetative state. Again, no mention of the person on the card, Agnes Klum.

The last folder was the same: strange news, note card, different names on the folder and card, no mention of the card name in the article. This was getting even more strange. My great-grandfather was obviously interested in these events and occurrences, some great accomplishments, and some tragedies. And even though the articles didn't mention them, the people on the cards obviously had something to do with the events in the newspaper articles. So, was it some sort of strange witness protection program? It seemed logical that the notecard name could be the alias these people were hiding under. Otherwise why wouldn't the name on the folder match the card? But why would you need to hide someone like Tim Cross, who obviously had a bright future ahead of him?

And did the "D" on the notecard stand for death? It seemed reasonable that it could be the date of their death recorded on the note card.

Were these people some sort of strange criminals? Witnesses? Victims? The records started right after World War II ended and my great grandfather returned home. Looking down at my wristband, I wondered again why I didn't know about any of this. It sure seemed like I was supposed to. Given the laptop, it was obvious that my parents were active in whatever was going on down here in this cellar. I closed the folder. It was a lot to take in, and I didn't love what it was doing for my opinion of my parents. Why hadn't they trusted me with the knowledge of what they were doing out here? It seemed like it had been some sort of family legacy. Why not clue me in?

And the kids were involved in all of this, I felt sure of it now. Did it have to do with everything that had happened here in southern Illinois? That certainly fit the profile of inexplicable events and disasters contained in these folders, taken to an extreme. What happened in the first place that Jessica and the others were pulled from their home? Did they have a folder of their own in the cabinets? What article would my parents have included for them?

I walked to the last file cabinet in the row and checked the years in the drawers. It ended with the year 1992. No answers about the children here, but what about on the computer? I turned to the desk, for once glad that my mother had never been diligent at being creative with her passwords.

Chapter 4

I was surprised to find that the password to get into Mom's account on the laptop wasn't any of her three usuals; not one of our three birthdays got me in. Looking at the user profiles closer, though, I realized one had my name on it. My skin prickled with goosebumps again. A hint under the password box read "your first kiss." I shook my head and smiled a little. It was an old family joke that my first kiss had been with one of the baby goats that had been born when I was five. I typed in "baby goat," and the screen dissolved as the desktop loaded.

There were only two items on the desktop. One read "Safeguard Record Database" and the other... A video file titled "To James." My mouth was dry, and I shook with shivers that started in my gut. My fingers tremored so badly that I had to stand up and take a few deep breaths to calm down. I was going to get answers. I double clicked the video, only to have a small query box pop up. A question and a text box for the response; password protected. The question: what was your favorite sandwich as a child?

I smiled as I typed in my answer: peanut butter and pickle.

The video played. It showed my parents, both

sitting at this desk. The filing cabinets behind them were unmistakable.

"Hey, James."

"Hi Jamie, Sweetie." Mom was the only one who ever called me Jamie.

"You have no idea how many of these videos we've made for you over the years." Dad's tone was tired.

"But we've never minded, because we love you." Mom punched Dad's arm teasingly. I smiled.

"Right. But—" Here Dad looked directly into the camera. "If you're watching this, it's because something's happened to us and there are kids who need your protection."

What were they involved with if they made regular "if you're watching this, the worst has happened" videos?

"Sweetie, we really hope you never see this, because we've worked really hard to keep you out of all this." Mom choked a little bit and looked down at her hands. Dad took one of Mom's hands and leaned over to whisper something in her ear. Mom looked at him and said something the microphone couldn't pick up. Dad shook his head slightly and Mom looked back at the camera.

"Your father and I are part of a network. We work with people across the country to relocate kids in trouble. Special kids. Kids who need our protection."

"Son, it's absolutely critical that these kids stay here. You need to make sure that they stay on the farm." Dad leaned down on his knees, looked directly at the camera again. "Son, you need to know, these kids' father, the man we helped rescue them from, he's a bad man. His name is Julian Danton, and he's killed people. A lot of people. I hope to God that you won't find this out this way, but he's the reason all of this happened. Everything that tore this area apart over the last few weeks, he made happen. I know that's going to sound crazy, but it's the truth. He's the cause of all of this. Our network, Safeguard, already took the kids away from him once. Our friends, the Miltons, he killed them to try and get the kids back. That's why they're here. The farm has been a haven of last resort for kids like them since it was founded."

"Honey, we hope that you don't have to learn any of this. We hope that we can either stop him or tell you all of this ourselves. But, if we can't..."

"That's why we've made so many videos over the years. James, you have got to stay on the farm, and don't trust anyone you don't know who comes looking around. We're asking for your help now because Safeguard has been compromised. We've never had anyone who shouldn't find kids who we've rescued. None of the people we've liberated kids from in the past have ever even gone looking for them. Your mother saw to that."

Mom saw to that? What did that even mean?

Mom nodded with Dad. "If Danton found the Miltons, it means that someone in Safeguard betrayed us. It's important that you get in touch with a man named Roger Caplan. He can fill in all the holes where

Safeguard is concerned, okay, Sweetie? But please, don't tell even him that the children are here. We still aren't sure who we can trust."

"We can only hope that the children are still here when you get here, and that you aren't too late."

Mom and Dad looked at the camera again, both smiling. "We love you, son."

"Be strong, Sweetie."

The video ended. For the second time in less than two weeks, I'd lost my parents, and Mom's last words to me both times were to "be strong." More fodder for the black pain in my chest.

I closed out the video player and sat there for a moment. So many questions were still swirling around my head. My parents were members of a secret society? How had I never known that? Suddenly every work trip and trip out of town, every time they sent me away from the house to a friend's for a sleepover or to run errands held new meaning and significance.

Suddenly the old radio blared to life.

"James?"

I stared at the radio. What was even happening? How was this even possible? This radio was so old. The speakers made the voice sound like one from the old radio shows I'd seen in movies, all tinny and distorted. This thing was probably still my great-grandfather's original radio.

I sat back down in the chair and my fingers hovered over the broadcast button on the microphone for a moment. Whoever this was obviously already knew who I was, somehow knew I was here, and wanted to talk. I certainly couldn't make the situation worse by answering.

"Who is this?"

There was a pause of several seconds, then the voice blared out again, "James? This is Roger Caplan. I've automated that broadcast to be sent out every hour on the hour in hopes that your parents called you in and I could catch you while you were in their, uh, library."

A lull. I didn't know how to respond to that. I reached out to reply, but Roger cut me off.

"Are they dead?"

Each time still felt like the first time. I hadn't even thought about the fact that there were lots of people out there in the world who cared about my parents, who didn't know they were gone.

"Yes."

Another lull.

"Are the kids there?"

I hesitated. Recalling perfectly what my parents had instructed, I replied, "What kids?"

A pause.

"I'll be there tomorrow afternoon. Don't shoot me."

My parents had said not to let anyone know the kids were here. I had to keep him away.

"No, Roger, I buried my parents last night. I don't want any visitors right now. I'll call you back on the radio when I'm ready to talk. I have some questions for you, but not right now."

There was a pause for a moment, then Roger crackled over the radio again.

"Fine, I'll give you a week. Don't go anywhere; I'll be there Monday afternoon."

The radio stayed silent. I didn't bother to tell him that I had no intention of sticking around for that long. These kids needed something stable. They needed to be kept away from their parents and with someone who knew how to care for them. We'd leave first thing in the morning for the nearest functioning Division of Child and Family Services office.

***

After crawling into bed, among all the remaining questions and things that bothered me in what my parents had said, one detail stuck out above the rest. Dad had said that Mr. Danton was responsible for all of what had happened; how could that be possible? Storms, fires, floods, all of those were natural disasters. They certainly happened in a way that seemed highly unnatural, but caused by one man? How could that even be? And the illness? Unless you gave credence to a whole ton of Internet conspiracy theories, it was highly unlikely. But the simple fact remained that Dad had said that this guy had killed people, that he'd killed the Miltons, who apparently were part of this Safeguard organization. That was a real threat. Domestic violence, abuse, murder, those were threats I understood.

So, did Danton know the kids were here? Was he the one who killed my parents? It was almost a sure thing if what my parents said was true. He had somehow found the children at the Miltons'. Apparently, he'd been told where to find them. My parents had trusted Roger Caplan, but not enough to tell him the kids were here. I needed more answers, which it seemed Roger Caplan could give me, but I also couldn't entirely trust the source. *Yikes*. My head was spinning. I needed sleep.

I needed sleep, but it didn't come. Thinking over and over again about some unhinged abuser tracking his kids to the farm made me paranoid. Every creak and groan of the house I grew up in, which I once found funny and calming, became suddenly menacing and ominous.

***

Waking up at 6 o'clock when Elizabeth decided she was awake for the day was excruciating. The breakfast of champions around the house that day was good old-fashioned oatmeal. I tried to smile at Elizabeth, aka Bethy, as I glooped some of it into a bowl for her, letting it fall from the big spoon from a foot above the bowl. She barely made eye contact with me, but I'm sure I saw the foundation of a smile in her cheeks behind the placid smile of her teddy bear. I took it as a win.

Jessica stumbled into the hallway from the guest

bedroom, Mary on her hip. It only surprised me for a moment that they had all ended up in the same room overnight, after all they'd been through. I should have figured that.

I could tell that Mary on Jessica's hip was an arrangement they were both familiar with, but Mary clearly wasn't as small as she used to be. Jessica lugged her into the kitchen and heaved her into a chair at the breakfast bar. I repeated my oatmeal-dropping trick for Mary, who was a much more appreciative audience; she squealed and giggled, clapping her hands. I scooped brown sugar into the two bowls and scooted Mary's to her, then finished by sprinkling some raisins onto Elizabeth's.

I held up the pot of cereal to Jessica, asking her with my eyebrows if she wanted some. She tried to stifle a sigh, then nodded. I felt the same way.

"Where's Steven? Still asleep?" I asked.

Jessica nodded.

"He'd better hurry, or he won't get any oatmeal."

Jessica actually laughed.

I didn't want to, but I had to ask Jessica about their history, and maybe her father, if I could do it without retraumatizing her.

"Jessica, can I talk to you for a minute on the back porch?"

I could tell she wasn't thrilled, but she came anyway. I closed the sliding glass door and made no move beyond that except to take a few steps away from her.

"I only want to talk to you out here so that we don't

upset your sisters. And, so you know, you don't have to answer if you don't want to, and you can go inside any time you want. Okay?"

Jessica nodded, but didn't say anything else.

"Did anyone from Child and Family Services ever come to your house, when you were with your dad?"

"What's that?" she looked genuinely confused.

"Well, it's people from the government who come to a house to check on the children to make sure they're safe. Did anyone ever come to see if you and your brother and sisters were safe?"

"Yeah, I told you about them. The Miltons."

"Did the Miltons say they were from the government?"

"They said they were there to help us. When my mom heard that, she packed us each a bag and sent us away with them."

I could tell she was getting upset.

"Got it. I have a couple of more questions, okay? And again, you don't have to answer. Do you know what exactly happened to the Miltons?"

Jessica looked down at her feet and crossed her arms tightly over her chest. "He made them sick, and they died."

"Who? Do you mean your dad? And what do you mean he made them sick? You mean he was sick, and he gave them something that killed them?" I thought they'd said the illness down here wasn't communicable.

"No, I mean he made them sick, and they died! It's

what he does! But we didn't have anything to do with that!" She was shouting. I glanced inside at Elizabeth and Mary; they were both watching us, concern and uncertainty on both their faces.

"I understand. I'm sorry. I didn't mean to upset you. I have one last question, and then I'll be done, okay? Did you see or hear anything the day—,"My voice cracked slightly. "The day my parents were killed?"

She thought for a moment, then said, "Not really. I mean, a few minutes after they put us down in the cellar, we heard some gunshots, and then later we could hear someone in the shop walking around, and it sounded like they were banging and throwing things, but then they drove off."

My hopes fell. I had really hoped they would have seen or heard something that would tell me who it was that had killed my parents.

"Okay, thanks, Jessica. You okay?"

She shrugged.

I laughed. "Okay, go ahead back inside."

I stood on the porch for another minute or two, trying to piece together everything I'd learned since last night, entirely absorbed in my thoughts. Jessica had verified what my parents had said about Safeguard searching out and helping kids in trouble. She'd also corroborated what they'd said about her dad being responsible for making people sick. How did that work, exactly? How did some abusive father have access to whatever it was that had caused the illness? And how did that relate to the fires, storms, and flooding that my parents also blamed on him?

"James Strader?"

I nearly fell off the porch as I turned around, looking frantically for the source of the garbled, digitized voice.

I spotted a person sitting on their heels on my parents' roof. He wore a black jacket with a deep hood and a face covering over his mouth and nose. He also wore some sort of crazy goggles or a helmet of some kind.

"Who are you?" I felt more than a little foolish that I had nearly fallen off the porch, and that I didn't have Dad's revolver to defend myself, if need be. I'd put it back in Dad's safe in his bedroom closet after burying my parents.

"Names are arbitrary. Calling something by a name doesn't change what it is. Yet some call me Heretic. I find it suits me. You may refer to me as such."

I glanced down at the girls through the glass, all three now sitting at the bar, eating oatmeal. I stepped off the porch, out of view of the girls, and looked back up at the figure on the roof.

"And what exactly do you want with me, Heretic?" Did he know the kids were here? Was he a friend or foe?

"I offer counsel. I know you shelter four children. They cannot be allowed to return to their father. You must keep them here on this farm, at all costs."

If he knew about the children, and why they were here, he must be a part of Safeguard. "So, are you with Safeguard?" Although, even if he was, my parents had said not to trust anyone.

Heretic stood up sharply. "I'm no child-snatcher!"

I instinctively brought my hands up, preparing for an attack. So, not a friend, then.

Heretic dropped from the roof, landing silently on the ground. He was short. When he stood up, he was probably only as tall as my shoulders.

"Why do they matter to you? Why do they matter to any of you? Why does Safeguard even exist? This is basically a really messed up DCFS case and a case for the Police or the FBI!" I shouted.

Heretic humphed, then muttered under his breath, "What can I say?"

"Would you just lose the theatrics and tell me what's going on?" Without thinking, I took a step toward him, my hands still up.

Heretic suddenly burst into motion and planted a kick straight to my chest, leaving me flat on my back and gasping for air.

Heretic sighed, stood over me and cocked his head down at me.

"Are you really the best chance the children have? Would they not be safer with me?"

There was no way I was going to let him take the kids. I wrapped one arm around both his ankles and kicked as hard as I could at his head. Because of the height difference between us, my kick caught him right in the side of the head. As he pulled one of his legs to catch his balance, I tightened my grip, grabbing my fist with my other hand and locking it to my belly.

Heretic went down but twisted in midair to catch himself squarely on his hands. As soon as the changing angle broke my grip, he whipped around, driving one leg down right across my chest. It felt as if I'd been hit with a baseball bat. Heretic stood up and took a step back.

"Pleasantly surprising. Perhaps the children do have a chance." He turned to look out at the woods and cradled his hands behind his back. I sat up, rubbing my chest, and wincing in pain.

"Pay attention, James, because I will not repeat myself. The children in your care are what we call Mythics. They represent a rare, extremely powerful and therefore dangerous, manifestation of Mythics in ages past known as Elementim. You might call them Elementals. Together, they hold mastery over the four elements, wind, fire, water, and earth. The Elementim represent significant risk, because they bring with them the unpredictable side effect of creating Aberrations, beings who are neither fully Mythic, nor solely human anymore. The duality of their new natures is often more than the individual can handle, and madness is an inevitability. The children's father is one of these."

"Hold on, what's a Mythic?"

Heretic looked back over his shoulder, silent for a

moment or two. I heard him sigh, and then he said, "So slow. And thick."

He turned back to face me, emphasizing with both gloved hands. "Look, keep the kids safe at all costs no matter what it takes, okay? And stay. On. The farm!" He made a noise of disgust as he turned away and I heard him mutter to himself, "That was a beautiful speech! Why'd he have to go and mess up my speech? Friggin' idiot."

As he started walking toward the woods, I called out to him, "Hey, where are you going? If this is gonna' be so dangerous and if it's so important, don't you think you should stay and help me?"

He turned around to face me again but started running backwards. "Nope! This is all your show, rookie! I'm more of a spirit guide than a guardian angel. Do me a favor, try real hard not to die, all right? And I'm serious about the farm—stay put!" He turned around to run forward and leapt impossibly high into the nearest tree, then quickly disappeared in the thick bare treetops.

I kept staring at the spot where he'd disappeared, my mouth hanging open in absolute disbelief. What was happening?

Chapter 5

With the addition of Heretic, that made three different parties who all agreed on the fact that I should stay on the farm. I didn't understand why, but I decided to take the advice, if only long enough to meet with and get Roger Caplan to fill in some more details.

The next week passed quickly, for a lot of reasons. It was more difficult than I realized it would be to take care of four children entirely on my own full time. It was a world of difference from taking care of twenty children in a classroom with two other adults, like I was used to. There was no break, no reprieve. When something happened, it was up to me to deal with it, period.

There were a lot of opportunities for the kids and I to interact closely. As the National Guardsman had promised, things like electricity and internet were in shambles with the fires and storms. Living in a house that only had power from a generator (when I felt like using up the gas) and some small solar panels meant that we had a lot of tasks to take care of by hand. I tried really hard to have everyone take turns doing everything; I wasn't a huge believer in strict gender roles when it came to jobs around the house. But try as I might, I learned quickly that each of the children had tasks that they enjoyed more than the others.

Jessica, who was ten, loved hanging the laundry to dry. I really hated the repetitive, slow task of picking up an item, pinning it to the line, and doing it over and over again. Out in the yard, Jessica seemed thrilled. She took her time; sometimes I caught her standing there simply staring beyond the clothesline into the trees, smiling. I tried help her out with it once or twice, but I didn't have the patience to hang in there the whole time with her. But I made a point of folding the clothes and sheets with her every time. We made small talk, but she was short with her answers. She was polite: she even said, "Yes, sir," or "No, sir," when I would ask a yes or no question. I didn't think anyone taught their kids that anymore. That didn't do much to change my opinion of Mr. and Mrs. Danton, though.

Ever since that first afternoon in the shop, I'd been careful not to raise my voice if possible. Even so, I could tell that, whenever I was around, Jessica was watching me out of the corner of her eye. I almost felt like I had to behave around her like I would around a wild animal: slow, big movements, and a quiet, calm voice. Any time she made a mistake or dropped something, which was often, she would tense up and hold stock still, like she was waiting for me to do something. When that happened, I tried especially hard to be non-threatening in my demeanor. I couldn't imagine what she must have experienced to react that way.

***

She could not have been more different from Steven. Steven was an eight-year-old powder keg. It felt as if he were always yelling at someone. I had to step in to break up arguments that consisted of him yelling at Elizabeth multiple times a day. Multiple times an hour, it felt like.

The slingshot had to go. I told him that firearms had to be locked up in the house to protect his little sisters. His reaction was:

"Fine. Whatever, you pansy."

He'd threatened me daily with everything from hitting me with a pipe to bashing my face in with a plunger. Some of his threats I had to fight harder not to laugh than to stay calm. He hadn't really tried truly getting physical with me since the shop. So far, he'd been nothing but a whole lot of talk. I'd learned quickly that asking him to do anything was like spitting into the wind: it didn't do any good, and you knew the outcome before it happened.

The one exception to this rule seemed to be the old cast iron wood-burning stove. The first time I asked him to help me light a fire in it, he just about smiled. That was when I knew I had him. Since then, I'd dubbed him official Fire Keeper, and he'd been nothing but happy about it. He was still surly and mean to the rest of us, but the talk was getting less directly violent and more evenly cantankerous.

He loved taking care of the fire. Every morning he'd coax the coals from the night before back to life and keep careful watch over it all day. I was a little hesitant at first about showing him how to cut the wood for it, but he insisted, telling me that I'm so old, I'd probably break something. I had to remind myself daily, where he was concerned, that the things he said to me weren't personal. He'd taken to the woodcutting with a will and a level of responsibility even better than I'd hoped for. I still watched him closely, but he was especially careful with the small hatchet I showed him how to use to split all but the biggest pieces.

Every night, he would sarcastically check in with everyone to see if anyone was cold. He tried to make it seem like he didn't care, and it was a burden to do anything about, but when anyone said yes, he gleefully brought the fire roaring to epic proportions. If not, he would carefully (dare I say lovingly) stoke it to leave him workable coals for the morning when he would wake up to do it all over again.

***

Six-year-old Elizabeth was still a bit of a mystery to me. I hadn't heard her speak yet. I knew she could; I'd heard her whisper responses to both older children, but her replies always seemed to dry up when I entered the room. In fact, I couldn't even look directly at her for long without her getting up and leaving the room, teddy bear clasped in both arms. It wasn't until the night that I asked for help doing the dinner dishes that she even acknowledged my existence, by volunteering.

With the water being shut off like the power, we had to do things old school. Our water every day had to be pulled from the well on the property. My parents had a decent hand pump installed several years ago, but it still took a good while to get enough for the whole day. I was excited that Elizabeth chose to stay within six feet of me while working it. The fact that she did so continuously for 20-30 minutes was nothing short of a miracle. And that was to draw the water for only the next day.

Doing dishes consisted of more of the same. She'd place her bear carefully out of reach of the splashing water and stand there at the sink, dutifully and carefully scraping all the scraps into the bucket for Mr. Urnck later, then scrubbing them off with a cloth in the left side of the sink before transferring them to the right side for a rinse. She'd then hand them to me, and I'd lower them into a tub with a mild bleach solution to sanitize them. While I waited for all the dishes to sanitize, Elizabeth would play quietly in the deep sink, drawing water up in her hands to watch it fall back into the bottom or pouring water from container to cup or into her hand. When we were done, she'd pull the plug and watch until every drop had drained before silently climbing off the stool, retrieving her bear, and disappearing to another part of the house where I was not.

***

Mary, at two-and-a-half, on the other hand, was an absolute joy, and surprisingly, the first to warm up to me. She was still young enough that I didn't really expect or even encourage her to take part in the chores (which were many), but she took an active part in it, nonetheless. She'd often follow me around, watching everything I did with big, quick eyes and the satisfying gasps and giggles of a child who was still discovering the world. She absolutely adored Mr. Urnck, in all his fat, prickly grandeur. She'd taken it upon herself to personally deliver him his morning scraps and his afternoon feed. She called him "Mr. Uck," and she wasn't wrong. He was a huge, fat thing, one of the biggest I'd seen my parents raise, and he was sour as chunky milk (which he also loved).

Yet when Mary came out of the house and bounced toward his pen, he bellowed at the fence and stood appreciatively still for her as she patted his sides and rubbed his snout. She talked to him non-stop, telling him everything she did the night before or that morning, and always ended the conversation by saying, "Okay, Mr. Uck, good eats! Smell you later!"

The rest of her time, all day, every day, was devoted to rocks. And dirt. And mud. It got to where I dressed her every day in my old yellow rain slicker on top of her other clothes and coat, with the sleeves rolled way up, to try and cut down on some of the laundry. She was perpetually filthy.

And yet, from day one, aside from the initial meeting in the shop, she greeted me by latching onto my leg and saying, "I yub you, Dames!"

So, a week into my new role as full-time caregiver, I felt like we'd established a pretty good routine and sense of new "normal," but how long could that truly last? I'd been told twice now to stay on the farm at all costs. But how feasible was that, really? The food storage would last for a while, but it was finite. And even though there were moments where I felt like the kids and I were connecting well, was that really my responsibility? I was only 21. I was no foster father or therapist. These kids needed permanency, they needed professional help; so did I, for that matter.

I had moments where I could feel my patience and caring thinning. The weeks of anxiety worrying about my parents during the outbreak, fires, and floods; the pain of losing and burying my parents; and the betrayal of trust at discovering an entire world my parents kept hidden from me pressed down on my every breath. I felt like the caring and the patience were a veneer over the geyser of my emotions. The black in my chest hadn't gone away. If anything, it had been pressurized. I'd never experienced hurt and betrayal, pain like this. I worried about having a come-apart constantly. Monday came far sooner than I was ready for.

***

"Morning, Jessica; is Steven up yet?"

"I think so. How come?" Jessica turned to look at me. We were around the breakfast bar, again. Oatmeal, again.

"I think I may need you guys to spend some time in the cellar again this afternoon. Someone who knew my parents is coming over some time this afternoon, and my parents said not to let anyone know you're here to keep you safe."

Elizabeth looked up from her bowl and made firm eye contact with me for the first time in a week. "I don't wanna' go back in the hole."

I tried to swallow my shock at her talking to me directly. "I know, Elizabeth. I wish you didn't have to. But my parents said not to—"

"Every time we go in the hole, the people die, and I don't want you to die."

Oof. I hadn't thought about that. It was true. Every time they'd been hidden in the last two weeks, people had died. Who knows how long they'd been in the hiding spot at the Miltons' before my parents had shown up? And then again for three days when my parents had been killed. Now here I was asking them to go back in the hole again. How could I keep them hidden from Roger, while simultaneously not recreating such an awful experience for them?

The closet in my parents' bedroom. It might not have been a secret bomb shelter, but it was the safest place in our house, and far off from anywhere I would expect Roger to be. I certainly wasn't planning on giving the man a tour. Plus, it had the distinctly positive note of not being a creepy, secret bomb shelter.

"Elizabeth, I have exactly the thing for you. Come with me. Jessica, you and Mary, too. Follow me."

We met Steven coming out of his room. Stretching and yawning, he asked, "What's going on?"

"I'm showing the girls my parents' closet. This is where my family used to go when there were tornado warnings when I was a kid. My dad built this part of the house before I was born." Steven followed us into my parents' bedroom. I went on, "He always said that, if there were ever an emergency, this was the safest place in the house to come."

I stopped dead in my tracks, repeating what I'd said aloud in my head.

"What's wrong?" Elizabeth looked up at me. I half-smiled and rushed the last several steps into the closet.

"Nothing's wrong. I'm just..." I trailed off as I lifted laundry baskets and pushed aside boxes.

"What are you looking for?" Elizabeth again. These were more words than I'd heard from her all week.

I looked up at her and grinned. "I'm looking for a symbol like this." I showed all three kids my wristband.

"Why?" Jessica asked.

"Well, if there's one in here, it might open a door or something."

"To where?" I could tell Steven was as interested as the rest of them.

I laughed. "I don't even know. Just help me look!"

"Cool." Steven pushed past his sisters and started throwing things around.

"Now, it'll probably be on the floor, or one of the walls, or something more stationary." As I said it, my eyes fell on the gun safe. I could remember Dad talking about how he preferred the combination safes over the electronic ones, because there was less to go wrong. Steven saw where I was looking and rushed over to it. He scoured the bottom half while I checked the top. I inspected every seam, every rivet and surface. I came up with nothing. Steven took my hand again, looking at the wristband.

"Find anything?" I asked.

"Nah. Just wanted to make sure I remembered it right."

The girls were busy combing the other parts of the closet. Jessica was even lifting Elizabeth up to inspect the closet shelf brackets while Mary opened every drawer. The floor was a messy jumble of shirts, pants, dresses, and socks.

Mary opened one drawer and shouted, "Hey, panties!" We all had a good laugh; it was a drawer of my dad's boxer briefs.

Five more minutes of searching and we still hadn't

found anything. I was extremely let down. I'd felt certain we'd find something. That line, which I'd heard Dad say so many times growing up, had felt so significant given what I'd learned over the last week.

"Hey, what's the number for this safe? What kind of guns does your dad have in here?" Steven reached up to spin the dial.

"It's not one number, it's three. And it's called a combination." I took over spinning the dial; I wanted that revolver out, anyway. "All right, no touching anything without asking first. These aren't toys." I turned the big wheel lock that disengaged the bolts and pulled open the door.

It was a big safe. There were eight different firearms in it: various calibers of rifles and several shotguns. My dad's revolver was the only handgun. I pulled it off the top shelf and flipped the cylinder open, then flicked it back in. It was a seven-round, .357 magnum with a four-inch barrel. I had a lot of memories of "wood-walks" Dad called them, with him, traipsing around the woods on the farm and plinking at cans and bottles he'd set up. We'd spent hours at a time out there, just wandering around the property, him letting me carry, load, fire, and maintain every firearm in the safe. Each one was a placeholder for a hundred memories, lessons, and conversations with Dad.

"Hey, look! We found it!" Elizabeth pointed up at the underside of the shelf in the safe. I bent down to look and, sure enough, a small metal piece, engraved with the symbol, fixed to the underside of the shelf near the back plate. I never would have seen it. I'd been into this safe with my dad a thousand times, and I'd never even noticed it.

Knowing exactly what to do, I pushed my wrist up against the piece. There was the now-familiar slide-click, but nothing else. I pushed on the back panel. Nothing. I lifted upward on the shelf. Nothing. Gripping one of the barrel supports, I pulled outward experimentally. The whole back panel pivoted on silent, invisible hinges outward. The safe had a false back.

All three of the older kids exclaimed in appreciation simultaneously. "Whoa!"

Mary jumped on the band-wagon with her own breathless, "Wow!"

I couldn't believe it. Another secret, right under my nose for all these years! The black twisted and writhed.

I opened the panel as far as it would go. Behind it, there was a metal chute, with a ladder descending into darkness.

"You've got to be kidding me," I breathed.

"Dude, your dad is so cool!" Steven yelled. "I'm gonna' go first." He stepped in to climb onto the ladder, but I stopped him with my hand.

"Stop. I'm going first. We have no idea what's down there, plus, I need you to stay here and keep an eye on the guns. Make sure nobody touches them."

Steven smiled at me so big, I thought his lips were going to meet his ears.

"You got this?" I asked.

"I got this," he said back to me.

I clapped one hand on his shoulder. "Good man." I then turned my head to look at Jessica and mouthed, "He doesn't touch them," shaking my head and smiling. Giggling quietly, she nodded.

I grabbed a flashlight from Dad's nightstand and shone the light down the shaft. It wasn't deep. I should say it wasn't endless, or anything. It was probably between eight and ten feet to the bottom.

Leveraging myself onto the ladder, I reached the bottom quickly. I turned around to face away from the ladder and shone the light that way. A large metal door was mounted into the concrete walls, floor, and ceiling. The metal only lined the chute. Getting closer with the light, I could see there was one small fingerprint scanner, aside from a thick metal bar handle down the length of one side on the otherwise smooth surface of the door. What were the chances? I put my thumb to the reader and there was a slight beep, then a loud hissing as some seal broke around the door.

My dad had built a hermetically sealed secret bomb shelter underneath our house. I was beginning to doubt that I knew anything at all about my parents. But now, it was clear my parents had planned on including me in the secrets, otherwise why allow my fingerprint to get me in? So, why hadn't they told me? Unless the plan was always this crisis version where I find things accidentally. The black pushed on my heart and it beat faster.

"Hey, what's down there?" Steven called. "Where'd you go? What was that sound?"

"Give me another second, guys, and I'll come back and tell you, okay?"

I heaved on the bar handle, and the huge metal door swung surprisingly easily and smoothly outward. I walked through the threshold and must have triggered some sensors, because automatic lights slowly winked on and brightened gradually around the ceiling perimeter of the room. What a room—everything was stainless steel, glass, or brilliant white.

On the wall to the left, in the far corner, hung several bunks that would fold down when needed. Also in that space were several folding chairs and a collapsed table that fit snugly into slots in the wall. At least, those were the symbols etched on the sides of the panels in the wall. Table, chairs. There was a much bigger section of the wall that showed a sink and a pot with steam rising from it. I assumed that was some sort of kitchenette. The next wall panel had a plate of food on it. Pantry?

Turned out, my parents were totally preppers. But why hadn't my parents put the children down here in the first place? This seemed not only more secure, but also a much better, more comfortable space for the children to have been left in.

At this thought, I felt my chest begin to tighten with anger when the symbol on a wall panel opposite me, next to the wall on the right, caught my eye. It was the now familiar shield with crossed sword and axe. I walked to it and touched my wristband to it. No sound. There was a small indentation in the panel with some grooves for fingers to fit in. I pulled on the handle, and the whole wall section pulled out, rolling back along the wall toward me. When it extended halfway along the length of the whole right wall, it stopped and pulled no more. Taking a few steps toward the back wall, it was suddenly clear why my parents had opted to put the children in the shop cellar, instead.

Nearly the entire section, from the far wall toward the center, was filled with weapons. Some I recognized, like the sword and axe on the far left, and there were two different versions of similar AR platform rifles, one with a shorter barrel and a red dot sight, the other having a significantly longer barrel with a large scope.

Although I could tell they were obviously some sort of projectile weapons, the rest resembled no other firearms I'd ever seen. One of the pistols caught my eye, and I took it down from its pegs. Examining it closer, I could see no magazine release, or even a magazine, for that matter. I was trying to figure out what kind of projectile it fired, but there were no clues about it that I could see. Short of pulling the trigger, I couldn't see any way of figuring that out. Somehow, I didn't think that was the best idea. And yet, I couldn't deny that it felt extremely good in my hand, heavy enough to compensate for recoil, but not so heavy that it felt awkward when I held it out in front of me.

I hung it back up on the rack but made a mental note to take it with me when I went back up.

The last section of the rack held a series of armor plate, and a set of pants and a top that looked like a bulletproof vest, but thinner. There was a helmet, as well.

"Whoa! Your dad was a badass!"

I whipped my head around; Steven stood in the door, and I could see Elizabeth standing right behind him, with Jessica helping Mary finish down the ladder behind them both.

"Hey, language, Steven!" I said, nodding my head toward Elizabeth, whose bear had stopped hiding her face. Then, under my breath as I pushed the wall section back in place, I said, "My dad *was* a badass." I unhooked the pistol I'd held and liked so much, placing it down the back of my pants for a moment while I finished closing the section. When it was again closed, I looked at the gun even closer, this time looking specifically for a safety. I didn't want to take any chances with these kids around. Turned out a safety was a good idea according to whomever designed this gun, too. It was similarly placed to others I'd seen and was familiar with.

"Whoa, what is this place?" Jessica and Mary entered the space, both looking around in wonder.

"It's another cellar. My dad built this one, though. The other one was probably built by my great-grandfather."

Elizabeth took the whole room in with her eyes,

going over to the bunks on the wall and patting them with her hand. After making one more pass over with her eyes, she nodded a few times then whispered, "I like this one better. It's cleaner."

I laughed. "It is. We'll use this one, but only if we have to. I think things will be fine with this Roger." It was confidence I didn't feel myself, but it wouldn't hurt to give them a little peace of mind. Turning to face them and the open door, I saw a few more panels on the front wall next to the door. One was another shield with sword and axe—more weapons, probably —but one in particular caught my interest. A security camera symbol. My parents had security cameras? Then they probably had footage of the day they were killed. I could find out who was responsible for my parents' murders.

I pulled out the section. Several screens blinked on, each showing a different view of either the outside or the interior of the house. How had I never seen these cameras? There was a central screen that had several buttons on it. One of them was "review footage." I pushed the button, then quickly selected the date that I'd received the call from my mom. I paused. Actually, I had a better reference point. The date my parents put Jessica and the others into the cellar. By my estimate, that was the day after my mom called me.

"Jessica, do you remember what time of day it was when my parents told you that you had to hide?"

"It was after they fed us lunch."

"Okay, so right around noon." I dragged a slider on that date toward noon, then paused the screens. "Will you take everybody back in the passage, Jessica? I want to check something." There was no reason they needed to see this.

"This will only take a minute," I said when they were all safely out of sight.

I pressed the play icon and sped up the playback. I watched my parents walking around the farm with the kids, doing a hundred different things in a few moments. As time progressed, I slowed it down, knowing the time must be drawing near.

Then I had it. My parents walked the children, holding their bags, out to the shop and moments (minutes in reality) later returned to the house alone. Mere moments after that, a large old red Chevy pickup, one of the models from the 70's, pulled up to the house. I recognized the age, because my dad, as an auto mechanic and machinist—I thought, at least—especially loved working on vehicle models that predated any onboard computer diagnostics or other similar systems. He said he enjoyed the greater challenge of listening to the machine speak to him, rather than being told what to do.

I hit pause. My heart was racing. I was about to see the face of the man who murdered my parents. The shakes from my navel returned. I looked down at my trembling hands. The blisters had mostly healed, but I could still easily delineate the bright pink flesh of new growth. If I closed my eyes, I could still feel the cold wood of the shovel handle, look over the growing mound of cold black earth, and see the two sheet-draped forms of my parents...

I opened my eyes. They were wet with unshed tears and burning. My breath came in heaves. I needed to see his face—needed a target for all the rage, anger, and grief to be leveled at. The black was pushing up into my throat now, making it difficult to swallow.

I pushed play, slowed it down to real-time. The red Chevy's door opened, and a man stepped out. He was too old to be the children's father, I decided that right away. He was probably in his late 60's, early 70's, by my guess. He had a short-cropped white beard and wore a ponytail from under the back of his mesh-back trucker's cap.

There was nothing overtly menacing or even mildly threatening about him. I had grown up seeing men like this all over my hometown. Maybe this was the wrong person?

I watched my parents come out of the house and they greeted the man as a friend. Both gave the man hugs. I watched as all three of them walked up the steps of the porch and took seats, Mom and the stranger in the rocking chairs, Dad leaning against the railing. They were talking.

Audio! There had to be audio! Tapping the screen, I found the audio symbol and turned it up slightly, wanting it loud enough for me to hear, but not the kids.

"—Miltons. I can't believe it. How could—" I pressed

pause again. If there was audio, maybe they said his name when they greeted him. I backed it up to when the man stepped out of the truck and my parents exited the house to walk out to him. I could hear soft rumbles, but nothing clear. I backed it up again, and cranked the volume, hoping for a clue to his identity. No good. It was still too far away for any of the microphones to pick it up. Maybe they'd say his name later. I turned the volume back down to its previous level.

"Yeah, no, I came as soon as I heard. It's a real shame, what happened to the Miltons. I didn't know 'em *that* well, but they seemed like decent folk." Even the man's voice had the hometown, good-old-boy familiarity to it. It was heavy, guttural, and gravelly. It was obvious he'd smoked a lot of cigarettes in his lifetime.

"They were. We loved the Miltons. I can't believe it. How could something like this even happen?" Dad sounded tired again, like he had in my video.

"Well, that's what I don't understand," Mom spoke up. "Nothing like this has *ever* happened, that I'm aware of. Not in the entire Safeguard history, has something like this happened. There's no explanation for it. I mean, even when we've brought people who've been Swept into any of the houses of bricks, not even *that* has been enough for the effects of a Sweeping to be reversed. The only Reversals I've ever heard of have been the ones done by our people, by the Thinkers."

Dad was shaking his head. He looked disgusted. "There's no way that's what happened. It can't be. The thought that one of us could do that to the Miltons? No. No, I refuse to believe it." Dad crossed his arms.

"But Jared, there's no other explanation for it. I mean, think about it. You know as well as I do that the effects don't just wear off. And not after a single day. Unless you think the Miltons forgot to Sweep and Bit their own mark. Is that a mistake you think Brad and Lil were even capable of making?"

Dad sighed slowly, shaking his head. "No. You're right. I wish you weren't, but you're right." He looked and sounded so tired.

"Keys, you're being awfully quiet. What do you think? I mean, you're the one who found the man. Is there any other way he could have found the Miltons and have done what he did to them other than by a Reversal?"

Keys? Was that his name? A nickname, perhaps? The man pulled his hands from his knees and drove them into his pockets.

"Yeah, I—I gotta' be honest, Deby, I think we're focusing on the wrong thing here. I mean, there'll be a time to figure out what went wrong at the Miltons', but right now, we gotta' keep our focus where it belongs—where it's always belonged— on those kids. I mean, you haven't even assigned them to a new set of Hosts, have you? I don't think I saw a new assignment yet, anyway, on the database. Does that mean they're still here?" Keys looked in the windows of the house, like he expected to see the kids right inside.

Mom and Dad were both silent. They looked at each other, and Mom nodded. Dad nodded, too.

Suddenly, Dad's revolver was in his hand, trained on Keys' chest. "Hands, Keys. Where I can see 'em, nice and slow."

"Oh, Keys," Mom said. "Why? Lillian and Brad? For the love of God, why?!"

There was a sharp crack as Keys' jacket pocket exploded. Dad's right arm went limp, but he kept hold of the revolver.

"Deby, go!" he shouted.

"Jared!" Mom screamed.

"Go!" he shouted again.

Mom ran to the door and disappeared inside. She popped up on the screen showing the entryway headed toward the kitchen. Dad followed her and took the revolver with his left hand. Once inside, he fumbled with the door, not able to work the lock effectively with either hand, the left holding his revolver and the right limp and now slick with blood.

Keys, who'd struggled for a moment to get the gun out of his pocket, was now at the door and fired several rounds through it. None of them hit Dad, but he gave up on the door and ran toward the kitchen. Keys threw the door open and fired several more shots, one of which hit Dad in the back, and he went down.

Mom, who had stopped in the kitchen when she heard Dad fumbling with the lock and had turned back to help, screamed, "NO!" when the shots went off and Dad fell. She turned to run toward the hallway and the master bedroom, Keys again fired several rounds, and my mother dropped.

I'd forgotten how to breathe. I couldn't breathe, couldn't catch my breath. I paused the video and leaned up against the panel, my vision blurring and swimming. The black was a writhing, squirming mass now, nearly pushing out my mouth and barely contained behind my fingertips.

"Dames?" Mary poked her head around the corner of the panel. "You coming?"

I forced a smile at her, but it felt more like a grimace. "Yeah, Mary, I'm coming. I'll be right there."

There was nothing else for me to watch. I'd seen all I needed to see.

***

We finally decided and agreed that the kids would stay in the closet, where they could hear what went on, but could go down into the safe room if anything happened, or if Mary couldn't keep quiet.

We didn't know exactly when Roger Caplan would arrive; he hadn't given a specific time. In the end, we played Uno in the closet together until we all heard the front doorbell ring, and then I gestured for them all to be quiet.

I took the gun I'd brought up with me from the safe room. I switched off the safety. While half-playing Uno, I had been thinking. I didn't know who it was who would be standing on the other side of that door.

If it was Keys, if Keys was Roger Caplan, I wasn't going to let him do to me and the kids what he'd done to my parents.

As I approached the front door, I peeked out the blinds toward the driveway. There sat an old red Chevy pickup, parked next to my parents' SUV. The bottom dropped out of my stomach, and the black inside me simply exploded.

When the doorbell rang a second time, I threw the door open. When I took in the close-cropped beard, the ponytail, and the trucker cap, I stuck my gun in Roger Caplan's chest, and all of the black, all of the broken in me pulled the trigger.

Chapter 6

There was no report of a round going off when I squeezed the trigger. There was a deep whoomp, like a subwoofer bottoming out, but ten times deeper. It was the kind of deep that you felt, more than heard. The pistol kicked back in my hands like a shotgun, and Roger Caplan went flying backward off the porch. The rocking chairs scraped and shifted back across the boards of the porch and three of the hanging flowerpots my mom had loved pendulum-ed wildly on their ropes.

I looked at the gun in my hand, most of me completely sickened by what I'd done without even thinking, another small part betrayed that it wasn't a more traditional firearm.

I put the safety back on and tucked it in the back of my pants.

Roger Caplan, aka Keys, lay crumpled in a heap on the grass, his nose and ears bleeding. I wasn't sure if I should move him or not. At his age, there was every likelihood that he had several broken bones, possibly joints, maybe even a spinal injury. There were no compound fractures anywhere, at least that I could see. That was good, at least. He wasn't going to bleed out, unless there was something bleeding internally. I was able to find a pulse, and his breathing was shallow but consistent.

He needed a doctor, there was no doubt about that. But I needed more answers first. I ran to the shop and grabbed a handful of zip-ties. I knew it wasn't good, but I gently straightened him as best I could, gingerly. Guilt consumed me. If he did have a spinal injury, I had almost certainly made it worse, maybe even paralyzed him. I had to remind myself that this man had gunned down both of my parents, shooting them both in the back. My anger outweighed my guilt. I zipped his feet together, then his wrists, and finally put a couple of zip-ties through the loop on his wrists and zipped them to his belt on the far side of two different belt loops. If he was paralyzed, this was all overkill. But I knew this man wouldn't be able to hurt anyone else today. I patted his jacket pocket and felt the unmistakable bulk of his pistol.

I had a sudden thought. I went into the house and came back with a ziptop plastic bag, and a dish towel. Using the towel, I reached in his pocket and pulled out the gun, dropping it in the bag. Not sure how much longer I had before he woke up, I released the magazine and racked the slide on the gun to empty it, then tossed the bag up onto the porch. They could match the ballistics on his gun to the bullets that had killed my parents in the future.

Just as I looked back to him, Roger's eyes started to move back and forth beneath his eyelids, and he moaned softly.

It took him another minute or two to wake up fully. I took that time to take the gun inside, where I summed up briefly what had happened to the kids. I put the gun in the safe, and told the kids not to come outside, but that they were in no danger, and not to worry.

When I returned outside, Roger was still lying exactly as I'd left him, but his eyes were open and looking around.

I took a deep, steadying breath and returned to his side. I stared down at him, saying nothing. He chuckled slightly.

"So, you're James. What the hell'd you do to me, boy? Was that your dad's Concussive Cannon? The last thing I told you was *not* to shoot me, you little turd! I can't move; I think you broke my back. Why'd you shoot me? I was a friend of your parents. I-"

"Don't." I cut him off. "My parents have a security system. I saw the whole thing."

"Is that so? Well, I'll be. That tickles the old funny bone—a Technopath like me, getting done in by a tacky ol' security system. Figures. I always hated coming here. Hate feeling blind."

"Technopath? What does that mean?"

"Oh. Well, that's right, you're not one of us, are you? Being adopted and all, guess they didn't want to involve you in the family business."

My stomach rolled over on itself. "Adopted? What do you mean, adopted?"

Roger looked up at me, and a cruel smile lit up his

face. "No way. They didn't even tell you that you were adopted? That is *messed up!* Boy, they screwed you as bad as they screwed the proverbial pooch!"

I couldn't even handle that right now. "Technopath. What's a Technopath, like you read technology?"

"Are you kiddin' me? I tell you that you're adopted, which you didn't even know, and you just gloss over it? And what about how you opened that door without so much as a 'who's there', a 'howdy-do', or even a 'not by the hair of my chinny-chin-chin' and used your old man's con-gun to break every bone in my body?"

"For what it's worth," I interrupted, "I thought it would blow your head off." In my head, I was screaming. This wasn't me; this wasn't the type of person I was. And yet, the black and broken thing inside me answered Roger's cruelty, his malice, with cruelty and malice of its own.

"Is that right? Well, you could not be less like them, now, could you? They were all over that touchy-feely crap, but you, oh, you're as cold as a mud-sucking catfish, aren't you?"

His words twisted a knot in my gut that seared my insides. Before I even knew what I was doing, I was holding what he'd called the con-gun against his forehead.

"I didn't know what it did before. If it did this to you then, what do you think it'll do if I fire it point blank, where you have no room to move with the blast? What do you think will happen to your brain?

You keep talkin' crap, and I'll do it once. Then, when you wake up, *if* you wake up, we'll try it again. If all I get is more crap, I'll do it twice. How many times do you figure you have before your bones are dust and your brain is mush?" I was repulsed with myself. These words were not mine. I couldn't claim them. This wasn't me.

The cruelty in his eyes had turned to fear; I could see it. It made me want to vomit. Bile climbed my throat and pooled on the back of my tongue. I choked it down.

"And here I thought Julian was a sick dude. You need professional help, kid. What do you want to know?"

"Everything."

"That's a little broad, don't you think?"

"Fine. Start with you."

He harrumphed. "Well, son, that's my favorite subject. Why didn't you ask? First off, my name's Roger Caplan, nice to meet you. As far as first dates go, this isn't the worst I've been on, but you might want to dial it in some, son; you come on a little strong."

I pointed the gun at his truck and fired. The truck rocked sharply on its suspension, and all the windows shattered.

"Clementine! Ooh, boy, you made the biggest mistake of your life. That truck is the one stabilizing and calming influence in my life. You best leave her alone."

I pressed the gun into his forehead. "Less. Crap."

Roger's eyes narrowed. "We're Mythics. All of us. Every last one of us self-righteous, self-loathing Safeguard prudes. We track and hide every Mythic who don't work for us. How's that for a paradox?"

"My parents were Mythics?" I asked. "What does that mean? That they had... powers?"

Roger nodded. "Yep. The both of 'em. Your dad came from a long line of Tinkers, we call 'em. Best one I ever saw, matter of fact. He designed and built that little ditty you're holding in your hand." He nodded at the Concussive Cannon. "Along with several other little toys over the years."

"And my mother?"

"Thinker. She could get inside a person's head and make 'em forget they were wearing stripes while looking at themselves in the mirror. They were the leaders of the outfit. Kind of a family business, like I said. Safeguard was started by Jared's grandfather. In Europe they're called the King's Men, poor dumb Monarchists. You ever heard Humpty Dumpty? Same group."

He saw my face furrow in confusion and continued. "Oh, yeah. All those things, the nursery rhymes, tall tales, fairy tales, legends, myths, most religions, pretty much all based on Mythics. Yeah, the Grimms?" He swore. "Really terrible secret society historians who decided to cash in."

"So, why betray them? Why kill my parents? And the Miltons? And what did you do to Julian Danton?"

"How do you know about all that? I thought you didn't know about any kids?"

"I saw and heard it on the security footage," I countered. I couldn't give up that the kids were here.

"No kidding? He's wired for sound here, too? Paranoid SOB. Guess that brings us back to me, which, as I said, is my favorite subject. I never really fit in too well with Safeguard. Self-righteous? Not really my problem. Self-loathing? Never an issue. And yet, their whole goal is to hide us, to hide Mythics from the rest of the world."

His eyes lost focus and I could tell he was remembering something vividly. "As a Technopath, I can control technology. If it's got a computer chip or electricity flowing through it, it's as good as mine. Back in my prime, I could have forced government transparency, brought entire oppressive regimes to their knees! I could have redistributed wealth so that there was no inequality, no selfishness of any kind!" His voice trailed off, and he stared up at the sky for a moment. Then he blinked and glared back up at me.

"I could have done that! Instead, what did Safeguard have me doing? Sending inane encrypted emails and tracking databases! You think I signed up for *this*?! Now, I've gotten to where's I'm tired of it. The only joy I take is when I'm driving in that truck, and all I hear is quiet. I used to have to drive hours into the country to get far enough away from all the buzz, the noise of technology. I hear it, ya' know. But, recently, it's been downright nice. It's quiet down here since Julian and his kids danced their little number. So, you wanna know why? You want to know why I'd help jog his memory after Lil Milton Swept him and remove the Bit from his abilities with a hard reboot? That's why. Julian and those kids?"

He smiled, revealing his chipped front tooth. He coughed, and I heard something grate together. He grimaced, then the forced smile returned. "They represent the coming of Spring. A chance to start over from all this mess, with Mythics in charge and alone? You bet. Is Julian crazy? Oh, like a rabid dog, my cold little friend. But he'd get a kick out of you, right before he rotted your body from the inside out." He nodded again, the cruel smile coming back to his face.

"That's right, Jimmy-boy. You don't make the cut. Your parents cut you out of their lives because you ain't no Mythic, and Julian's gonna' do the same thing: cut you right out of life."

I tried to ignore the panic his words about my parents drummed up in me. They felt truer than I cared to admit. One thing I still didn't understand. "Why didn't you know about my parents' security system, if you're such a tech pervert?"

His eyes glared around the property, as much as he could without being able to move. "It's this place. This cursed farm. It shuts down powers of all the Mythics. I can't stand it. I've learned to appreciate the quiet of the woods, but this, it's like one of those sensory deprivation tanks. It's enough to drive you mad. They call this place, and the few others like it we know about, a 'House of Bricks'. Yeah, I know what you're thinking." His eyes rolled, and he licked his cracked lips. "Well, where do ya' think the idea for the three little pigs came from, brother? They're all about us."

"You probably feel pretty safe right about now, don't you?" he asked, looking me in the eyes. "Yeah, I can see it. You're probably thinking, 'Boogeyman can't catch me if I pull up the covers' – pretty sure he's one of ours too, by the way. But *you'll* never have the chance to worry about him. Well, son, you go right on thinking you're safe here. 'Cause while we may not be able to bring the pain with our powers, we still got the numbers to take you down, and when we come, we're gonna' walk right over your cold corpse, and we're gonna' take those kids—"

I glanced at the house, and Roger smiled.

"Oh, yeah, I know you got 'em in there somewhere. It's the only reason I'm here, Junior. Figured I'd try the easy way, get you to hand 'em over to me. But the hard way suits me fine. It suits me just fine. We're gonna' take those kids, and we're gonna' make 'em finish what they started weeks ago!"

I stood up when he started cackling and walked back inside, leaving him on the ground. He wasn't going anywhere, and I had a lot to think about. But before I did that, I vomited into the kitchen sink.

Chapter 7

I spat one more time and rinsed my mouth, walking shakily to the hallway. There was too much. The world had somersaulted to its head, and everything was lies, deceit, and betrayed trust. Was I really adopted? How much could I trust what Roger had said? How much could I trust my parents, after how much they obviously hadn't said?

I staggered to the door of my parents' bedroom, entirely flummoxed. I leaned against the doorframe, carouseling about what to do next.

The black in my gut squeezed my insides, and a thought bubbled up through my consciousness. *They're not your kids. They're someone else's problem. You have no responsibility for them. You have no obligation to your so-called "parents."*

The words stung to even think, but they also calmed the raging inferno of my nerves down to an angry smolder.

Just like that, I knew what I wanted to do.

I opened the door of the master bedroom and barked to the kids, "Pack your bags. We're getting out of here."

"James, what do you mean? Where are we going?"

Jessica followed me outside. I grabbed my bike and threw it onto the roof of my parents' car.

"It doesn't matter. Go pack your stuff and help the others with theirs, then get it all in the car." I stormed into the shop. I yanked some twine from its drawer and returned to the car. Jessica still followed me.

"Where ya' headed, Catfish?" Roger calls from the ground in front of the vehicles. "You gonna' try and hide with them kids? You can't hide from us, boy!"

"Unless you want me to finish what I started with your back, I suggest you shut up!" I shouted at him. To Jessica, I snapped, "Go get your stuff! I'm serious. Now!"

She shrank and looked away, but said again, "I want to know where we're going."

I whirled on her. "Away, okay?! We're getting out of this hellhole, going back to civilization, and turning you over to DCFS! I'm done! I didn't ask for any of this, didn't ask for any of you, and I'm done!"

I could see tears in Jessica's eyes, but I didn't stop. Something broke, the dam holding back all my pain finally gave way, and I didn't stop the furious flow, wasn't sure it *could* be stopped.

"I lost my parents, literally buried my parents, only to find out that they *never* ever trusted me with anything! Not even with the fact that they aren't my real parents! They lived a completely secret life, and never even considered letting me in! Only when the whole thing blew up in their faces, blew a quarter of the state all to hell, did they call me in to fix up their mess. And what do they leave me with? With the four kids who, according to every psycho who keeps calling, are the ones responsible for it all in the first place!"

Jessica's sobs cut into me like broken glass, but I shoveled pain on the guilt, and it burst into more angry flame.

"You're not my problem, you're not my responsibility. Just get your stuff, get your siblings, and get in the car."

Jessica fled, tripping up the stairs and scrambling back into the house.

Roger swore. "That was cold, even by *my* standards. You certainly ain't no hero, are you, Catfish? I'm probably doing those kids a favor gettin' 'em back to their old man."

While Roger railed, I tied the bicycle down, then returned to the shop for one more thing.

"You know, I don't think Catfish does you justice. I think I'll call you Iceman. I think—"

The duct tape trapped whatever Roger thought in his throat.

"I'm tired of your crap," I said.

I slunk back inside, rushing past the guest bedroom door to the master bedroom. I avoided looking at Jessica, who choked on her sobs when I came in, watching me in terror.

I walked straight into the closet and spun the dial on the safe. After tucking Roger's gun in the baggie into my jacket pocket and leap-sliding down the ladder, I scanned my thumb and yanked open the door to the safe room. If Roger was telling the truth about there being others who were all after the kids, there was one last thing down here I wanted. I shucked my coat and pulled out the long wall section.

***

In the end, my guilt held at least a little sway on my actions. I didn't yell at the kids any more than I'd already let loose on Jessica. Instead, I limited myself to terse, one- or two-word commands.

Mary wailed as I carried her to the car with her bag. When I opened the door, Elizabeth was already inside and silently scrambled over seats to be as far from me as possible. I set Mary roughly down in one of the seats, which made her cry the more loudly. By this time, I had shut down all feeling. I was an observer in someone else's life now, detached from everything. Steven kicked me roughly in the shin as he climbed in. I was past caring. Jessica entered from the other side, sitting directly behind the driver's seat. No one even asked to sit up front with me.

I squatted down next to Roger. "I'm not even sure which would be crueler: to leave you here, or to risk moving you to load you into the back of the car and bring you with us."

Roger made no sound, only glaring.

"Well, if you have no opinion, I guess I'll bring you with. I can dump you off at a hospital somewhere. Even if you don't survive, my conscience will be clear."

I ended up improvising a shoddy stretcher board from an old door, some rifle rests, and several tiedown straps. I knew it was probably a moot exercise at that point, but it helped keep my guilt at bay.

With Steven's and Jessica's begrudging help, we managed to get Roger onto the door, secured, and into the back of the SUV with only a moderate amount of jostling.

With Roger in the back, we had to put the third row of seats down, meaning all four kids were crowded onto one row. Still, no one brought up the empty seat in shotgun.

Saying nothing else, I retrieved the keys, locked up the house and shop, and climbed into the driver's seat.

I turned over the engine, checked the fuel level, and rolled away down the long driveway toward the road. I put in my address at USI. Estimated travel time, one hour, twenty-three minutes. That would put us there at about 6:30 this evening. Not too late to find a hospital, but probably too late to find anyone at a DCFS office. The kids would probably have to stay the night with me. That was going to be uncomfortable, in every sense of the word, for all of us.

We drove in silence for the next several minutes. I weaved my way through town and toward the

Interstate, navigating around fallen trees and downed power poles carefully. Obstacles like these hadn't been a huge deal on my bike; I'd just gone around. Getting back to USI in a car might be a little more difficult and would take significantly longer than the navigation system estimated.

At one point, the GPS announced that it was re-routing. Receiving a GPS signal in all this mess must be difficult, after everything that had happened.

At the Interstate on-ramp, the navigation said to continue straight, past the entrance and down the county road we were currently on. Knowing that would take significantly longer, I pressed the brake pedal and signaled for the turn. Nothing happened. The car didn't slow down. I pumped the brakes, but it felt like the car was only picking up speed.

"What the hell?" I grunted. I pulled the shifter into neutral. Again, nothing happened. I tried to downshift to slow the car down. Nothing worked.

The radio flicked on, and Roger's voice snarled through the speakers. "Iceman, Iceman, Iceman. Did you really forget about me already? I told you: if it's got a computer chip or electricity flowing through it, I can make it my bitch."

The car swerved wildly to the far side of the road, then corrected sharply. All four kids screamed.

"Not only that. Did you know that these kids are also like big, obnoxious batteries? They amplify the power of any Mythic around them. Right now, I'm the freaking Energizer Bunny!"

The engine roared and the car lurched forward. Roger's voice boomed over the children's screams, "It's a good thing your parents opted for the model with the front camera, otherwise I'd have to be doing this in reverse, and I've never been great in reverse."

I had zero control over what was happening. I could barely believe what my eyes were telling me. All the curtains of disbelief in my head came tumbling down. It was all real. This was all real. Everything everyone had said was true. The only insane thing was me: I had loaded us all into a cell and handed Roger the key.

I scrambled for solutions. Stopping the car didn't seem to be an option; Roger had total control. Escape? I yanked the door handle and threw my weight against the door, but it remained locked. Pulling up manually on the lock didn't work, either. I tried the windows. No luck.

"I'm sorry, Iceman, but there'll be no leaving the train until it comes to a full and complete stop!" Roger's cackle filled the SUV.

I reached around and drew the Con-gun out of my waistband. It had blown out the windows on Roger's truck, Clementine, but it had also nearly thrown it on its side. Plus, I had absolutely no idea what the effect of the gun would be when fired in an enclosed space like this.

"Oh, are you thinking of using your dad's little pea-shooter to get out? I told you, I can hear tech, you little cockroach. You can pull that trigger all the livelong day; out here, I'm the big, bad, mother-lovin' Wolf, Iceman!"

I pulled the trigger. He was right: nothing happened. It was no more useful than a paperweight now. Then I remembered. I jammed my hand into my jacket pocket and drew out the bag with Roger's pistol. I reached in, drew out the pistol and magazine, rammed them together, and racked the slide.

I unbuckled and wriggled around in the seat. Looking past the kids to where Roger lay, I shouted, "Move!" then climbed between the children and into the cargo area. I shoved the pistol against Roger's forehead.

"Stop the car!" I screamed.

"James, you know it's dangerous to distract the driver. Why don't you go ahead and climb back up front and relax a little? You look stressed, son. You rest easy: Roger's gonna' take care of everything, and it'll all be over for you soon."

"Stop the car!" I shouted at him, spit flying from my lips onto his face. I pushed the gun harder into his forehead.

"I think I misjudged you, James. I don't think you're actually as cold as I thought. I think you're really a coward. You were a coward when you shot me at the door, you were a coward when I told you we were coming for you, when you yelled at that little girl, when you decided to bring me with you, and I think you're a coward now, James. You're no cold-blooded killer. You're a frightened little boy with a gun."

Roger stared hatefully up at me as his voice on the radio dropped to a hiss. "If you think you're man enough to do it, go ahead. You shoot me, you send these four children to their graves. So, go ahead. Do it."

My hand holding the gun whipped and jerked in barely contained rage. I gritted my teeth and sucked in a cold breath, then dropped the gun, lowering my face to Roger's and screaming at him until my lungs and my abdomen clutched my spine.

Then I sank down next to him and sat, my back against the side of the car, my knees pulled up to my chest. My head sagged onto my arms, and I wept.

Roger's voice had his cruel smile even through the radio. "That's what I thought. Buckle up, Buttercup."

We drove only for another five or six minutes before we stopped. I looked up from my hands to see a few trucks and a van stopped in the road ahead of us. There was a large group, several men and a few women, gathered around the rear truck. In the bed of the truck stood a man wearing a white dress shirt, a navy blazer, and a tan wool overcoat with khaki slacks. Surely this couldn't be the kids' father, Julian Danton? The man's sandy blonde hair was slicked back and his wide mouth pulled back in a smug smile.

I heard Jessica and Steven both confirm my suspicions.

"Oh, no," Jessica breathed.

"It's Dad." Steven groaned.

As Danton climbed down out of the back of the

truck, the group surrounded my parents' car and opened all the back doors nearly at once. As several hands pulled the children out one by one, Danton said, "Load them into the van. Take them back to the house."

The children all looked at me, inert in the back of the car, and screamed my name. Every cry lacerated my heart and paralyzed my lungs. I couldn't do anything as they disappeared into the van, and it drove away. I couldn't even look away. I could only watch as the van grew smaller and smaller, then disappeared around a bend in the road.

One of the men standing at the back of the car, looking in at Roger and me, said, "Hey, Julian, you better come take a look at this."

Danton walked around to the rear hatch and looked in.

"Kid busted me up pretty good, Julian." Roger's voice sounded over the car's speakers, but it sounded tinny and thin now, like he was talking over a small handheld radio. "I can't move anything below my neck. I need a doctor."

Julian looked on, now unsmiling and expressionless, and asked, "The kids all right?"

"Oh, yeah. Not a scratch, and potent as hell! I had no trouble wrapping this entire car around my little finger with them around. It's waning now, though. My strength's fading fast, Julian. I need a doctor!"

Danton turned his head slightly to look at the

man who'd called him over and said, "Leave him." He turned and walked away, having not even looked in my direction.

"What about the kid?" The man asked, pointing at me.

"Kill him," Danton didn't hesitate or even turn around.

The man motioned for me to climb out as Roger's voice started screaming obscenities over the radio.

I had stood up into a crouch to climb out when the vehicle suddenly turned over and lurched forward, sending me tumbling forward, landing heavily and partially upside-down on the bumper with my chest, then rolling on out in a complete somersault, landing heavily on my back. The breath knocked out of me; I couldn't focus my eyes. I raised my head slightly, trying to stop the world spinning.

The man who'd ordered me out of the vehicle, seeing me still conscious and looking around, drew a pistol from its holster under his shirt, pointed it at me, and said, "This is nothing personal. Honestly, it's probably easier for you this way."

Then he pulled the trigger. A new pain exploded in my chest and my head whipped into the pavement. Black.

Chapter 8

I woke up to competing agony in my head and in my chest. I opened my eyes gingerly. *I was lucky to be opening them at all.* Moving my arm up to my head sent shockwaves of pain radiating from my chest. I brushed the back of my head with my fingertips, feeling an open wound and coming away sticky with partially clotted blood. I must have hit it pretty hard on the asphalt when I'd reflexively jerked back after being shot.

I sat up, carefully unzipped my jacket, and pulled up my shirt. The armored-vest suit that had been hanging in my father's arsenal had stopped the bullet from penetrating; the projectile's flattened remains fell down to the road between my legs with a quiet "plink." It may have stopped the bullet from going through me, but that much force, even distributed across a large area, still hurt. My chest felt like I'd been hit by a bowling ball, but I clearly wasn't dead. *Thank you, Dad.* I'd never seen armor like this but decided then and there that this stuff wasn't coming off any time soon.

The sun was going down; I must have been out for at least an hour or so. The quiet crackle of flames drew my attention. Sitting slowly up, I turned my head and could barely see, out of the corners of my eyes, my parents' SUV, blackened and burning in places. Smoke poured from the rear hatch. I was glad I couldn't turn far enough around to see well inside. I was sure Roger hadn't made it out before it caught fire.

There was another vehicle in front of the SUV, one of the trucks. Roger must have rammed the truck in an attempt to run down Danton, then the SUV must have caught fire somehow.

What now? Go after the kids, or return to school as if nothing had ever happened, and pretend I'd never learned anything about Safeguard or Mythics or any of this? Well, realistically, I had a more immediate problem; I was probably 20 miles from home, with no transportation. Groaning to a standing position, I glanced back at the SUV. Maybe my bike... Nope. The wheels were bare, blackened metal. I hobbled to the vehicles, every breath and shuffle sending a new wave of pain through my chest. *Maybe the truck will still run.*

I turned the keys in the ignition, but nothing happened. Too much under the hood had probably melted from the heat of the other car fire.

I shuffled off, walking my only option. It didn't take me but five minutes to realize that there was no point in leaving now; I needed to find somewhere to spend the night. As long as the interior of the truck wasn't too damaged, it would be easy enough to spend the night in the cab and probably be significantly more comfortable than I would be on the ground.

Luckily for me, the owner of the truck kept a box with a winter car emergency kit inside. I had everything I needed for a not-altogether terrible night. I fell asleep mentally thanking the owner of the truck and inwardly laughing over the possibility that the owner could very well be the same man who had tried to kill me.

***

I woke up the next morning before the sun rose, stiffer and sorer than I'd been yesterday, but in considerably less pain, overall. There was a bruise the size of a dinnerplate in the center of my chest that started angry red in the center and gradually darkened to a deep purple on the edges. I loaded a small backpack I found in the truck with the rest of the water and food from the kit and started out for home before dawn, the wool blanket from the kit wrapped around my shoulders for extra warmth.

The closer I got to home, the more I dropped and abandoned. The wool blanket went first, when I realized I'd easily be able to make it home without having to spend another night outdoors. Then, when I was only a few miles from home, I left everything aside from a single water bottle.

I passed my great-grandfather's mailbox around two-thirty in the afternoon. Strangely enough, that old familiar feeling of coming home and being all right was back, but I sure couldn't give any reason for it.

After taking a good long drink from the water cooler that Elizabeth and I had worked so hard to keep filled, I sat down in the living room and stared at the big black stove, cold and dark without Steven to prep and pamper its coals. I looked across the room and saw a laundry basket, still full of towels that had been fresh from the line, filled with the scent of Jessica's wind. I glanced toward the back door, where my old yellow slicker hung, caked and crusty with dirt that had once been mud from Mary's constant playing.

Elementals. Mythics. Powers. I could hazard a guess at which child held mastery of each element. It seemed fairly obvious, now.

I carted enough water to bathe in into the house and heated it on the stove. Walking into the bathroom, I peeled off my clothes and the body armor suit. Already, a huge ugly bruise was forming where I'd been shot. I pushed on the edge gingerly. That was going to be sore for a while.

Climbing into the tub, I turned my attention to the wound on the back of my head. After washing all the blood off, and exploring with blind fingers, I decided that the wound wasn't nearly as serious as it had seemed. Like most head wounds, it had bled like crazy, but the actual injury itself seemed fairly superficial. I didn't think it would need anything but a good washing and monitoring.

Sitting in the tub, the thought I had staunchly been avoiding for hours finally made it past my defenses: *it was my fault.* It was my fault they were gone. My fault they were back with their father, who had done terrible things to them long before he was a disease-ridden inhuman Aberration. What would happen now that he had them back? Whatever did happen would be on me. I'd done this. I'd left the farm, when everyone who'd had an interest in helping the children had told me not to. Now that I was back on it, back in the place where I'd spent a week caring for them, where I'd been instructed, in my parents' antemortem video, to protect them and look out for them, there was really only one option. *I had to rescue those kids.* Not only was it what my parents had died doing, but, apparently, it was also what they had spent their whole lives doing.

I'd failed my parents, and I needed to make it right. I also needed to make it right to Jessica, Steven, Elizabeth, and Mary. They'd begun to trust me, and I'd betrayed that trust in the worst way possible. *I was going after the kids.* My parents had lied to me for twenty-one years. How many days was that? Thousands, multiple thousands. They'd had literally that many opportunities to tell me, to be honest with me about who I was, and they'd passed on every single one. I had one opportunity here to not be like them. To not betray the trust of someone who had chosen to implicitly trust me. *I would not betray that trust again.*

After drying off and dressing again, I went back down in the safe-room. I had to decide what I needed to take with me to rescue the kids. I really wished that I still had the Con-gun, but it had been in the SUV when it burned. Looking at my dad's rack of armaments, I wasn't sure what to opt for.

The doorbell rang upstairs. I had no idea who that could be. It couldn't be anyone involved with Danton; they wouldn't bother ringing the doorbell. So, who could it be? Climbing the ladder, I picked up my dad's revolver on my way out of the safe and crept to the front door. Peering through the peephole, I saw two people I didn't recognize standing on the step: a man and a woman, both probably several years older than me. *Mid-thirties, maybe?*

"What do you want?" I yelled through the door.

There was a look of confusion and concern on the couples' faces, then the woman called out, "Are you James? We're friends of your parents. Are they here?"

The ruse with Roger was up. Surely this couple wasn't with him? Could they actually be some of my parents' other associates from Safeguard?

"Roger Caplan killed my parents, and now he's dead!" I decided to try to knock them off their game if they were pretending.

They looked at each other in horror, then the man pulled out what looked like a small silver flip phone and started talking into it. Did he have service? The woman looked back at the door. Her dark brown hair was pulled back in a short ponytail at the back of her head. Everything about this woman spoke of efficiency; her clothes, her makeup, even the way she carried herself. Everything seemed intentionally simple but effective and ready for action.

"James, are you okay? How do you know Roger Caplan?"

For the second time in two days, I opened the front door and shoved a gun in someone's chest.

"The question is, how do *you* know Roger Caplan?"

The woman looked at me, down at the gun, and sighed curtly. Then in one smooth painful motion, she wrenched the gun from my hand, took a quick several steps away, and held it back on me.

"If you're holding a gun on someone, James, always maintain your distance; don't be the one to close it." She flipped the revolver back around and offered it out to me. "I'm so sorry about your parents. Truly. May I ask, how much do you know about how and why they died?"

"Roger Caplan killed them. He was after the kids. Julian Danton's got them, now," I stated.

"So, you know about Roger and Julian Danton; do you know about..." The woman waited for me to fill in the blank.

"You're with Safeguard," I guessed.

"So, they told you. Okay. I know they didn't want to. Wanted to keep you out of it, since you aren't a Mythic. Wanted to keep you out of our problems, I suppose; a shame they found you anyway."

"I'm Clara Walker," the woman introduced herself. "I was your parents' second-in-command. Well, my husband and me. He's Pat. You said the kids are back with Danton, their father? When did that happen?"

"Yesterday," I snapped. "Where were you? Why didn't you come for the kids earlier?"

"Your parents put us all on lockdown. They said that something had happened, and that none of us was to make any sort of move until they gave the order. I think they weren't sure who they could trust. We thought we were taking a huge risk coming here like this against their orders, but we were worried. We hadn't heard from them for almost two weeks."

Clara's tone softened significantly, and she looked me in the eyes. "James, I'm really sorry about your parents. I don't think you know what great people they were."

I looked away and nodded. I didn't want to hear this right now. "So, what now?"

"Now, we go after the kids." She called, "Pat!"

Her husband jogged back over, the phone still in his hand. Where everything about Clara seemed streamlined and ready, Pat seemed her polar opposite: everything he did seemed relaxed and calm. Even his jog was somehow easy and casual.

"The kids are back with Danton," she explained. "We gotta' act fast. Call in everyone within a six-hour radius. Any larger than that is too long. We're a step behind Danton as it is. Tell them to come locked and loaded, prepped to scrap with Tinks, Tanks, Think-ers, Techs, and Tamers. We have no idea who else Danton's swung over to his cause."

Pat nodded and started talking into his phone again, turning and walking back toward their vehicle, running a hand across his close-cropped hair, scratching his scalp.

"I want to help." I interrupted Clara as she was about to say something else to Pat. She turned and looked at me.

"Look, James, you have helped. You told us it was Roger who betrayed us to Danton. Now that we know that piece, we can scour out the rest of Safeguard and clear this nasty little chapter from the books. I'm sorry about your parents, and I'm sorry you had to get involved. Your mom and dad talked about you a lot, and they were always so proud of you. And, believe me, coming from them, that means a lot. They were some of the most brilliant people I've ever known."

She looked back to Pat, who was pacing back and forth on the phone. "Pat, we gotta' get off the Brick." He gave her the thumbs-up sign. She turned to me again. "James, jump in the car. We've got a few things to take care of first, and I'd feel better about things if you came along for now."

"Where are we going?" I asked, suddenly suspicious. Just a moment ago, she hadn't wanted my help.

"Just off the property. There are a few things we have to do that require our powers, and we can't do that here. Do you know about the House of Bricks?"

"Yeah, Roger mentioned it. Said it made him feel blind," I spat.

"He really did hate it. But right now, we need to be out from under it."

I nodded and walked to their vehicle.

"No, James, here, climb up front with me. Pat's gonna' be on the horn for a while."

I shrugged and took shotgun.

Pat climbed in the back seat, behind me, still talking quietly. Clara started the car and shifted to Drive, taking us back up the driveway and toward the road. A few yards onto the pavement, Clara pulled over and stopped the car.

"This is good right here. We're out from under the Brick." She looked behind me at Pat and nodded.

Suddenly Pat's hands pressed on either side of my head.

I ducked and swatted his hands away. "What are you doing? Don't touch me!"

"The hell?" I heard Pat mutter, and his hands reached for my head again.

I pressed to the dashboard and turned around to better face Clara and Pat. I raised the revolver, holding it closer to my body this time. I fumbled for the door handle, but Clara held the lock button down.

"James, calm down. Pat, what's wrong?"

"I don't know; it's like I can't read him."

Clara looked at me, her face confused. "James, are you a Mythic?"

"No. I never even knew there was such a thing until a couple of days ago!" I shouted.

Clara's face furrowed and her gaze quickly gravitated to my wrist.

"Your wristband!" She reached out to grab my wrist. The moment our hands touched, she gasped.

I pulled my hand away from her touch, and her eyes went wide in surprise. This time she held out her hand. "James, may I see your wristband?"

"Why? What's going on? What are you doing?" I was rattled.

"I'm a Tinker, like your dad. It means we can see things; how they're put together and work. I say 'see', that's part of it, but it's more than that. As far as your wristband goes, it's almost like you're your very own House of Bricks. My Mythic power doesn't work when I touch you, and it seems to be generating from your wristband. I can see it."

I rubbed the wristband hesitantly.

"I'll give it right back. May I see it, James?" She held out her hand again.

"No. You were going to have Pat Sweep me, weren't you? If I give it to you, you'll have him finish it. Let me out of the car."

Clara nodded. "Fine. Or, you stay in the car, lock us out, and hand out the wristband for me to examine. I just want to study it."

Eventually, I agreed. Pat and Clara climbed out, leaving me inside with the keys. I locked the door and passed out the wristband through a gap at the window.

Clara held it for a moment, and she frowned again. "I don't understand," she said. "It's harmless now." She put it on her own wrist, and nothing happened. She looked at her husband. "Pat, can you read my head?"

Pat pushed back the sleeve of his hooded sweatshirt and put a hand on Clara's cheek. "Like a dirty book," he said, smiling slightly.

"Huh." Clara ignored his comment. She removed and turned over the wristband, looking closely at both sides. "Well, this is your dad's personal mark. Almost like a signature. He put it on all his inventions. But, looking at this, it's a metal I don't recognize, and it's got no internal workings that I can see. Here, you put it back on."

I replaced the wristband on my wrist.

"It's back up," Clara said. "Hold your fingers out."

I put my fingers out the window so she could touch them. She did and shook her head after only a moment.

"I don't understand it. The effect is as if your dad figured out how to take the Bitting procedure our Thinkers use and built it into a piece of tech, which shouldn't even be possible."

Pat looked at Clara, then at me, then back at Clara. "So, do we Sweep him now? This is awkward."

Clara looked at me through the window, clearly thinking. Finally, she spoke. "No. I don't think we do."

Pat must have tracked her thinking. "You think he can get close to Danton?"

"I think that whatever this device is, it's a unique

gift from Jared that can help us out of the spot we're in."

I opened the car door and stepped out to stand with them. "What do you mean? How can I help?"

Clara crossed her arms. "How long were you with the Danton kids? You had them for a while, correct? So, they know you? Trust you, maybe?"

I cringed. "Maybe. I was taking them out of the impacted area and to DCFS when Roger— when we—,"

She nodded. "I get it. James, I think you're our best bet at getting in there and getting the kids out. If they know you, they'll likely follow you out without much fuss. I'm thinking we have our team engage Danton and whatever other flunkies he has from the front, while you sneak around back and get the kids out.

"When the Miltons got the kids the first time around, they were able to catch Danton unawares, when he wasn't expecting it. This time around, we won't have that advantage. He'll be expecting some kind of attempt to get the kids this go around. But, with your dad's wristband, James, he won't be able to touch you. Not with his powers, I mean. You'll still be vulnerable to any good, old-fashioned violence, so we'll send one of ours in with you for protection. We've been holding our own for a long time; we can take care of you against any Mythics you run into."

I waved off her offer. "I'll be fine. I was gonna' go without you guys, anyway."

Clara actually laughed. "You think the events of the last few weeks were bad? I'm pretty sure that was

Danton testing the waters. The truth is, we don't fully understand what we're getting ourselves into here."

"What don't you understand?" I asked.

"Well, for reasons unknown, those kids suddenly manifested having powers we've never seen before, and when they did, Danton did, too, shortly after. We'd never even heard of him or them before this. We're fairly certain none of them was a Mythic until a few weeks ago. We have no idea why they've all started manifesting so old. We usually catch Mythics when they're younger. The kids, we don't really understand, and Danton is a complete mystery. We've never seen any of these types of powers, either. The truth is, we have no idea what their limits are, or if they even have any. They represent a complete unknown."

I was confused. "Wait, but I thought they were Elementals, or something. And that they're really rare Mythics who create Aberrations, half-Mythics or something?" I suddenly remembered Roger's comment in the car, when he'd taken over. "And apparently, they work like some kind of batteries, adding power to other Mythics around them?"

"Where did you get that information?" Clara asked, visibly shocked. "I've never heard any of that."

"Well, the battery thing I heard from Roger when he took over the car we were driving yesterday. The other parts, that Heretic guy told me that, I think," I nodded. "Did he used to be one of you? He didn't seem too fond of Safeguard."

Clara's eyes narrowed. "Heretic? What involvement do you have with Heretic?"

"He showed up at the beginning of the week and told me to protect the kids. Also, that stuff. Why? Who is he?" Her reaction made me suddenly nervous.

Clara gritted, "He's essentially a terrorist. He's been sabotaging our efforts for years. He's been kidnapping Mythic children from our custody for nearly that long. Some he manages to obtain during our ops, others we suspect he located and abducted after they'd been removed and Hosted. They just went missing. We don't know what he does with them. We've never recovered any of them."

Pat frowned and spoke up. "If Heretic's involved, this whole situation just became a whole lot more complicated. That psychotic ghost is a wild card. We've had what should have been absolutely flawless ops go so far south they hit penguins, as soon as Heretic shows up.

"Clara, I've been on the phone with everyone, checking in. Pulling in everyone six hours out will only give us an eight-man squad. That's only two fireteams, counting us, which puts us down to seven, if we send a man in with James, and no Tech. We have no idea how many other Safeguard members Danton turned, you said it yourself. Are you sure you don't want to wait a little bit longer?"

"I don't think we can afford to," Clara huffed. "That's my opinion. What do you honestly think?"

"I think that we should call in at least one more Tinker-Thinker team, and a Tech. They'll come in handy if Danton has a security system or another Tech.

Clara seemed to think on that for a moment, then nodded. "All right, call it in. How much further behind does that put us?"

Pat smiled. "I already did. They'll be here in seven hours."

Clara gave Pat a look that said, *"Really?"* then smiled and laughed. "You're an idiot. And I love you."

"Love you, too." Pat smirked.

Chapter 9

Having not slept well during my night in the truck, nor the night before, for that matter, I knew exactly what I was doing with my seven hours. After driving back down the driveway to the house, I walked down the hall to my room, closed the door, fell into bed after removing my shoes, and slept. I didn't even bother removing the armor.

It was altogether too soon that Pat was shaking my arm. My eyes were leaden and gummy.

"Time to go. Everybody's here. We gotta' get you ready. Where's your mom and dad's Closet?"

"Their what?" I couldn't focus. Is there another place where you would find a closet?

"Their Closet. You know, where they keep all their stuff?"

"Oh, it's in their bedroom," I slurred.

"No, not their actual closet, the *Closet* Closet, ya' know?"

"Yeah. Their room." I sat up on the edge of the bed and put my face in my hands. I blinked heavily several times. Sleep was not letting me go easily.

"Yeesh. You are absolutely no good to anyone when you first wake up in the morning, are you? You need my 'Pick-me-upper.'"

I blinked up at him. "What's that?"

"Essentially, it's a slap in the brain. Figuratively, I mean. I do it for Clara all the time. She's won a lot of drinking games that way. I mean, a lot of drinking games. Like, probably an unhealthy amount, now that I think about it. It's great for the hangover, too. Remind me when we get off the Brick, and I'll give you one." Pat was a bit of a chatterbox.

"Closet?" Pat smiled, gesturing out the door.

He followed me down the hall to my parents' room and into their closet.

As we lowered ourselves down the ladder and crossed into the safe-room, Pat's eyes went wide.

"Now, this... This is a Closet! Look at this stuff! They went full-blown Panic Room down here! Y'know, I keep tellin' Clara we gotta' step up our game. She does really well; I mean, we got all these little hidden compartments and guns and gear stored in all sorts of cool little stashes. But this!" He walked to the center of the room and turned around in a full circle, arms outstretched. "Hashtag relationship goals."

I looked at him, genuinely confused.

"Nothing. Never mind. It was a social media thing when I was a teen. Don't worry about it. These the armaments, I'm assuming?" Pat glided to the wall section near the right wall. He sighed when he opened it.

"Your dad was such a badass," he gushed.

The similarity between his and Steven's reactions was almost funny. Pat was a big kid. "That's what I'm told," I grumbled.

"Oh, yeah? Well, did you know that your mom was an equal, if not, some may reasonably argue, more of a badass?" He pulled out the second section with Dad's symbol I'd noticed yesterday. It was an identical array of weapons and armor. I never would have guessed. I'd seen Mom in an apron far more often than I'd seen her hold a gun. And yet, here she had a whole row of them, all for her.

"You're already wearing your dad's liquid armor, then, I assume?" Pat asked, pointing at the empty rack.

"Yeah, it's a good thing I was, too. It saved my life yesterday. Did you say liquid armor?"

Pat grinned and nodded enthusiastically. "I know: cool, right? You know the slime you make from corn-starch and water? Think that, but in impregnated Kevlar fibers. Very cool. And fashionable!" Pat pulled down the neck of his own shirt to show a similar suit.

"Huh." I picked out the now-familiar shape of the Concussive Cannon on my mom's wall rack.

As I retrieved it, Pat said, "Hey, nice choice. I've always been partial to a good Concussive Cannon, myself."

"So, we ready to go, then?" I said, tucking the cannon down the back of my pants.

Pat groaned and bit his fist when I did that. "That— That's not a good idea. I have a buddy who nearly lost a butt-cheek and a decent rental car on an op that way. Try this, instead." He took the Con-gun from me and held it to his hip, then took his hand away. The gun stayed right where he left it.

"What the—,"

"I know. Cool, right? Micro magnets in the suit. Totally holster the gun wherever you want it." Here he took the gun and left it placed in the middle of his chest. "Plus, they work to deactivate the weapon, so it can't be fired until your hand is back on it. There are proprioceptive sensors throughout the suit that tell it when your hand is aligned with the weapon and de-activate the magnets when you pull." He removed the gun. He returned to the wall, where he proceeded to attach gun after gun to his body in various places and positions. He waddled over to me, rifles and pistols protruding from all over his body.

"Go ahead, try and take one. Or better yet, pull the trigger. Any trigger."

I looked at him, covered in weapons, and I shook my head slowly.

"Pat! Are you covered in weapons again?" Clara's voice echoed down the shaft.

Pat's eyes stayed locked on mine, and his smile turned to a grimace. "No, Dear. You know me better than that," he called loudly. Then to me, in a whisper, he said, "We tell her nothing of this. She's a soldier, I'm a geek! What does she want from me?" He re-placed all the firearms then grabbed down the plates from my father's side.

"No, I'm fine, I have this stuff, remember? I'll be fine." I retrieved the Con-gun and tried out the holstering effect for myself, figuring out where I wanted it to ride.

"Yeah, that's great for bullets, being punched by a Tank, all that good stuff. It's the Tamers you gotta' watch out for. You ever been bitten by a bulldog before? It's the slow chomp you gotta' watch out for. Corn starch and water, remember? Nope; if Tamers are out and about," he knocked on one of the plates. "Old school is king. Here, I'll help you get 'em on. It's tricky the first time. And let's go under the street clothes, so you don't creep out the kids."

As I took off my shirt and pants, down to the liquid armor suit, I asked, "Okay, so Tamers and Tanks; what are those? My dad and Clara are Tinkers, you and my mom are Thinkers, Roger Caplan was a Tech." Every time I said the words "mom" or "dad" now tasted like bile in my mouth.

"Right." Pat started buckling plates onto my legs. "So, Tanks are like, well, tanks. They're big and slow, but can pack a wicked punch, and are super strong. Plus, when they're all hot and bothered, their skin is pretty much impenetrable. The Con-gun was designed with them in mind. Doesn't hurt 'em, but it does knock 'em on their asses for a bit. Arms up."

Pat buckled plates onto my arms and shoulders, over the top of the liquid armor. "Tamers, as their name implies, connect with animals. They can get a porcupine to supply them with quills, talk a turtle out of its shell, even convince a housecat to actually let them pet it and like it. They're that powerful.

Seriously, though, they can control any animal around them and have them do whatever they tell them to."

Pat went on. "I heard, back in the day, there used to be more of both of them with Safeguard. But, as technology became more sophisticated and common, it became more and more important for operations to be efficient, effective, and not noticeable. I mean, the whole point is to keep Mythics hidden, right? It's a little hard to do that when you have people who are knocking down entire buildings or driving huge rat armies like the Pied Piper, ya' know? Those are the sorts of things that people tend to notice. So, I guess they stopped recruiting them into Safeguard. They're still out there, we've still gotta' deal with 'em as kids, we don't really have a use for them on the inside, ya' know? There; you're good to go." He patted me on the shoulder. "How's that feel?"

The armor was obviously noticeable to me while wearing it, but not as bad as I'd have thought. It left my joints pretty much free to move around if a little bit squeezed when I flexed them to their extremes. Only the large fleshy parts of my limbs and torso were covered by the plate. "Fine. Surprisingly light." I remarked.

"I know, right? Let's hurry upstairs before Clara asks if I'm trying to stick to the walls. Don't ask, okay?" he interjects when I open my mouth. "It's a theory. You can't cover me in magnets and expect me *not* to play with them..."

***

We started from the house with the now twelve of us divided into three vehicles, headed toward Springville. I was riding with Pat and Clara, along with another couple, Mark and Tina, and the Tech, an absolutely gorgeous girl whom I guessed to be about my age whom I couldn't stop looking at.

When she first arrived, she was wearing tall brown riding boots around her wide calves, form-fitting dark jeans that showed off an ample bottom and a flattering lavender blouse that was form-fitting across her chest but flared outward in some slight ruffles from about the middle of her ribcage. She was pleasantly plump, and absolutely beautiful. After arriving she changed into a suit and armor combo nearly identical to mine and both Pat and Clara's, with her reddish-brown hair pulled back into a high ponytail, leaving her bangs hanging down over her forehead.

It got easier not to look at her after Pat noticed me staring and asked me if I'd like a napkin for all my slobber. Clara reached over and slapped his leg, while a moment later he started dancing all around because the seat warmers had inexplicably turned on and wouldn't turn off. The Tech, Sammy Charleston, looked at me and winked when that happened. I tried not to look at her at all after that.

Pat snapped his fingers, then turned around in his seat to look at me.

He reached down and removed my wristband.

"No way! Give it back!" I leaned away from him and swiped for the wristband.

"Calm down. I'm giving you the 'pick-me-upper'. Ready?"

I hesitated, then nodded, and he stretched to place a hand on the back of my neck, near the base of my skull. Suddenly my eyes flew wide, my mind cleared, and my heart started chugging in double time.

"Whoa! What did you do?" I demanded.

"Slapped you in the brain, I told you. You feel alright?" Pat was smiling broadly.

"Yeah, fine. Thanks."

I peered out the windshield, suddenly far more aware and awake. "So, if you guys find Mythics when they're kids, then who are all of these people with Danton? And we're all geared up for anything. Who's he got working with him?"

Sammy spoke up. "It's a big world. There are a lot of people. We don't catch everybody. I mean, it's definitely gotten easier over time. In the olden days, they had to wait for newspaper articles and everything to locate them. Nowadays, with social media, it's a hell of a lot easier than it used to be, but still not foolproof. Especially in rural areas like this: not everyone is on social media, or even connected to the internet. More conservative, too." She smiled. "Gotta' watch out for Big Brother, ya' know?"

The rest of the hour to Springville passed quickly, and soon we were unloading from the cars onto a quiet, dark country road a mile or two outside the city.

"All right, everybody, listen up. The Danton property is a mile due north through these woods." Clara pointed behind us. "The ten of you will be approaching the house via the driveway from the northwest. Exercise extreme caution: Sammy's been trying to run digital recon, but with the power out, there's not a lot of digital activity, which means we're essentially going in blind. Not ideal, but if we're blind, it means so are they. We have no idea how many Mythics to expect. According to James, he saw between ten and twenty individuals with Danton yesterday. We don't have confirmed how many there will be total, and we don't have the time to do thorough recon. Our best chance is to attack now, while most of them are hopefully asleep, and catch them off guard."

Pat took over. "Right. So, because we don't know exactly which variants of Mythics we'll encounter, we want everybody sporting arms to incapacitate at least two variations. Stan, you'll be our designated Caveman. If Sammy lets you know there's a Tech, you take 'em out, copy?"

A heavily bearded man at the back of the group nodded, then traded his futuristic weapons for an AR and a tranquilizer gun.

"Everybody remember our overall mission: subduing and peacefully relocating all Mythics for whom it is possible. Non-lethal is our first and foremost, 'kay people?" Pat finished, nodding to Clara, who took things back.

"Stay safe out there, people. Keep your comms

active and secure. Move in on my mark, then James and I will move in through the back door to extract the kids. If we can subdue all Mythics on the premises, we'll Sweep and Bit the lot. If we can't, we pull out and regroup until we have a larger force and can take them all later. For now, our main priority is the kids. Questions?"

No hands went up.

"All right. Let's do this." Everyone put on their helmets, and the other ten headed off down the road, while Clara and I entered the woods.

It took us under half an hour to get to the point where we could see the house through the trees. There was a large, cleared area around the perimeter of the house, enclosed by a high metal fence. Clara took a device from her belt and used it to cut through the bars. I couldn't see what it was. When she'd cut through three in a row, enough for us to easily come and go through, she put away the tool and we both lingered beneath the shadowed canopy of the trees.

"This is Bravo Team, checking in. We're in position. Tech, are we secure?"

"We're secure," I heard Sammy's voice come over my headset in my dad's helmet. I wondered where she was from. Her accent sounded like maybe it was somewhere out West? *FOCUS!*

"I'm not picking up any tech activity inside at all. No electricity, no security system, at least not an electronic one. I don't pick up any other Techs, either. What about you, Thinker One? You getting any other

Thinkers, or a read on how many people we might be dealing with?" Sammy sounded like she'd done a hundred of these things. My heart, meanwhile, was beating in my chest like it was trying to run away for me, where my legs obviously weren't doing their job.

"That's a negative on the Thinkers," I heard Pat say. "So far, at least. Distance is still too great to determine number of individuals."

"Alpha Team, are you in position?" Clara broke in again.

"Affirmative. Awaiting your signal, Tinker One."

"Copy. Three, two, one, Mark! Move in, now!"

I heard and felt faintly several deep thwumps and recognized the effects of the Con-gun and saw several bright flashes.

Clara and I watched as several electric lanterns, flashlights, and even a few small flames—candles and lanterns, I assumed – lit in several of the windows throughout the house, then disappeared in the direction of the front.

"Let's move," Clara said to me. We left the trees and made our way to the expansive back face of the house.

This place was huge! Between how he was dressed and the size of this house, I guessed that Julian Danton was extremely well-off, which I had not expected. Before yesterday, I had pictured him as some tweaker, or an alcoholic roughneck. Neither his dress nor the house pointed to either of those being true. *I guess you can't judge a book by its cover.*

The back door was locked, but Clara took a small device from her belt, stuck in into the keyhole, and the knob soon turned. She repeated the process on the deadbolt, and soon moved through the open door. As I followed, she turned and handed me a small handgun. "Con-gun may be a little much, indoors. Use this tranq gun. Think paintball gun, but with a potent sedative that can be absorbed by the skin."

I took the gun, looked it over to become familiar with the safety features, and nodded, holstering the Con-gun on my hip.

We advanced through the house, clearing each room quietly as we worked our way upstairs.

Alpha Team outside gave periodic updates over the comms. It sounded like they had things well-in-hand.

One door had a faint bit of light coming from under it. Clara pointed at it and gestured for me to take up a position behind her, along the wall. She opened the door from the side of the frame, and several gunshots fired out the open entryway. Clara removed a small orb from a pouch on her belt and rolled it into the room, then clicked a small button on her glove. A jolt rocked my body when I thought she had detonated a bomb in the room. Instead, I heard a high thrum, then a yell and a few sharp cracks.

Clara burst into the room, and I followed closely, my knees nearly giving out beneath me. Two men stood staring dumbly at their handguns, both of which had a bright yellow goop coming from the barrels and several fractures along the length of them. Before they could even react, Clara took down both men with a single shot apiece from her rifle. They each sprouted a single, blinking syringe dart and fell to the floor, unconscious.

Suddenly, Clara dropped the rifle and her hands fought at her helmet, clawing at the release. It barely cleared her mouth before she spewed vomit on the floor, crumbling to her hands and knees and gagging, retching repeatedly, her breathing diminishing to short little pops of sucking. I took off my helmet and knelt beside her. There was nothing I could do for her.

I turned to look toward the far end of the room. Julian Danton sat in a large leather armchair, one leg casually crossed over the other and one hand lazily lifted up from the arm of the chair, palm pointing toward Clara and me. In a corner of the room, behind Danton's chair, I could see the heads of the four children huddled together and shaking.

"Interesting. Why aren't you a putrid mess of regurgitation like your lady friend, there? And aren't you the young man I told Barnes to shoot yesterday? You came back for the children, didn't you?" He glanced behind him at the children, who were huddled together, trying to disappear into the corner. "James, isn't it? They told me about you, you know." He adjusted himself in the chair, sitting up straighter. "They said you were kind, patient." He scoffed. "In other words, weak. The only reason I haven't already killed you with a different strain of virus is so I can enjoy the look on your face when you realize that you've lost

them again. You looked so pathetically broken yesterday. I look forward to seeing the hope leave your eyes
as one of my viruses boils your insides and leaves you
a simpering vegetable."

His eyes narrowed, and he waved his hand several
times in front of him. His eyes narrowed even further
to barely slits. His hand waved faster, and then his
eyes bulged as his teeth ground together. He leapt to
his feet, yelling, "Why won't you die?!"

My mouth had gone dry as he'd waved his hands,
trying his very best to kill me. I silently blessed my
father's ingenuity housed on my wrist. There were a
thousand things I wanted to say, a million more I
wanted to do to this man who'd ordered my parents'
death, who'd spent years mistreating his own children. The darkness within me shouted, *Blast him to
pieces! Make him suffer! Use the Con-Gun to liquify his
insides!*

I had put the tranquilizer gun on my hip and had
every intention of drawing the Con-Gun, when my
eyes darted for a moment to the figures huddled in the
corner. My eyes connected with Jessica's, which were
staring from their sockets as she buried Mary's head
in her stomach. I glimpsed Steven standing in front of
his sisters, pushing them further into the corner, his
body faced outward, putting himself between them
and danger, but his feet constantly pushing back, trying to get away himself. I could only just see Elizabeth,
standing blank and pale behind her brother, eyes not

focused on anything, her faithful teddy bear clutched tightly at her throat.

I saw those kids, and my own pain stilled in my head. My own gut turned hard with resolve, and I released my grip on the Con-Gun.

"You're a sick man, Danton." I fired three shots in quick succession. One hit the chair back, one spattered on Danton's shoulder, and the last connected directly with his neck, blue liquid blossoming up his throat.

"What is this garbage?!" He put two fingers to his neck and brought them up to his eyes, which by that time had rolled back in his head, and he lapsed into unconsciousness.

My arms shaking, I turned back to check on Clara. She was burning up and shivering uncontrollably, lying on the floor in her own vomit.

"Jessica, Steven, bring the other two and let's go! We've gotta' get outta' here!" I shouted.

I put my helmet back on and rolled Clara onto her back, then pulled her into a sitting position and leveraged her onto my shoulders in a fireman's carry. "Jessica, Steven, help me stand up!" With the two older kids' help, I was able to get my legs underneath me. I wouldn't be running anywhere, but I could move, for now.

"We need to leave," I panted. "Take us to the backyard. Shortest route. Hurry!" Jessica nodded and bent down to help Mary onto her back, and Steven took Elizabeth's hand.

We had gotten to the top of a staircase and were about to head down when another door opened, and a woman stepped out into the hallway. I knew who she was as soon as she turned toward us. She looked exactly like Jessica.

The children's mother looked first at the children then at me, face hidden again beneath my helmet and carrying Clara. Lastly, she glanced at the crook of my elbow, which Elizabeth had reached up to hang a hand in protectively.

The woman didn't say anything for a moment, then she said simply, "James?" All of us nodded, the children smiling largely. She walked directly to me, held the candle close to my helmet, and brought her face in close enough to touch the helmet's front. I could smell her perfume, subtle and flowery.

"Save my children, James. Don't ever let him hurt them again." I could see a bruise on her cheek and a fat, split lip. She had whispered the words, but I felt like she'd yelled them at me. "Help them live a happy, full life, one where they can forget all of this."

I nodded again, not knowing what else to say. Then she kissed each child on the forehead and gave them all hugs. She looked behind us, at the room we'd come from, and started walking toward it, her pace getting quicker with every step.

The children and I clambered down the stairs. Clara was beginning to breathe easier, but she was also beginning to weigh heavily on my back; my legs were shaking with every step now. I wasn't going to last much longer.

"James Strader."

I turned and saw Heretic standing in a doorway at the end of a hallway. "How the heck did you get in here?" I shouted at him. "And why now?" I stepped in front of the children, remembering what Pat and Clara had told me about Heretic.

"We have no time for your questions, James. Behind me is the door to the garage. In it, you will find a camper van. I have already destroyed or disabled everything in it that would allow a Technichim to track you. The keys are in it. Take it and go to the location on the map. There is no time for argument. Go now!"

Looking back upstairs, I could see a flickering glow and hear a growing roaring noise. The house was on fire! There was yelling from outside and the sound of running feet from somewhere else in the house.

"But Clara, she's so heavy," I said. "I can't."

"Give Clara to me. I'll see that no harm comes to her." Heretic approached me and easily transferred Clara to one of his shoulders. The sound of running feet grew louder, and there were more shouts, this time from inside the house.

"James, please, you've got to hurry! There's no more time to waste! Be strong!"

I stood there in shock as Heretic disappeared toward the back door. The kids pulled me in the direction of the garage, starting to scream at me.

I shook my head, unable to think. *Be strong.* Every muscle in my body went rigid and my breath caught in my throat. I picked up Elizabeth and ran through the door. The garage was dark. I fumbled with the helmet and found the switch to turn on the lights on the faceplate, illuminating the way forward. We filed past a Porsche, a Ferrari, and an old battered Toyota minivan before we got to the Mercedes Sprinter Van at the far end.

I hustled the children inside, moved aside the map on the driver's seat, got behind the wheel, and started the engine. Scrambling for a garage door opener, I couldn't find one anywhere. Finally, I reached to my hip, pulled the Concussive Cannon, lowered it out the window as I shifted out of Park, and blew the garage door from its tracks. As soon as it fell free, I gunned the engine, driving past several bodies, whether dead or unconscious, I couldn't tell. Several coyotes and a veritable pack of large dogs scampered out of the path of the van as it hurtled down the driveway. Over the comms in the helmet, I could hear various voices asking if that had been one of ours in the van; were the children safe; were Clara and I clear of the house? Finally, Pat's voice came over the speakers.

"James? Where are you, man? I found Clara in the bushes outside the fence. She's fine, but she's still unconscious. What happened to her? Do you have the kids? Was that you in the van?"

All the voices blended together, a cacophony of verbal nonsense. All I could hear, replaying over and over in my head, was that digitized, altered voice, saying repeatedly, "James, be strong!"

Chapter 10

The rest of the night passed, not in hours, but in miles on the odometer for me. When we reached the border of the affected area, we passed through the checkpoint where they were making sure everyone had somewhere to go, providing information on several evacuation centers nearby. I made up some story about catching up to my aunt and uncle to take their kids to them. I'd already forgotten the details of the conversation with the National Guardsman who checked us through.

I had Steven open the map while Jessica got the younger two settled into sleep on the bed in the back of the van soon after we'd gotten on the freeway.

In the folds of the map was an envelope. Steven opened it and read the letter tucked inside.

> *Go to this location. You'll find a log building in the town. If I am not already there, ask for Carly and tell her you're a waif seeking refuge and rest. She'll take care of you.*
>
> *The charge card in the envelope is one of my own designs. I call it the Infinity. It's designed to be untraceable.*

Any charges you make will be directed to one of any number of billionaires and appear only as a minor bank charge. Even to the bank, it will be indistinguishable from one of their own internally generated transactions. Untraceable.

Also find enclosed five small pins. As soon as possible, attach one to each of you and wear it any time you travel into the public eye. To any camera that catches images of you, you will appear blurred and out of focus. Not entirely invisible, but close enough.

Never travel a straight line. Any stop you make for food, fuel, or rest, when you begin again, identify six possible next checkpoints and roll a die to determine where you will next stop. The priority is unpredictability. Time is immaterial, so long as you remain hidden from those who will pursue you. Backtrack, deviate. Be unpredictable. It is imperative that they not be able to predict where you will next arrive.

I will meet you there.

Heretic

The map was an area of northern California. I only

recognized it due to Mt. Shasta's designation in the upper right-hand corner. The rest of the map was small towns, forests, and wilderness areas I had otherwise never heard of. There was a small area circled within "Marble Mountain Wilderness area." That, I assumed, was our destination.

Steven pulled the other contents out of the envelope. Five small pins in the shape of a dark raven or a crow of some sort, a black credit card, and one small die.

Here we were, on the run. From Danton, from Safeguard, from everyone. I had fully intended to take the kids outside and join up with the rest of the team. So, why hadn't I? When Heretic appeared in the thick of things, I had no intention of trusting him. It wasn't until the absolute last moment, when he had said those words, those two words, that my resolve crumbled, and I decided on a new course in the breadth of a single moment.

It was not my mother under the hood and mask. I knew that. Not only was it simply impossible, given I had put my mom in the ground myself, but Heretic was shorter than Mom. So why use those words? Out of all the words in the entire English language, why end his warning with those very same two last words as the woman I'd known as my mother?

Steven and Jessica both fell asleep soon after passing through the checkpoint. I was left alone with my thoughts. They weren't helpful.

***

When morning came, I was exhausted. We found a rest area and stopped for an hour.

"I have to sleep for a bit. We can leave in an hour, but I need to sleep," I told Jessica and Steven. "Don't let Elizabeth or Mary wander off. If anyone asks about you, or even looks too long at you, wake me, 'kay?" Both children nodded.

I went to the rest stop bathroom, taking off my clothes so that I could remove both the metal plate armor and the liquid armor, then putting my clothes back on. Once I was back in the van and lying on the bed, I fell asleep instantly. I was in the middle of a dream where I was being pursued by wolves, when Jessica shook me awake.

"James, you've gotta' come, quick."

I startled awake, kicking loudly against the side of the van from my back on the mattress.

"What is it? What happened?"

Jessica said nothing but led me along to the bank of a small stream flowing at the edge of the rest area.

A woman in a long skirt and a wool jacket held Mary in her arms. Mary, covered in mud, was struggling hard and crying to be put down.

"Hey!" I called out. "Put her down."

The woman looked at me and disapproval wrinkled her nose. "Are these children with you?"

"They are," I said, and took Mary from her arms.

"Well, why weren't you watching them? I pulled

this one," she pointed at Mary, "from the mud. She was up to her knees and sinking fast. And not one of them with coats, and in their pajamas? They're all going to catch hypothermia!"

I tried to speak, but she talked over the top of my muttering.

"How old are you? They aren't yours, are they?" She took her phone out of her purse and unlocked it, looking for who knew what.

I decided to stick with what I remembered of the lie from last night at the checkpoint.

"No, they're my cousins. I've been driving all night and I was taking a nap so I wouldn't be overtired. I was staying with them at their house in southern Illinois while their parents were on a business trip. After everything that happened, we're trying to get to my mom's house in Michigan. Thank you so much for catching her." The lie came surprisingly easily.

The woman's face softened. "Oh, my word, y'all were there when all that craziness was goin' on? It's a miracle y'all are all right! Well, do ya' need anythin'? Y'all eaten today? I got some oranges and muffins in my car."

"No, Ma'am, I think we'll be fine, just gotta' get back on the road."

"No, young man, I won't take no for an answer. I bought way too many oranges, anyway. I'll never eat 'em all before I get home to Georgia. Y'all follow me, we'll get you all fixed up."

***

When we got back on the road again, it was with an orange and a muffin apiece, plus several Moon Pies and half a pecan pie. It turned out Betty was a good old-fashioned, true Southern 'gal. Breakfast wasn't quite as nutritious as oatmeal, but I noticed that not one of the kids complained.

It was time to explain to them what was happening and what would happen over the next several days.

"We're going on a road trip," I said, pulling out into traffic on the freeway.

"Wussa road-tip?" Mary asked from where she was laying on the bed at the back of the van.

"A road trip is where you drive a long way, but you go to a lot of fun places along the way," I explained. How else could I explain a multi-day escapade of being on the run from several pursuers to a three-year-old?

"Ooh. Like Dissy-Land?" she asked, sitting upright.

"Sure, one of those could be Disneyland, I guess. What about the rest of you? Any place you've always wanted to see, between here and California? That's where we've got to end up."

"We've never been to the beach," Jessica shyly suggested.

"Sure, we could do that. Probably a bit too cold already this year to go swimming or anything, but we could go see it and maybe play for a bit."

"Where's Burning Man?" I saw Steven's eyes light up from the front passenger's seat.

Shock made my eyes go wide. "What do you know about Burning Man?"

"Nothing, it just sounds really cool. Is it like a circus show?"

"Yeah, but not the kind you're probably thinking of. How about Death Valley?" I suggested.

"What? That's a real place? Even cooler." Steven fist-pumped his approval.

"All right," I sang. "So far, California is our destination of choice all around. Elizabeth, do you have any other requests?" I found her face in the rearview mirror and we locked eyes.

She held my gaze in silence for several seconds, then asked quietly, "James, why'd you give us back?"

All of the air went out of my lungs in a low moan. I signaled and pulled over onto the shoulder, braking the van to a rocking stop. I flicked on the hazards and turned around in the driver's seat.

The passing traffic was the only sound, and the van rocked slightly each time a semi with a trailer passed by.

"Is that what you all think? That I gave you back to your dad?"

The three older kids all nodded slowly in agreement. Mary, seeing and feeling that something was off, laid her head on Jessica's shoulder and patted her arm.

I gestured to Steven to come and sit back with his sisters on the bed, then moved to where I could sit cross-legged on the floor in front of them.

"First of all, I am so sorry that it felt like that.

Taking you back to your dad was the absolute last thing I wanted to do that day. I was going to take you to people who know how to take care of kids who have been through what you guys have; it's their job."

"But you were doing a good job taking care of us," Elizabeth spoke up. "And it wasn't even your job."

"That's really kind of you to say," I attempted to smile at Elizabeth.

"So, is that where we're going in California? To someplace where they know how to take care of kids like us?" I could hear the hurt behind Jessica's words.

"I—I don't know, honestly. I came back for you because I couldn't stand the thought of you going back to living with your dad. You were right, Jessica; he's not a good person. I care about you guys; I care what happens to you, and I don't want you to be unhappy. And after what your mom said to me, I can't sit around and do nothing. So, for now, I guess you guys are sort of stuck with me. Is that gonna' be okay?" I tried to be as open and honest with them as I could, considering their ages.

I locked eyes with them, one by one. I started with Jessica, who nodded seriously. Steven nodded once and held up his thumb. Elizabeth sat with her hands clasped together in her lap around her teddy bear and bobbed her head up and down several times with a shy smile. Mary walked over to me and clasped me around the neck, then pulled back and asked, "We going to Dissy-Land?" I squeezed one of her pudgy little hands and said, "Yes, All the way to Dissy-Land."

***

The first thing we had to take care of was clothes. Nobody, including me, had any extras. The kids were still in their pajamas.

If we were going to be living out of the camper van for a long time, I wanted them to have good, warm clothes. Knowing that we would now most likely have both Safeguard and Danton and whatever Mythic followers he had on our tail, I didn't think staying in hotels or even in towns, where there were so many cameras, was a good idea. We were going to be spending a lot of time in the middle of nowhere, outside, when we weren't driving.

I knew there was an outdoor recreation superstore in St. Louis, having been there before. Without any kind of phone or navigation system, we were pretty much limited to places I personally knew, locations on the map, and roadside information signs. So, simply because there was no reason why not, I took the next interchange southwest for St. Louis.

Leaving the kids in the van, I went inside and bought us each a couple of changes of clothes, along with some good cold-weather layers, jackets and shells, shoes, even a pair of long underwear each. I bought a candy bar first to see if there would be any issue with the card Heretic had given me.

When the clerk swiped the card the second time, she said, "I've never seen a card like this."

I started lying again. "Probably won't ever again, either. My employer's a huge oil tycoon. The family's loaded. I'm their manny; I'm taking their kids out to Aspen to learn how to ski this winter.

"Oh, awesome! That's gotta' be the sweetest gig ever! So, you get paid to take them places?" She was envious.

"Yeah, pretty much," I lied. I wanted her to hurry. I'd realized that I'd forgotten to wear one of Heretic's pins, and the kids were still alone in the car.

"That's so cool. Well, have fun in Aspen!" she grinned.

"Oh, for sure," I said, gathering the clothing, shoes, other gear and odds and ends I'd decided on.

When I got back to the car, Mary was screaming and everyone else started talking all at once. I sighed. This was the new, new normal. We topped off with gas, then headed back on the freeway. I'd picked up a US road atlas at the store, and we'd rolled a six on the die. It was official: we were headed for California, aimed at Iowa, and Lady Luck was our navigator. All things considered; this wasn't the craziest thing I'd done this week.

Chapter 11

If taking care of four kids at home on several acres was challenging, taking care of four kids in a van on the road was insanity.

I learned a few things really fast, really painfully. Snacks were not simply a luxury. Neither were stretch breaks, meal stops, or naps for Mary. Luckily, the van had a small bathroom in it, or potty breaks would have been the biggest issue of them all. With four kids, it seemed like someone was always in the bathroom.

I realized it was a good thing we didn't need to hurry to get to where we were heading, because we were going nowhere fast.

I thought the first night would be a real challenge, with everyone sharing such a small space. I was shocked when the kids negotiated sharing a single full-size bed with efficiency and familiarity. This wasn't something new to them. That left me on the bed that converted from both front seats, a small couch, and a table surface that Transformer-ed into a single uniform sleeping surface.

That first night, we parked the van on a wide shoulder of an obscure stretch of frontage road, only a few miles from nowhere. We repeated this pattern every night thereafter, too.

Aside from that first night, I refused to drive while all of the kids slept. Without the constant need to referee fights, answer questions, and dictate whose turn it was to use the bathroom, there was too much time and silence in which to think.

The revelation of my being adopted, coupled with how little I truly knew about my parents was too much. I refused to give myself room to dwell on it. That was easy to do during the day. Night was a bit more difficult. On one of our first grocery runs, I bought a bottle of "sleep-aid" liquid to help me get to sleep faster. It was getting harder and harder to get to sleep each night.

The heavier I focused on the kids, the less time and energy I had available to spend on myself. Meanwhile, the black in my chest had started growing again. Now it felt like I had a full core of black, an oozing feeling of darkness and doubt. I could feel it swell every day. Moment by moment, it grew.

"Why are the signs different colors, again?" Elizabeth asked for the third time.

"The color tells you what kind of information or services the sign has on it." I snapped that time.

I began to picture myself as skin and muscle stretched over a balloon person filled with dark sludge that kept swelling and swelling. The smallest frustrations and irritations, things that even last week I'd been able to talk through with seemingly infinite patience, felt irksome, tedious, and insufferable now. Each draw on patience that was already running thin pushed me ever closer to bursting, exploding again, like pins pushed through, agitating and releasing foul little streams of black. I began to wonder about the wisdom of my choice in taking the children. I began to think often that I should have let them be taken by Safeguard. How long before their innocent pokes and prods caused me to simply rupture, spewing my black sludge and doing or saying something that I couldn't make right again?

There were several other things we had to figure out as we went, like the waste dumping, water resupplying, and fuel restocking for the stove/oven in the van. Talking to a few different people at rest stops in similar setups, I was able to pick up pretty quickly where to go, facilities to look for, and tricks and tips to follow.

The die became an interesting part of our day. "Whose turn is it to roll? I asked as we pulled off the exit to stretch our legs and buy some groceries. Breakfasts and lunches we prepared in the van. Dinner we stopped somewhere for.

"Mine!" Elizabeth shouted. She walked to the front of the van, and Steven pointed out the city we were approaching to her. With her fingers, she traced the main roads and highways branching out from the city on the atlas. Each time she stopped, pointing at one specifically, Steven would write it down in a small notebook. They repeated this wordless exchange six times, then Elizabeth kissed the die in her hand and rolled.

"Yes! Six!" she shouted.

I chuckled slightly. "You must really like that highway."

"Nope, I just like six. That's how old I am." She returned to the back of the van.

This made five days we'd been on the road, and the routines by then were familiar and comforting. I noticed that each day brought more and more lowering of defenses and guards from the kids. Jessica spent what felt like hours each day simply telling stories out loud to Mary, who ate up each word with a fork and spoon. Elizabeth spent a good deal of time looking out one of the windows, asking questions about anything she saw that she didn't understand. Even Steven had mellowed considerably, even smiling on occasion, especially when it was his choice to choose what to eat for whichever meal was his to choose that day.

I had been dubious when Steven had initially read Heretic's letter explaining how we were to proceed to California. I was convinced we would never get there. But we were making good time, all things considered.

Desperate to avoid thinking about the thoughts that plagued me day and night about my parents, about who that left me to be, I decided it was time to bring something up with the kids I'd staunchly avoided thus far. "So..." I found I didn't know quite how to begin.

Steven looked at me. "What?"

"Can you guys really," I had to word this carefully, "control things?"

The van filled with silence. I found a city park and a spot to park the van. Turning around in the seat, I looked at the kids. Steven, sitting in shotgun, was furiously distracted by the seam of the leather on his seat, frowning. The three girls sat together on the edge of the bed. Jessica was busily scooting backward, as far as she could, while Elizabeth stared solidly at the floor. Mary, on the other hand, stared at me, eager and grinning as she bobbed up and down.

"It's okay, you're not in trouble or anything. I'm just curious," I assured them.

"He made us do really bad things," Jessica whispered from near the back doors.

"We don't like hurting people. He hurt us when we didn't listen," Elizabeth said.

"He said he wouldn't hurt the girls if I did what he said. But he lied!" Steven hissed without looking at me.

"I don't blame any of you for what your dad made you do. None of that was your fault. You know that, right?" I spent time looking at each one of them until we'd each locked eyes for a moment or two.

I gave a tired smile. "So, what can you do? Who controls what? Can I guess?"

Small smiles started on each worried face. They all nodded.

"Jessica... you control the wind? Or air? Am I right?" Jessica started scooting slowly forward again. She nodded.

"Okay. Steven," I turned to face him. "I'm guessing

you're the one who has something to do with fire? Yeah?"

Steven quickly nodded a few times, looking shy for the first time since I'd met them.

"Elizabeth, you're really fond of water, am I right?" Elizabeth nodded eagerly.

"And Mary—,"

"I yub dewt!" Mary yelled, raising her fists as if in triumph.

I managed to produce a laugh, but it felt hollow. "You do love dirt. Wow. Okay. I've gotta' see it, now. Can I see it? Not here, obviously, but after we've stretched for a bit and finished our shopping?"

All four children nodded.

"Cool."

***

I rushed them through playing at the park for a bit and then shopping for the next day's groceries. I truly wanted to see it all in action. *How did it work?*

After we filled up with gas, we drove several miles down the highway Elizabeth had rolled on the die. We were miles from any significant town. We stopped near a stand of trees and a small stream. I was suddenly nervous.

As the children pulled on coats, I climbed out of the van and walked to the passenger side.

"How shall we do this?" I asked as they all climbed out. "I don't know how any of this works."

Jessica was about to speak up, when Mary sat down on the dirt and said, "Dames, wash!"

She proceeded to sink up to her waist in what had been solid ground. She plunged a hand into the soil and closed her eyes, frowning in concentration. I watched, wide-eyed, as she reached and moved around *in* the ground, as if it were no more solid than water. Finally, she drew her hand up, holding aloft a smooth stone, free of dirt. "Ta-da!" She stood up, stepped up out of the ground, and placed the stone into my hand as if she were bestowing on me the largest and rarest of gems.

I accepted it, noting with not a little surprise that Mary had not a single speck of dirt on her clothing or hands. Unbelievable.

"Thank you." I accepted the rock with a great show of gratitude and seriousness. Mary nodded serenely. The effect was comical.

"My turn," Elizabeth giggled. She took a few steps toward the stream, carefully set her teddy bear down on a rock, and bent down. I watched, fascinated, as a small trickle of water diverted from the stream, ran *uphill* toward Elizabeth, and pooled rapidly into the cupped hand she held to the ground. The pool quickly became a mound, which grew into a ball. Eventually, and entirely in defiance of physics, Elizabeth held a sphere of water in her hands. She brought it to me and set it gently on top of the rock in my hands. The water engulfed the rock but sat congealed and swirling slightly in my palms. An instant later, it splashed down out of my hands, as normal water would, then collected as a unit once again on the ground before it ran down the hill to rejoin the stream.

My eyes were wide. I had no words.

"I got next," Steven said, pretending to crack his knuckles. He picked up a thick branch from the ground and broke off the smaller twigs and shoots from the limb. He walked to the edge of the stream and held the branch underwater, making a great show of turning it, pushing it down and up in the water, making sure it was truly good and wet.

He brought it back to me, dripping wet, and put it in my hands. I pasted a questioning smile. Steven held up a single finger and smiled his own knowing grin.

The stick in my hands started to hiss, and I watched in amazement as steam emanated from up and down the stick as it grew warm. The end opposite of where I was holding started to glow, heat radiating from the inside out, and then small licks of flame appeared, licking the now-dry wood. The branch burst into brilliant flame, all along its length, except where I was holding it. I dropped it in panic. The flames disappeared, leaving the limb blackened and charred, but not even smoking. Steven picked it up and handed it back to me. It wasn't even hot. He grinned. I stared back in utter disbelief.

Jessica took a step toward the road, looking out over the empty, harvested field across from us. She simply stood there, when suddenly I saw husks, leaves, and debris from the field begin gathering into a circle, blowing across the ground. I watched in equal parts fascination and terror as a cyclone of vegetation, refuse, and dirt rose dozens of feet into the air, blowing toward us. It grew larger as it came, the circle growing wider and wider, until, as it crossed the road, it suddenly died, all the refuse showering down on us dully with only a small puff of breeze.

Jessica and the other three laughed as the leaves, husks, and dirt showered down over us all. It was good to see them so carefree and happy. It pained me that I couldn't share that joy. It felt like my heart was shrouded within the new darkness inside me, and not even these children, so pure and joyful and sincere, could break through it. Desperate not to put them off, I gathered a handful of debris and tossed it at the kids, forcing a laugh. For the next several minutes, we exchanged laughs, my counterfeit for their priceless giggles, throwing leaves and other debris and chasing each other around the van.

Later that evening, after we'd changed direction one more time, eaten dinner, then driven out into the country and fields, Jessica, Steven, and I sat in the front seats and the small sofa, Mary and Elizabeth already asleep in the bed.

"How does it work?" I asked quietly. "How on earth do you control the wind? Or fire?" I looked from face to face.

Jessica and Steven simultaneously shrugged, looking at each other.

"I ask the wind to do something, and it does,"

Jessica hesitated. "I can hear it all around, even when it's not blowing. Not *hear it*, hear it, like with my ears, but that's the only way I can describe it."

"Same here, only I feel the heat of things. Even when they aren't hot on my hands, I can feel the heat inside. Then, I ask it to come out. And it does," Steven added.

"Have you always been able to do it?" I asked.

"No." Jessica shook her head. "It wasn't until the last year or so. And it wasn't that easy at first. It took us all a bunch of months of practicing to do things like what we did today."

"Yeah, and Mary was really scary at first. Sometimes she'd cause these little earthquakes, or the ground would explode," Steven whispered.

"Huh." I thought for a moment. "And what about... Your dad? Has he always made other people sick?"

"No. That wasn't until after we'd discovered ours," Jessica shook her head. "There was one day we'd all been playing together with our special skills in the backyard, and Dad started screaming inside the house. He got real sick, with big nasty boils and blisters and sores all over him." She whispered, "We thought he was going to die, he was so sick. It lasted for weeks. Then, one day, he wasn't sick anymore. And he was worse, so much worse."

I didn't need to ask how he was much worse. Jessica had shivered as she'd said that. I could guess.

"And then that Caine guy showed up," Steven said.

Caine? I hadn't heard of a Caine yet, I wondered if

he was a personal associate of Danton's, or if he was somehow connected to Safeguard.

"Ooh, I forgot about him. Yeah, Dad went away for a few weeks after that. But when he got home, he was really mad about something, and it was right after that..."

"That *he* did all those things," I finished.

They both nodded.

"Huh." They'd confirmed what Heretic had told me about Elementals and Aberrations if nothing else. "Well, that was one of the coolest things I've ever seen, you guys. Way cooler than any magic shows I've ever seen."

"I know, right?" Steven gushed. "We should have our own YouTube channel. Or a streaming show, or something! Or we could even be superheroes!"

"Sssh!" His voice kept rising with every new idea he tossed out. I smiled thinly. "Maybe tonight, we get some sleep, huh?'

The two older Danton children nodded. They muttered quiet good nights, then jostled their way gently into the bed next to the younger two sleeping children. Suddenly Steven sat back up, wriggling his way back to the edge and off the bed. Walking right up to me, he said, "Um, James, I wanted to say thank you. For my sisters. I know they really like you, and they were really glad when you came back for us. So, you know, thanks for that. For them."

I should have been brimming with satisfaction and

pride. Instead, I felt nothing; it sickened me. "Well, tell your sisters that they're welcome."

Steven smiled briefly, then crept back to the bed. I followed him and pulled closed the large privacy curtain that enclosed the bed area.

I returned to my portion of the van and, after converting the seats and couch back into a bed, removed the liquid armor I was still wearing daily, sipped briefly from the sleep-aid bottle, and laid restless and still until I fell asleep.

Chapter 12

So far, on our little trip, Lady Luck had taken us on a solidly northern trek across several states, nearly to Canada on several occasions. I was starting to worry, though, about winter storms. I didn't know exactly when they started becoming a problem for travel, but I knew that I didn't want to be caught in one.

"Guys, we need to start making our way more south. I think we need to be out of these really northern states before we get bogged down by any serious winter storms. I want you to start loading your choices with more southern routes."

"Okay," Jessica spoke for all of them. "Hey, we've been talking, and we've been driving straight for a really long time. Can we have a rest day? What if we took one day in town, to play at a park for a while, then went to a movie or something?"

I thought about it. We'd been on the move constantly for days, now. And we'd been following Heretic's directions to the letter. Surely, we'd earned ourselves a momentary reprieve.

"Sure," I said. "What could one afternoon hurt?" We pulled into a small city in North Dakota around noon.

"All right, it's totally your call. We can do whatever you guys want for the afternoon."

"Yes!" Steven shouted. "Do you think they have a comic book store?"

"I'm sure they have something like that. What about the rest of you? What do you want to do?" I asked them.

"I wanna' go to McDonald's!" Elizabeth called from the bed. "I want a Happy Meal with a toy!"

"I wanna' toy!" Mary jumped on the McDonald's bandwagon.

I smiled sadly. I could remember when a Happy Meal at McDonald's with my parents was the most exciting thing I could think of, too.

"Sounds good. Jessica, you vote for a movie?"

Jessica nodded.

"All right; sounds like a pretty full day to me. We'll eat lunch at a park, play for a few hours, find a comic store or bookstore or something like that, head for dinner at a McDonald's, and end the night with a movie. Sound like a plan?"

"Yeah!" All four shouted in agreement

"Great. We need gas, but I'll get that on our way out of town tonight after the movie. Let's find ourselves a park!" I attempted a cheer that felt like it fell flat on its face.

It was a day we all needed. We all decompressed quite a bit after riding together on the road for so long. Even though it was cold, barely above freezing, we played tag and lava monster at the park for hours before we all finally called it quits. We found a fun little bookstore a few blocks away and spent a good two hours reading and browsing. Mary fell asleep on my chest while I was reading her a book of princess fairy tales. I kept thinking about what Roger Caplan had said and imagined how a Mythic could have inspired the original tale.

When we finished at the bookstore—really, when Mary woke up—we went to find a McDonald's. We found one with a Play Place and went inside.

"All right, I know what Mary and Elizabeth want. Jessica? Steven? What do you guys want?"

Jessica and Steven both started talking, but at that point, I was no longer listening.

Three men had walked into the McDonald's. There was nothing overtly out-of-place about them. They were dressed casually, nothing remarkable in boots, t-shirts, jeans, and jackets. It was something about the fact that they walked in obviously together, but not looking at or talking to one another at all.

"Sorry, say that again?" I asked Jessica and Steven. I listened but paid a lot of attention to the men in my periphery.

I still had the small tranq gun Clara had given me at the Danton's. I'd taken to wearing it magnetically holstered on my belly beneath my coat and shirt. I couldn't exactly pull it out and start sedating people, though. That was a good way to attract all sorts of the kind of attention we didn't need.

I tried to think, had I seen any of these men on the road with Julian Danton? Were they his men, or were they with Safeguard? It was no good; aside from the one man who'd shot me, I couldn't remember any of Danton's men well enough to possibly recognize them.

"James?" I realized Steven and Jessica were both watching me, waiting for me to respond.

"Sorry," I apologized. "Go ahead and order." After Steven and Jessica put in their order and I ordered the younger girls' Happy Meals and whatever a "Number One" combo was, we walked into the Play Place area. If the men followed us in there, they were almost certainly after us. Again, why would three men with no children choose to put themselves where there would be four screaming, playing children unless they had a reason to be there?

The kids threw their shoes off in the direction of the cubby holes, then disappeared into the Play Place, Jessica giving Mary an assist when she needed it.

I situated myself at a table where I was hidden from the view of others inside the restaurant by the garbage bins and cabinets. I took off my coat and sat down at the table. Pulling out the tranq, I held it in my right hand, then draped my coat over that arm, hiding the gun as it pointed at the door. I crossed the other arm across my chest and settled in to wait. My heart was pounding again, like the night of our assault on the Danton house. It jumped up even higher when the door opened, and all three men walked in. As the first man turned to hold the door open for the others, I caught the unmistakable glimpse of a futuristic fire-arm grip protruding from under his shirt. Safeguard, then.

I had a moment's hesitation, when I wondered why I was running from Safeguard in the first place. They had helped me get the kids back from Danton, hadn't they? All argument in their favor went out the window when they all three turned and started to draw on me.

At that moment, four things happened in rapid succession. I fired several shots from my pistol as I drew the coat off my right arm. A few of them missed, but several found their marks. The air in the Play Place seemed to condense, then implode inward on the three men, blowing all three off their feet and out cold on the ground. All three of their jackets burst into flame. Water burst from a pipe in the ceiling and showered the three men, dousing the flames on their jackets.

I stared up at the Play Place, where all three of the older children pressed their faces against and had fingers clasping onto the rope netting. I motioned quickly for them to come down, gathering up their shoes.

I picked up Mary and we ran for the doors of the restaurant, ignoring the bewildered looks of the workers behind the counter. Several patrons stood up and walked toward the Playplace, one man shouting, "Hey, man, what happened in there?" His cry broke a dam, and I heard voices rising, and someone screamed. As the door closed behind us, I heard someone call for an ambulance. As we loaded into the van, I looked around the parking lot. There were three other cars, aside from ours. There was no way of knowing which belonged to the men.

"Jessica, I need you to blow the tires on the cars. Can you do that? Or Steven, set the tires on fire? Somebody, do something fast so that no one can follow us!"

There was a series of loud explosions as all the tires in the parking lot but ours exploded outward, then caught fire, the rubber quickly melting.

Several of the people from inside who had begun following us out screamed, pulling the door closed and ducking. I heard someone shout "Gun, gun, gun!" They thought someone was shooting at them. I couldn't think about it. *Let Safeguard sort it out.*

We accelerated out of the lot and careened onto the highway Jessica had chosen earlier as the one we would next take out of town.

"How did they find us?" I asked out loud. "Is everyone wearing their pin?"

Everyone nodded, holding out the small black bird pins in confirmation.

"Good. I guess the how at this point isn't nearly as important as the fact that we need to lose them again. Jessica, I want you to watch out the back window and tell me if you see any headlights that follow us out of town, okay?"

Jessica nodded and clambered to the back window.

She kept watch as we drove into the dark and the town slowly disappeared behind us.

Large, fat snowflakes started falling all around us, quickly sticking, then accumulating rapidly on the ground. We made it another thirty miles down the road before the snow became too slick and deep on the road for me to drive either comfortably or safely.

I then remembered that we hadn't gotten gas before leaving town as I'd planned. I'd been so focused on what was happening behind us, I hadn't noticed when the "Low Fuel" light came on in the dash display.

I pushed my head into my palms. "All right, the good news is, I don't think anyone's going to be able to follow us in this storm. The bad news is, we're now caught in a North Dakota winter storm, which I was really hoping to avoid. Jessica, is there anything you can do to help us out of this?"

"Me?" Jessica asked, sliding to the front of the bed again.

"Yeah, you can speak to the wind and ask it to calm down, right?" I encouraged her.

"Maybe. I don't know, I haven't asked anything that big since..."

"I know, it's a big ask. But we need some serious help here, or we're gonna' find ourselves in big trouble."

"I'll try," she hesitated. She came to the front of the van and looked out the windshield, up into the whipping flakes of the storm as it howled around us.

She frowned as she stared up, furrowing her brow in concentration. "I can't. I just—it's like I can't quite understand it, like it's speaking a different language than I'm used to, or something. I don't know how else to explain it."

I looked around for Elizabeth. "Elizabeth? There's a lot of water up there. Can you help us out?"

Elizabeth looked up from where she sat, huddled against the wall of the van, holding her knees up to her chest, her always-present teddy squished between them. She whipped her head back and forth.

"No, huh? Okay." Inside I was screaming. This was a North Dakota blizzard! We needed help if we were going to make it through this. But, looking at Elizabeth, I knew she was in no shape to be pushed. Her eyes were frightened, her contracted little body spoke volumes of fear and uncertainty.

"Then we ride this one out," I said. There was nothing else to do. I turned the car off and climbed into the back. "All right, nothing to do now but wait," I said. I pulled the extra blanket that I slept with from a cabinet and shepherded all four kids together to huddle underneath both blankets.

"Won't we freeze, without the heater?" Steven asked, concern written all over his face.

"I don't know how much fuel we have left. It was pretty much empty when we rolled into town. We'll use the heater every half hour or so for as long as the fuel lasts. I don't know how long that will be, but we'll be okay, I'm sure." I wasn't sure, but I didn't need them panicking, too.

"Dames, I'n hongy," Mary piped up.

"I think we might have some granola bars and some other things left from yesterday. Let me see." I rummaged around the couple of cabinets and the small refrigerator and came up with three granola bars, four apples, a couple of juice bottles, and a half-eaten bag of beef jerky. I'd eaten worse meals in college. I divided the spoils out as evenly as possible. We all ate in silence, listening to the wind howl outside the van. There were light skittering sounds every now and then as a gust of wind blew the sharp flakes sideways into the van.

Mary was the first to nod off to sleep beneath the blankets, followed by Steven and then Elizabeth. I watched Jessica fight sleep, then quietly succumb as the day caught up with her.

The oozing, writhing black at my center pulsed and swelled. Staring out the windshield was a dark reflection of my thoughts and feelings. Cold thoughts flashed and darted in chaos across the bitter, black backdrop of anxiety: how had they found us? How would we get out of this? We weren't on a main Interstate. It was an obscure county road. How long before we would be found? How long would the fuel last? How much colder would it get? How far was it to the next gas station? My fear of being alone with my thoughts raged in battle with my anxiety over the storm taking place outside the van. Eventually, I swigged some sleep-aid and prayed for oblivion.

I don't know when I'd fallen asleep, but when I

woke, I was shocked by the cold. My breath billowed in shimmery whirls.

The wind outside was still moaning and gusting the snow sideways. Out the windshield, the road was simply a smooth path where the snow wasn't marred by the mounds of snow-covered bushes and grass. It looked deep.

I crawled into the driver's seat and turned the ignition. The starter chugged, but the engine didn't turn over. I waited a minute or two, then tried again. Still nothing.

I turned around to look back and locked eyes with Steven. I gestured for him to join me in the front seats.

When he was situated, I whispered, "How cold is it under the blankets?"

Steven's teeth chattered despite having put on his jackets and shell. "Not as cold as out here."

I nodded in agreement. I pointed to the bag where we all kept all of our extra layers. I helped him into his, then shrugged into mine.

We sat looking out the windshield in silence for just a moment, then I asked, "Anything you can do to help?"

His eyes bulged. "You want me to start a fire in the van?" He sounded horrified.

I laughed slightly in spite of myself, shaking my head. "No. But I'm glad to know you think that's a bad idea. No, you said you can feel heat inside of things. I'm wondering if you can ask the heat to come out without catching fire. Do you think that's possible?"

He frowned, obviously thinking deeply. "I don't know. I've never done something that specific before. Usually, I'm like, 'Burn!'" He threw his hands out like a magician casting a spell, to emphasize his point. "Plus, metal's weird. It's almost like it's sleeping, ya' know? You know how, when you talk to someone who's almost asleep, but they sort of answer back? Metal's like that. Foggy. Tired, almost."

"But can you try?" I pressed.

"I don't know. What if I do, and everything catches on fire? We'll be cooked alive!" He looked appropriately horrified.

"Well, then, don't let it. If you can't, we're gonna' freeze. It's too cold out there. I can't start the car, and we have no other options at this point. Can you try?" I pushed a little more. "But if you need a minute, that's okay. I know it's probably a hard thing I'm asking."

He nodded, and took a few deep breaths, staring out the window. After a minute, he turned back to me, and nodded. He was in.

"Okay. Let's start with something small that we can put out if it catches fire, okay?" I looked for something that fit the bill. I removed the key in the ignition from the keychain and held the fob out to him. It was a heavy metal circle with the letters "JD" engraved into it. "Try this."

He took it from me and held it flat in his palm. He looked at it for a solid minute, turning it one way and then another. He brought it right up close to his eyes, and I watched as it suddenly glowed a deep cherry red, then quickly went lighter and lighter until it abruptly burst into flame. I found myself yelling and swatted his hand instinctively, batting the metal piece to the floor of the van. I used the tranq gun to slide it to the door, which I opened, and flicked the fob into the snow, which sizzled and steamed as the keychain landed then disappeared beneath the powder.

I carefully reached for Steven's wrist, afraid of the horrific burn I expected to find. His palm was un-believably fine.

"What...?" I couldn't finish.

"Well, no, it didn't burn me," Steven shrugged. Like it was a given.

"Why not?" I wanted to know.

"'Cause I asked it not to," Steven said. His face said, "Duh!"

"Of course you did. Of course you can do that," I laughed, completely hysterical by this point. "Okay, let's try it again, can we?" I crept to the stove in the van and pulled out a small baking sheet. "On here, this time, for my sake." I handed Steven the sheet, then hung out the open door, shoving my arm into the snow after the fob. I was in up to my forearm before my fingers touched fob and asphalt.

I pulled myself upright and brushed as much snow off my arm as I could before closing the door. It was noticeably colder inside now. I looked back and saw all three girls staring at me from the wad of blankets.

"Sorry for yelling," I said. "We're trying to figure something out."

166 ~ JUSTIN K. NUCKLES

I placed the fob on the baking sheet. "Again?" I asked Steven.

He nodded and again stared at the fob. This time, when I could see a hint of red glow on the fob, Steven squinted harder, and the color faded. Finally, he sat upright, a satisfied smile on his lips. "How's that?" he asked.

I tentatively held out a single finger and held it close to the fob. I could feel heat, but how much? I quickly tapped the fob lightly. No pain. I rested one finger on it fully. The fob was warm. Warm, but not painfully or even uncomfortably so. I picked it up and held it fully in my fist. My hand, cold from the snow, felt much better.

"That's amazing," I gushed. "What else can we do it with?" I looked around for more odds and ends.

"I bet I could do it with the whole van," Steven said.

I stopped looking. "Are you sure? What if it went super-heated, like the fob the first time?" I was nervous. I felt justified.

"No, it'll be fine. I know what to ask, now," Steven said simply.

"Do it one more time on a smaller scale, for me," I said.

Steven rolled his eyes but complied. He held up the baking sheet, and it wasn't but a moment before he handed it to me. It was pleasantly warm. I unzipped my layers and hugged it to my chest, and warmth seeped into me. I sighed involuntarily.

"That's really nice." I handed it back to him. "You're sure you can safely do the entire car?"

"Yeah, yeah, watch." Steven grinned. He put a hand on the door panel and closed his eyes. I did the same. In a few moments, I could feel the metal start to heat beneath my fingers. Another several minutes later, the temperature in the car had risen considerably, and it was much more tolerable.

"Is that hard to maintain?" I asked. "Can you hold it like that for long?"

"No, it's not hard," Steven grinned. "I ask it to do something, and it does it until I ask it to stop."

I didn't understand any of this. Reason and logic were out the window. So long as the heat stayed inside the window, I didn't particularly care. "All right, I think that's probably good for now. Let's go back to sleep and figure everything else out in the morning, okay?"

Everybody got situated again, and it wasn't long until all four of them were again breathing deeply and evenly, their breaths contrasting with the irregular howling of the wind. Another chug from the bottle and I was hot on their heels.

***

When I woke up in the morning, the sun was shining brilliantly through the rear windows, basking the kids' legs in white light.

I rubbed the sleep from my eyes, wishing I had one of Pat's brain-slaps handy.

The temperature in the van wasn't bad. In fact, with the warming sun coming up, it was starting to get downright uncomfortable. I touched a piece of the metal of the van, and it was just as warm as it had been last night. It was extraordinary. And totally in defiance of the small understanding I had of physics. Maybe there was some obscure physical law or property rationally at work here, but, as far as I was concerned, it was nothing short of a miracle. Or magic. Or witchcraft. Boy, I was tired.

I took a more focused look out the windshield of the van. The level of the snow seemed a foot or two below the hood of the van; it was hard to estimate in the brilliant white, but I estimated maybe two feet of snow. Even if the day was warm, that amount wasn't going to melt away any time soon. I wondered if this stretch of road was even plowed regularly during the winter. It had felt remote last night as we'd driven out this direction, and it still looked it this morning.

The dark anxiety and swelling in my chest ebbed its way in earlier than usual this morning. If Safeguard was after us, and closely, they must have someone more local who might either have or know someone with a plow that attached to a truck. If they could possibly be moving while we were stuck, we were going to have a problem. Fortunately, I had several potential secret weapons on my side.

As soon as the kids were up, we finished the left-overs of our makeshift meal last night, and I began problem-solving with them.

"So, the snow stuck quite a bit last night, as you can see, but we need to get moving. What are our options, guys? What can you do for me?"

I looked at Elizabeth. "Elizabeth, that's a lot of water out there. It's cold, but it's water, and it's in our way. Can you ask it to move?"

Elizabeth pursed her lips and put her hands on her narrow little hips. I knew that look; I'd seen my mom —adopted mom, the blackness reminded me— wear that look hundreds of times. That was the look of a woman who was about to have her way, come Hell or high water. We had the high water. The only question was how much Hell she was about to give it.

She walked to the side door of the van and heaved it open. We all shivered as the heat of the van rushed out and the temperature plummeted an easy dozen degrees. Elizabeth picked up a heaping handful of snow and hefted it, as if testing its weight. The snow turned to water in her fingers and dropped to the ground. Elizabeth then wrestled the door closed and marched to the front of the van, where she leaned against the dashboard. A moment later, I could think only of the story of Moses as the snow directly in front of the van parted, curling perfectly away toward the sides of the road in crunchy cresting waves. About twenty feet from the front of the van, the waves faded away, leaving the road glistening but free of obstacle. Elizabeth turned to us and, with a satisfied smile, gave a thumbs-up.

"That takes care of that!" I shouted. "Nice work, Bethy!" Her smile widened. "That leaves us with..." I got behind the wheel and turned the key. Like last night, the starter whirred, but the engine stuck. "Steven, any chance you can give us a general, all-over flame-free engine warming? On the off-chance that it's the cold?"

Steven nodded, then closed his eyes and I saw his hands extend out some at his sides. He stood in silence for several seconds, then his hands laid flat, and he opened his eyes. "Try that."

I turned the key once more. The starter whirred, the engine heaved, churning and churning, then finally caught, turning over and purring to life. The gauges all maxed out and the indicator lights flashed as the system came on, then the fuel gauge plummeted to below Empty and the light stayed lit.

"Well, everybody strap in. I don't know how far we'll make it on this tank, so we gotta' make good use of what we have. Bethy, you're riding shotgun this morning: keep us dry and rolling, Little Moses Plow!" I laughed. The black in my chest shrank somewhat.

Elizabeth smiled again as she took her seat. The snow started curling back again in front of us, and I sent us rolling, gaining speed as the Moses effect surged off ahead of us.

We made it about fifteen minutes down the highway before the engine sputtered, then stalled and died. We'd run out of fuel. I pumped the brakes to stop us and wrestled the steering wheel to take us to the shoulder.

Out of habit, I put the van in park and turned back the key. I sighed heavily. It was getting hard to breathe, and my head was swimming with the pressure I felt from the bursting black inside me.

"Let's see the map," I said. I was curious about roughly how far we might have to go before our next fuel opportunity. I checked where I thought we might be, based on the most recent crossroad we'd passed.

I sighed again. "We've got probably twenty or thirty miles to gas, I'm betting," I said.

"Twenty miles? That's a long way to go on foot!" Steven exclaimed. "How are we gonna' get there?"

"Not we, me. And I'm gonna' hoof it on my good old 'Chevro-legs'," I said bitterly.

"You'd think the people out here would have their own gas or something," Jessica piped up. "It's so far in between stations."

I looked at her. "That's a really good point. We don't have to make it to a gas station; we only need to get to the next farmhouse! I bet they'll have some gas. You're a genius, Jessica!"

Jessica smiled.

I looked around. "Okay, you guys sit tight in the van, and I'll take off for the nearest house. The sooner I leave, the sooner I can be back." I didn't see any other way of making this work.

"Dames, I'na come wif you," Mary said, wrestling with her coat.

"No, Mary, you can't come. It's safer, and I'll be faster, if you stay here." It was the truth. It was brutal. It was the absolute wrong thing to say.

"NOOOO!" Mary burst into tears and screamed, furiously pulling at her coat and trying to get the side door open, proving to me that she was going with me.

I gave up. I couldn't leave Jessica and Steven to try and manage that. What if Mary managed to get out and really tried to follow me? Leaving was apparently a no-go.

"Okay, Mary, I'm not going anywhere." Therefore, none of us were.

We sat in silence for a minute, then I spoke up again. "Jessica, how strong and focused of a wind do you think you could get for us?"

Jessica blinked at me. "I think I had the same idea. Were you thinking I could have the wind push the van?"

"That's exactly what I was thinking," I nodded.

Jessica bit her lip. "I can try."

"Do it," I countered. What an interesting day this was turning out to be.

Thirty minutes later we were clipping along at about twenty-five miles per hour, which was as fast as I was willing to travel without power steering or braking. Jessica rode at the back of the van, focusing out the back window as a pin-pointed, jet-stream of a wind rocked against the rear doors of the van, while

Elizabeth rode shotgun, Moses-clearing the snow from the road ahead of us.

A farmhouse up ahead on the right looked promising, with a large outbuilding or barn immediately behind it on the property.

I pumped the brakes to slow us down for the right turn, and we coasted up the long drive to a stop.

A man wearing insulated coveralls and a cowboy hat walked out of the outbuilding, wiping greasy hands on an oily rag. "Well, look what the wind blew in! I didn't see the plows come by. You havin' some trouble?"

I snorted. "You have no idea! We coasted in on fumes and a good tailwind. You haven't got any spare gasoline we could buy off you, do you?"

Chapter 13

We didn't deviate from Heretic's instructions after that. The states and the days flew by quickly and without further incident.

As we crossed the state line into California, I had to break the news to Mary that we wouldn't be stopping at Disneyland.

"It's too risky. We still don't know exactly how Safeguard found us, but it's too big a chance to take. I don't think we'll be deviating to see the beach, either, Jessica. And Steven, Death Valley is gonna' have to wait."

I don't know if it made it easier or harder when all of them simply accepted it and moved on. I was simply another entry in the long list of broken promises in their lives. I wrestled with annoyance and revulsion within myself.

Northern California was incredibly less populated than I expected. I'd always thought of California as being so absurdly crowded and overpopulated. But I realized that must be in southern California, for the most part.

We pulled into a nearly empty gravel parking area of the building Heretic had mentioned and indicated to us on the map. We all piled out of the van, stretching and groaning. We'd done the last eight hours without breaks or rest stops and all of us were ready to arrive and be done with the trip.

I was confused. The "log building" was actually a bar. How was I supposed to take four children into a bar?

"I hate to do this to you Jessica, but can you keep everyone in the car while I run in and see if I can find this Carly lady?"

Jessica nodded, her eyes tired.

"I know. We're almost done. Help me keep everyone hanging in there for just a bit longer," I pleaded.

The kids clambered back into the van, Mary loudly protesting and going full limp-fish to try and avoid containment again. Jessica ladled her back into the car, one limb at a time, with Steven's help.

I entered the bar, not knowing what to expect. It was a bar, totally unremarkable. It was early enough in the day that the regular evening crowd must not be in yet. Either that, or it wasn't very busy. A woman, probably in her late fifties, stocked bottles behind the bar.

"I'm gonna' need to see your ID!" she called to me, both lazily and slightly annoyed, by her tone.

"I'm actually looking for Carly?" I asked it as a question.

"And now that you've found her?" The woman's voice took an edge, and her body stiffened. I noticed that one hand dropped beneath the counter.

"I'm a poor waif... and I—" I struggled to remember the rest of the phrase.

"Yeah, yeah, Preacher send ya'?" she visibly relaxed.

"Preacher? You mean Heretic?" I asked, confused.

"Are they that different? Little guy, got a flair for the dramatic and a thing for ninja wear?"

"Uh, yeah. That's him." This was not at all what I'd expected.

"Cool. You here alone, or you with somebody?" Carly asked, returning to her box of bottles.

"With somebody. Four kids, actually."

"No kiddin'? Gonna' be a tight fit, then," she shook her head slightly.

"Sorry? What's gonna' be a tight fit?" I asked, suddenly wary.

"The room. There's only the one room, and one bed. It's too late tonight for Preacher to send for ya'. I'll radio and let him know, though. He'll likely be here first thing in the morning." Carly emptied the box and broke it down, then gestured for me to follow her.

She led me through a door at the back of the bar, then down a narrow hallway stacked tall with boxes of alcohol and cleaning supplies, to a small office buried in papers and lousy with stale cigarette smoke. Carly pushed a button under the desk, and a small fuse box on the wall opened. She fiddled briefly with the dial inside, then opened the door of the small safe and yanked on a large lever inside of that. A large section of the tile flooring slid aside, revealing a staircase into darkness.

"What is it with these people and their secret rooms?" I asked out loud.

"Didn't I say he has a thing for the dramatic? Get your kids. This is where you'll be staying the night," Carly directed. She exited the office, and I followed her back down the hallway.

"Just the night? You mean this isn't where we're hiding out?" I pressed.

"Nope." Carly didn't offer any more.

"So, then what? Where to tomorrow?" I demanded.

"Look, kid. Preacher runs the resort, all right? I never been, I just run the front desk, as it were" Carly sighed. "Don't go gettin' a knot in your shorts."

"Do I need to park the van somewhere to hide it?" I asked, remembering what had happened the last time we'd stopped for any significant amount of time close to town.

"No, I'll have somebody take care of it; go ditch it somewhere it won't be found for a while," Carly said calmly.

"Ditch it? Whoa, no, won't we need it when we leave tomorrow?"

"Nah. Preacher will have you covered for rides. Now get your kids and your stuff while I radio Preacher."

I left the bar and went back to the van. I heaved open the sliding door. "This is the right place. Get everything you need out of the van; apparently, they're going to ditch it somewhere."

"What? They can't ditch our van!" Steven shouted. "This is ours!"

I sighed. I was exhausted. Even thinking right now was mental torture. I wanted to go to sleep and let someone else have to make all of the decisions after I woke up.

"Steven, this is happening. I don't like it, either. But I genuinely think this Heretic guy—Preacher, whoever he is—is going to take care of us. We just need to trust him right now." *Because trusting people has worked out so well for me, lately.* The black sludge balloon inside me swelled slightly in agreement.

Steven settled slightly. "Okay, if you trust him, I trust him." He went to work gathering clothes and the last of the food into a large duffel.

I gathered my own change of clothes and layers to clear out the van. I hesitated when I looked at my dad's helmet and the rest of the plate armor on the floor between the seats. Should I take it, or leave it? I took it with. *You never know…*

I corralled the kids into the bar, where Carly was waiting. She led us down the hallway and into the office, then gestured down the hidden staircase, which was lit now by lights from the room below.

Elizabeth looked back at me, disappointment on her face, and I could easily imagine her thoughts: *"Another hole?"* I tried my best to smile encouragingly and held up my own stuff to indicate, *"I'm coming, too."*

She turned, tightened her arms around her teddy bear, bounced her shoulders up and down in a visible sigh, and descended the stairs.

There was an air mattress, queen size, which visibly sagged, and an old wooden-frame cot. The room was thick with the smell that somehow manages to permeate all basements everywhere, dusty and musty.

"The cot's mine from upstairs. Don't break it," Carly said simply. When we were all situated, she looked around at the kids and asked, "You kids hungry? I flip a mean burger." The kids all nodded. We hadn't stopped anywhere for dinner on our sprint to the finish line at the lodge. Carly looked at me, and I nodded my head. She nodded back and left without any more chatter. She was *not* a talker.

Carly was right; she did flip a mean burger. Delightfully greasy and tastefully simple, it sat heavy and full in my belly. After we all finished eating, I blew some additional air into the mattress and the kids all situated themselves on it. It took a while for them to really settle in, especially once Mary learned that when she jumped up and landed on her bottom, it would throw Steven to the ground out on the edge of the bed. She squealed and jumped two or three times before Jessica managed to coax her down.

"Mary, can I tell you a story?" Mary was a sucker for Jessica's stories. All three of the others fell asleep before the end, and even Jessica fell asleep mid-sentence.

And then it was only me. I toyed with the idea of staying awake and wading through some things, but I eventually chickened out and chugged some sleep-aid.

Sleep came slowly, just as my brain began to dance with images and faces, figures that waited impatiently to be addressed.

***

I woke in the morning to Mary playing with my face.

"You havva big nose! And you bref is stinky!"

"Yes, thank you, Mary."

"You weckum." Sarcasm was completely lost on her. I rolled out from under the covers and sat up. The other three were sitting quietly on the blow-up mattress, waiting for me to wake up, probably.

"What time is it?" I mumbled. I looked down at my watch: 7:15. "How long have you guys been up?" I asked.

"Not very long," Steven offered.

"Forever," Elizabeth moaned at the same time.

I smiled. "Well, which is it?"

Jessica pointed to the corner. "Long enough for Mary to make a whole tea set out of dust." Sure enough, there in the corner lay a complete tea set, four simple cups, saucers, and spoons, complete with teapot, sugar bowl, and cream pitcher, all formed roughly and simply out of the dust and dirt accumulated in the cellar.

"I hadda tea pawty!" Mary gushed, proudly displaying the set.

"You certainly did. I'm impressed," I smiled.

Suddenly the door opened, and Carly poked her

head around the edge. "Let's move it! Your ride should be here any minute, and I've heard from some of the folks in town that they've had some men looking for you, knockin' on doors and such. Bold bunch, ain't they? Not sure how they're tracking you, but it must not be precise, if they're canvassing the neighborhood." She paused, looking at us one by one. "Why aren't you moving? Let's go!"

The kids and I scrambled to gather our things, trying to fold sheets and blankets.

"Just leave those! I can fold, I can't keep you from Safeguard thugs on my own. Come on!" Carly gestured impatiently.

We all filed out of the cellar, belongings in hand. Carly closed the trapdoor behind us, then led us out into the hallway, this time leading us further toward the rear of the building. She pushed open a door and let us out into the cloudy gray of a mountain morning. She pointed toward the line of trees growing several yards from the building.

"Your ride will find you in there. Head into the trees toward the mountain, and don't stop for nothing. If those goons show up here, I'll do what I can to slow them down and put them off your trail. You catch your ride, and they won't be able to touch you. Go!" She closed the door behind her.

I had so many questions, but Carly's no-nonsense attitude left no room for argument. We jogged into the trees and the bar soon disappeared behind the wall of green pine needles.

"James, what did she mean, we'd find a ride in here?" Jessica wondered.

"No, she said the ride would find us," Steven corrected her. "That's different."

Any further conversation was cut off by a high, piercing bugle that came from startlingly close ahead of us. I'd never heard it in real life, but I'd heard it in enough videos and TV episodes to recognize the bugle of a bull elk.

A moment later, seven of the massive mammals pranced through the trees in front of us, huge, spear-like antlers, expansive back and up from their heads, clicking together occasionally as they jostled each other.

"James?" Elizabeth squeaked. She clung to my side like a baby chimp, all grasping hands. I was entirely preoccupied with the teenager, a Black girl, who rode on the back of the animal in the lead.

"I'm guessing you're our ride? You're a Tamer, aren't you?" I asked.

The girl smiled. "I'm Shanice. You James?"

I nodded.

"Preacher sent me to get you guys. You got what you need?"

The elk stamped and shifted rapidly on their feet, a few of them walking around behind us. One of them stuck its nose boldly into Mary's face, sniffing and blowing out loudly. Mary giggled and put her hand on the long muzzle casually. The elk tensed visibly for a moment, then leaned carefully in and placed its forehead directly against Mary's head, fitting her easily between the two more forward-facing spikes on its rack.

"Yeah, we're good," I whispered, finding myself needing to remember to breathe.

"Well, help them up! We gotta' go!" The elk Shanice rode on whipped around and I noticed for the first time that she had her feet in some simple stirrups cinched around the elk's belly. No saddle, but some stirrups to help her stay in place. I looked at the others and noted that all but one had similar straps. The last one had some rudimentary saddle bags cinched to his back.

Shanice noticed me looking and nodded. "Throw your stuff in there, then help the kids get up an adjus' the stirrups. You can fix the length on 'em by rotating 'em up. But y'all gotta hurry." Shanice glanced toward the road. "Safeguards'll be here soon."

"Yeah, on it," I replied. I loaded my bundle and the duffle with the kids' things in it into the saddle bags on the one elk, then lifted each of the kids up onto the back of an elk and adjusted the straps on the stirrups to fit them.

"You'll want 'em a bit shorter, so they're long enough to more stand in 'em, than sit and rest your legs in 'em. These elk'll put up with the stirrup strap, but not a full saddle. So you gotta' sorta' stand to stay on," Shanice offered.

I made an adjustment to Steven's, then finished with the others. "I really doubt that Mary's gonna' be

184 ~ JUSTIN K. NUCKLES

able to stay on alone. Do you have some rope that I could ride with her and tie her to me? And I don't know that the others will be able to stay on, either, without anything else to hold onto."

"Oh. Right, I totally forgot," Shanice said. She looked at the elk with the bags, and he stepped over to her side, peering at her with one eye while standing close enough for Shanice to reach into the bag closest her and pull out a rope and several belts with sturdy loops attached to them.

"Here's a rope, and these are handles to hold onto. They belt around the neck, and you can hold on there. But you gotta' hurry. You do half, I'll do half." Shanice slid easily off one side of her elk and handed me the rope and two of the belts. Then she showed me how the belt cinched around Steven's elk's neck and allowed Steven another point of contact in staying astride the elk.

"That seems better, but don't we need reins or something to steer?" I asked.

Shanice cocked an eyebrow and frowned at me. "You ain't in charge. He's letting you ride, and he's choosing to go where we need to. You don't need to steer nothin'." She was disgusted with me, I realized.

"Sorry, I just—" She interrupted me, pointing to the other elk and making the universal "hurry" rolling motion with her hand.

I buckled my two belts around the elk Mary and I would ride and Elizabeth's. Shanice finished with Jessica's elk, then remounted her own elk, who angled

his head backward so she could grab onto his ant-
ler then pulled her up onto his back. They'd been
through this together a time or two.

I adjusted the stirrups on Mary's elk to where I estimated my legs would fall, then pulled myself onto his
back with only a few failed attempts. I situated Mary
in front of me, then lashed our thighs to each other,
finished with a loop around both of our middles right
under her armpits. That would have to do.

"All right, le's go!" Shanice leaned forward and
patted her elk's neck. He bugled once, then loped off
into the trees. The others echoed his call and followed
close behind. We'd managed to catch our ride.

***

We rode for several hours in a close line through
the trees, following a trail only our mounts seemed
to be able to see. I could only occasionally catch a
glimpse of what I recognized as a trail. The rest of the
time, it seemed like untouched, virgin wilderness.

"How ya' doing, Mary?" I asked. So far, the rope
tether system I'd rigged seemed to be holding her secure. Secure was one thing, comfortable was another.

"These deew aw stinky!" she giggled, holding her
nose. If that's as much as she had to complain about,
we were doing pretty well.

I checked on Elizabeth, Steven, and Jessica. They
all looked tired, but still positive. I called ahead to
Shanice, "How much further?"

Shanice shouted back, "Hang tight! Jus' a few more minutes! We almost there!"

I turned to make eye contact with and offer an encouraging thumbs up to the other kids. They all offered tired smiles and their own shaky thumbs in confirmation.

A short while later, with little warning, Shanice's elk drew up short, slowing to a jerky trot and finally stopping altogether. Shanice dismounted and removed the collar and stirrup belt with a practiced hand.

"Hop off and undo the belts. This here's far as they go."

I untied Mary then let myself down. My muscles and joints screamed from being locked in one unfamiliar position for so long. My legs felt wobbly and uncoordinated. As I lifted Mary down, she simply started screaming as her legs adjusted. Our elk ride looked around uneasily and began side-stepping quickly to get away from Mary's screaming. He turned to face Mary and me, craning his neck downward, forcing his sprawling, spiked antlers in our direction.

Just as his bunched muscles started to propel him rapidly forward, Shanice was suddenly there, a hand on his crown and speaking quietly under her breath. I couldn't hear what she was saying, but the elk beneath her hand instantly froze, then slowly began to relax, drawing his front legs back beneath him and raising up his head once more. He turned his head to one side and extended his neck, accepting a vigorous chin-scratch and rub from Shanice, who then slipped beneath his neck and deftly removed both straps.

I slowly walked toward Elizabeth and Steven, who were both still astride the elk. I helped them down, one at a time, then slowly removed the belts and collars.

Shanice did the same for Jessica's and the two others, then made a stop for each elk, again offering quiet words and neck scratches for each of them. When she was finished, she picked up each of the belts, slung them over a single shoulder, and handed me the saddle bags. Then she turned and walked away. The elk all stood, silently watching, until one moment, as if on some silent signal, they all wheeled quickly about and loped off independently.

The kids and I followed after Shanice, with me again carrying a now drowsy Mary, along with the saddlebags.

A few steps forward, Steven, in the lead, shivered slightly and said, "Whoa. Did you feel that?"

Jessica, following right behind him, said, "Yeah, like at the Straders' farm."

"You guys can't use your powers?" I guessed.

All three of the older kids shook their heads.

"Huh," I grunted. "It must be another thing. Another House of Bricks, or whatever."

"It is. Tha's why we couldn't ride no further. I can only talk to the animals outside. Once we get in here, they're wild as anything," Shanice called back to us.

"But don't worry, 's only a bit further to the cabin. Preacher and Rachel should have lunch ready in jus' a bit. We gotta' hurry if we want any. The food don't last too long up here." She laughed, good-naturedly.

"So, Preacher is here?" I asked. It took a lot of effort to refer to him as "Preacher" and not "Heretic."

"He's here. Least he was, when I left to come get y'all. He's coming and going all the time. Sometimes he more ghost than guardian." Her words were similar to what Heretic had said to me that first meeting: more spirit guide than guardian angel.

"So, where are we? What is this place? How did you end up here, Shanice?" I fired.

"Ain't got no name. We jus' call it home. We all got here the same way. We all got taken by Safeguard from our family. Some of us been placed with Hosts, others Preacher caught us before they got that far. But all of us been rescued by Preacher, brought here to live."

"Wait, you keep saying 'all of us'. How many of you are there? And you're talking kids, right?" I couldn't believe what I was hearing. I guess I'd found out what Heretic was doing with all the kids he'd taken from Safeguard custody over the years.

"There's twenty-eight of us. An' yeah, we all kids. Or were kids, least. I'm one o' the oldest. I'm eighteen."

That surprised me. Maybe it was because she was small for her age. She wasn't very tall. Looking closer at her face, which I hadn't really done up to that point, I could see it. She was quite good-looking, too, which I felt awkward about when I noticed. She was eighteen,

I guess, but still, she was only eighteen. I shook my head. She was still talking.

"There're a few others around my age, then it goes on down from there. We got some as little as Miss Mary, there." She looked back and smiled at Mary, who looked around when she heard her name, then buried her face in my shoulder.

"And you're all Mythics?" I asked. The thought of so many children in one place, with so little supervision, appalled the professional in me. The thought that they were all Mythics terrified the rational in me. The thought that they were all stolen from their families angered every part of me. But I wasn't sure if I was angry with Safeguard, or with Heretic. Both, maybe? It was hard to tell. I wondered which was more painful, to know who your family was and not be able to return home, or to find out you were adopted, and your whole life was a lie. My insides curled and my head felt hot. I knew what one of those felt like, at least.

"Yup. Every one of us. Most of us are Tamers and Tanks, but we got a few Thinkers, and one or two Tinkers and Techs each. Preacher's got fancy names for all of our abilities, Latin or Hebrew something, but we usually stick with what Safeguard refers to us as. Easier to remember."

We rounded the corner of a large boulder and I stopped short. It was beautiful. A large alpine lake, a sprawling meadow with tall grass, and a huge building, built into the side of a large hill near the north edge of the meadow.

"That's the cabin?" I asked.

"It looks like something from Star Wars!" Steven yelled.

"No, it's like a Hobbit-hole, but with more windows," Jessica countered.

"I love it here," Elizabeth breathed.

"It's pretty great, isn't it" Shanice was grinning again, that smile that seemed to come from her toes. How long had it been since I'd felt joy like that? It seemed like a lifetime ago, those weeks ago when I'd returned home and found my parents murdered. It felt like a switch had been thrown off inside me and hadn't come back on since. All I'd felt since then was fear, doubt, anger, rage, anxiety, the list of negative emotions went on. I realized that Shanice was looking at me, as if waiting for an answer. What had she asked me?

"Sorry, what was that?" I fumbled.

"I asked if you're okay? You look like someone jus' killed your dog," Shanice said.

"Yeah, sorry, it's—it's been a crazy couple of weeks for me."

"Hey, I get it. It took me a long time to come to terms with what Safeguard did to me, to my family. What's your skill, anyway?" She changed the subject. Maybe she really could see how broken I was inside.

"Nothing. I mean, I don't have one," I stumbled. Shanice looked at me in surprise.

"He doesn't have a superpower, but he's really nice," Elizabeth said, patting my elbow.

"Yeah, we wouldn't be here if it weren't for James," Jessica offered in support.

Shanice looked at me again, and I couldn't tell what it was in her expression. "Really? No powers? How did y'all manage to stay away from Safeguard, if you don't got no powers?"

"We all had to work together," Elizabeth said. "I had to move the snow, and Steven had to keep us from freezing, and Jessica pushed us like a sailboat, but it was all James' ideas."

"Well, maybe he's just super-awesome, then," Shanice said. She looked at me out of the corner of her eyes, eyelids half-closed, with a smile that made both my heart and my stomach flop like a bullfrog. For having worked around women and girls for so long, I sure was uncomfortable when they decided to flirt with me.

When we were within a few yards of the structure, it was easier to tell what it was. I'd heard of these types of buildings, these earthships, I think they were called. Made from recycled materials like tires and bottles, they were supposed to be entirely self-sufficient, using solar and rainwater and the heating and cooling effect of the earth, along with a greenhouse in the front, which was what we were looking at. A great wall of windows, behind which was a space entirely filled with greenery, plants that should not have been so vibrant this time of year.

A door opened at one end, and a woman came out. She was probably in her mid- to late-forties, I guessed.

She was tall and slim with dark brown hair in a close, short haircut. *A pixie cut,* I thought absently. She carried herself with the confidence of someone who had probably been an athlete when she was younger.

"You're back! How'd it go, Shanice, did you have any trouble?" Her voice had a motherly tone and lilt to it.

"Nope, everything went jus' fine," Shanice smiled. She walked right into the woman's arms, who put a small kiss on Shanice's hair and rubbed her shoulder. Everything this woman did was so motherly and full of love. I'd worked with several women like her over the last several years. Not all women had this much natural nurturing instinct and demeanor, but I could tell, instantly, that she did.

Shanice released her, and they exchanged one last look before Shanice turned to face the children and me. "Rachel, this is James." Shanice smiled at me again. I looked anywhere but at her. "And Mary, and Elizabeth," she pointed at each of the children. She hesitated when she got to Steven. "Steven, I think? And this is Jessica."

Rachel came and stood in front of me, Mary still held in my arms. From several feet away, she bent down so her face was on Mary's level. "Hi Mary, I'm Rachel. Welcome to my home." To my surprise, Mary didn't hide, but smiled back at Rachel.

Rachel moved down the line, slowly and respectfully introducing herself to each child. Then she came back to stand in front of me.

"James, thank you for bringing them here. Preacher told me a little of what you've gone through and done for these children, recently. I appreciate your effort. And I'm so sorry for your loss." Her face was so open, showing first gratitude, and then such grief as she expressed them, that I was taken aback. I'd never met anyone who was so easy to read.

"Thank you," I managed. Rachel nodded slowly, then turned and welcomed us inside.

Behind the wall of plants, which actually spanned two stories inside, there was a large open area where the longest table I'd ever seen was laden with huge pots of steaming soup and huge brown sliced loaves of bread and surrounded by a couple dozen children who all sat in chairs, dishing out portions for each other and passing bowls and bread slices up and down the table.

"Please, find a seat and join us," Rachel invited. "Such as it is, our mess is your mess, if you want it."

Chapter 14

After dinner, Rachel showed us to a room at one end of the home.

"You can stay here; I've already had the other children clear out their belongings."

"Oh, no, we couldn't do that. We don't want to displace anybody," I protested.

Rachel held up a hand. "It's already done, and it's no trouble. We're used to it here. This is what we do: we make room for newcomers."

I continued to protest, but Rachel insisted. The Dantons had already settled in, lying down on the rough mattresses in obvious relief. It wasn't long before they were all asleep, tired out by the morning elk ride.

"If you're feeling up to it, Preacher would like to see you. He said to have you check in with him after you ate and got settled," Rachel said.

"So, he's here, then? Where do I find him?" I badly wanted to talk to him.

"He's outside. On the roof. Just walk around the side of the house and on up to the top. He's waiting for you."

I followed Rachel's instructions and found Heretic

tinkering with an array of solar panels. He straightened when I approached.

"James. I'm glad you made it. Did you have any trouble on your drive out?"

My throat constricted in anger and my hands clenched involuntarily. "Are you serious right now? What do you think? You tell me, based on how many different people we had chasing us, do you think we had any trouble driving across the continental U.S. in late fall?

"That probably depends. Did you follow my instructions?" That was all he said.

I couldn't help myself; I stepped forward and swung at him. He didn't even try to block it or move. My fist connected with the side of his head with a clang and an explosion of pain. I'd forgotten about his headgear.

"Son of a—" I shook my hand, eyes watering with pain.

"That was foolish, James. I would advise you not to do anything like that again. More for your benefit than mine." His tone, even behind the voice scrambler he used, was flat, detached. How did he do that? At times he sounded like he was reading from a script, other times he sounded like one of my peers from school, and others, he spoke like someone from my parents' generation. It was grating. I hadn't recognized what irritated me so much about his speech until now.

I turned to face him again, cradling my throbbing hand. "Who are you?" I shouted in his face. "The only reason I decided to go along with your plan was because of the last thing you said to me at the Dantons'. Do you remember what you said that night?"

Heretic's shoulders visibly slumped and his head lowered slightly. "I do. I told you to be strong."

"Why did you say that? Did you know what that phrase meant to me?" I peered into the shadow of his hood.

"I do. It's the last thing your mother said to you. It's something she said often."

I took a step back, surprised. "How do you know that? Who are you?"

"I can't tell you that, James. Not yet, at least. Just know that I was profoundly influenced by your parents. I would have done everything in my power to protect them if they'd let me."

"What does any of that even mean? Who are you? Let me see your face!" I reached out again with my good hand and tried to push back the hood. Heretic caught my hand and twisted it back, driving me to my knees as he leveraged it back and then down.

"I warned you, James Strader, do not attempt to touch me again." It was the scripted voice again. He let me go and took another step back.

I stayed on my knees, gasping up at him and holding both hands gingerly in front of me. "Who are you?" I asked again.

"I am Heretic. I am Preacher. To you, James, I am friend," he said quietly.

"Were you in Safeguard, too? I know you think

they're child snatchers. Did you used to be one of them? Are you a Mythic? You know they call you a terrorist, right?"

"One man's terrorist is another man's freedom fighter. Do you think I mean you or the children harm, James? Would you even be here if you thought that I meant you any harm?" Heretic cocked his head slightly, looking at me.

"I don't know what to think. Safeguard says they're protecting Mythics with what they're doing. What makes them any different from you and what you're doing?" I shot at him.

"Safeguard snatches children away from their families and hides them from the world. I rescue those children from Safeguard and hide them until they're old enough to control their powers and return to the families they've been denied. It's not ideal; far from perfect, but, for now, it's the best I can do. At least here, these children are allowed to be themselves, to grow unhindered by false pretenses and narratives."

Heretic couldn't possibly know about the fact that I was adopted, could he? He couldn't possibly know what his words did to me. All the thoughts I'd been pushing back into the night, keeping at bay with the sleep aid syrup, came crashing in on me. I realized *that* was what I mourned most: the knowledge that I was adopted had stolen from me the order, the calm, the assurance of who I was. I wished, more than anything, that I could go back to before I'd known that.

"You're right," I said aloud, my voice trembling.

Every muscle in my body tensed and flexed, until I was shaking head to toe.

"Jamie, are you all right? You're shaking." Heretic took a tentative step toward me, one hand extended. Fury over being called that, being called Jamie, filled my insides. The black clawed up my throat and left my mouth in a roar:

"You don't call me that! No one but her ever calls me that!" I batted his hand away roughly. "I don't know why I came here. I thought maybe you knew something more about my parents, but if you won't tell me anything, there's no reason for me to stay. I promised my parents that I would keep those kids safe, and that's what I'm going to do. But not with you. I don't know what your game is, I don't even know who you are. I have absolutely no reason to trust you.

"And as for your drivel about letting them keep their narrative, let me tell you, I have my new narrative, and there's nothing I wouldn't give to go back to before I knew that. It broke me! I'm broken inside!" My eyes filled with water, and I couldn't even see Heretic clearly right in front of me, but I pushed on. "You think you're doing these kids a favor by reminding them every day of the trauma you and Safeguard have inflicted on them? You inflict that level of pain and grief and you call it mercy? Well, at least *they* have the decency of Sweeping the kids. They don't have to live with the pain, with the loss, with the grief of what they can never have back. You call what you do here kindness? It's not kindness. It's cruelty!"

I looked away, down the valley back toward where I knew the town and the road to be, blinking tears from my eyes but refusing to let him see me wipe them. "I promised these kids' mother that I'd keep her children safe, and that I'd help them forget all of this. I was stupid to come here. Why I thought I could trust someone who isn't even honest enough to show the world their face is beyond me."

I turned away and stomped down the hillside.

"James!" Heretic called after me. "James, come back here. James, what are you thinking, son?"

I ignored him. His manipulation, using phrases, nicknames, terms that my parents used to use repulsed me. I hated him. Heretic was a hypocrite. A hypocrite and a liar. He, like Safeguard, cut into others' lives like a surgeon. But whereas Safeguard seemed to do so with a purpose, and with mercy, removing the memory of the trauma and abuse, loss and separation, Heretic operated without anesthetic, and had the gall to call it mercy and kindness.

The Danton children were still napping lightly in the bedroom when I got back to it. I closed the door softly and sank to the floor, tears falling freely from my eyes. My body still shook with suppressed anger and pain. I trembled against the wall, biting back sobs in silence, as the children slept. My entire chest felt like a rubber-band-wrapped watermelon, on the verge of splitting wide open, it was so tight. And my eyes pushed against their sockets and lids as if they'd burst.

After several minutes, there was a quiet knock on the door. It was probably Heretic. I did nothing. The knock came again, and this time Rachel's voice came muffled from the other side of the door.

"James, are you in there? I heard what you said to Preacher. It was hard not to."

I said nothing, trying to cut some of the bands on my chest and breathe again.

"James, I don't have all of the answers, but I'd like to help. Even if that means simply listening."

I stood up shakily against the wall and fought for breath and calm, willing my muscles to relax from their rage-induced tremble. Every moment they stopped quivering, I felt exhausted, and I had to fight to keep them from starting again. I opened the door and stepped out into the hall.

"Not here. Somewhere else; anywhere else," I pleaded.

Rachel quietly nodded, then led me down the hall and deeper into the hillside. She opened a door at the end. We stepped into the dark room, and she used a flashlight from her pocket to locate an electric lantern in the dark and switch it on.

We were in what must have passed as the cold storage for the home. It was quite cool in the room, being so far into the hill, and there were stacks of dry goods and shelves of cans and bottles. She pulled up a bucket and patted it, then brought another for herself.

"Sometimes I come in here to be by myself," she

laughed quietly. "Twenty-eight is a lot most days." She looked at me and put a hand on mine. Her hand was warm and rough from hard work. "I know what happened to you, James. Preacher told me. It's a terrible thing to lose people close to you."

I sighed. "I was dealing with their deaths. It was hard, but I was dealing with it." It was a lie, and it tasted like one as it left my lips. "But—" I took a steadying breath. "To find out they weren't even my real parents? I can't even..." I struggled to find words and failed. I sat for a few moments and Rachel sat with me, saying nothing, waiting.

I started again. "It's like, before Roger told me that I was adopted, I was part of a puzzle that was missing a few pieces. That was it. It sucked. It sucked hardcore. But then, finding out I was adopted, it's like I don't even know what puzzle I belong to anymore. I fit into the old one, but it's not even the puzzle I came from, you know? I just feel so lost. The only thing that's keeping me upright is those kids. I know that I care about them now. I care about them and what happens to them. So, I'll do whatever it takes to keep them safe and see that they make it through this horror show that's happened to them."

I stopped talking and we sat in the light of the lantern and the quiet of the dark around us. Finally, Rachel spoke.

"I know how you feel, James. I'm an awkward puzzle piece, too. I had my own children once. But that's all I know. I can't remember how many, I can't remember if they were boys or girls. I can't remember how old they were when I lost them, what they looked like, their names, nothing. Just this sense of loss and sorrow, every time I saw someone else's child. I wouldn't even know why; I'd just start crying. I floundered in that limbo for years. I was homeless, I was strung out on drugs and liquor. I had nothing and no one, because I was so focused on those missing pieces I had lost, that aching pain of something I couldn't even remember."

I watched Rachel's face travel back over the years and age as she talked. Lines of worry, concern and pain creased her forehead and around her mouth. She sat there for a moment, feeling the years, then her face suddenly relaxed, and the years fell away again as she spoke.

"Then one day, Preacher found me. He found me, and he gave me a purpose again. He found me a new puzzle to fit in." She looked at me, her eyes earnest and wide. "There isn't a day that goes by that I forget what I can't remember. But, if you were to offer me the chance, would I ask you to help me forget about them, to forget that hurt? Never. It's not what I remember that haunts me; it's the parts I can't.

"I know you wish you could go back to a time where you never knew what you know now. But that's the thing about us as humans, James. It isn't a puzzle with one simple picture. We're part of an elaborate tapestry, a thread in a much bigger design. Even though we may lose some of the threads we felt most defined us, there are always others around us that need us, just like we need them." She reached out and put her hand on top of mine, squeezing gently with those long fingers.

"I know you're hurting, James. But don't make any permanent decisions based on that pain. Feel it, poke it, find out all you can about it, but then, when you're ready, move away from it. A piece of it will always come with you, but that's okay, because it's that memory that will help you find the place where you can best shine, for you and for others. You don't have to be alone. That's never been the plan."

She stopped talking and simply watched me. When I didn't say anything for a minute, she sighed. "I did it again, didn't I? I spoke up with solutions too soon, didn't I? I always do that. Sometimes, it's not about the nail, Rachel!"

"Huh?" I grunted. "What nail?"

"Oh, nothing. It was this stupid video when I was a teenager. Do you want to talk any more about it?" she asked.

"No, I'm done," I said, feeling a little embarrassed about what had transpired. I hardly knew Rachel, and yet here I was pouring my heart out to her. I stood up and walked out with a hurried, "Thanks," to Rachel as I left.

***

The next couple of days went by quickly. The Danton children spent a lot of time playing with the other kids, going out of the House of Bricks for a few hours each day to play with their powers. But even in all this pleasure and enjoyment they were taking in their newfound friends, I could still see the pain and terror of their lives with their father hanging over them. Jessica still fled the room any time someone in it raised their voice. Steven's first response in a disagreement was always to throw the first punch. Elizabeth still froze any time anyone became upset with her for any reason. Mary didn't faint often, but I was partially certain that was because she had so much dirt constantly caked to her that she couldn't even hear what was going on around her.

They'd fallen in love with Rachel, though. It was difficult not to, honestly. She had one of those personalities where, when she was speaking with you, or even around you, she could make you feel like you were the most important person in the world. The other kids all loved her, too. It was obvious. They all responded to her and treated her with the same care and concern that I'd seen Shanice treat her with that first day.

But, even with all that positive, I couldn't help but feel like the Danton kids needed something different. Their mother's words kept coming back to me, over and over again: "Help them live a happy, full life, one where they can forget all of this."

Here, they would constantly live with the reminder that their father had been a monster. Every argument, every disagreement, every yell would transport them right back to what they couldn't forget. But I kept thinking, what about with Safeguard? With Safeguard, their memories could literally be Swept of their own traumatic history. They could be rid of all the bad and keep all the good parts. The longer we stayed, the more certain I became that we should reconnect with Safeguard.

It seemed like all the kids here could benefit from Safeguard. All the kids, even Rachel, I was sure. And me. I was starting to think that, despite what Rachel had said, the best thing for me would be to have Pat or another Thinker help me forget that I was adopted. It was such a simple fix. It would probably be easy, and God knew it would help me.

I wasn't sleeping anymore: my sleep aid ran out. I couldn't eat and I was losing weight. This pain wasn't something I was getting to know; it was eating me up from the inside. I had to do something, or I was seriously and irreparably going to lose it. I had to act.

Heretic and I hardly spoke after that first afternoon. He was constantly in and out of the house and the Brick, coming and going often. One of the afternoons that he was gone, and the Danton kids were off playing, I pulled out my father's helmet. I had no idea how the communicator in it worked, but maybe it was worth a shot.

I pulled the helmet on and spoke. "Hello, is anybody listening? Hello?" I waited for a few seconds and a voice crackled in my ears. It was faint, and it broke up a bit, but I thought it said, "This... a secure... device. Who... this? How did you access th—"

"Hello? Is this someone with Safeguard?" I figured maybe I wouldn't completely out them in public, if this was basically a public radio frequency.

"Yes, this is Tinker One with Kilo Bravo Unit. Who is this?" came the voice. It was much stronger and clearer now.

"This is James Strader. I need to talk to Pat or Clara Walker."

There was silence after that for a full minute. A couple of times I heard something click, and each time I said, "Hello? Pat?" But there was no response. I was about to take it off and try again another day when Pat's voice shouted in my ears.

"James? Where the hell have you been, man? It's been weeks since we lost contact with you after the Danton op, and nobody has seen or heard anything about you since the McDonald's debacle in North Dakota. Are you okay? Are the kids okay? Where are you?"

"Yeah, we're fine. We're all fine. I'll answer all of your questions, Pat. But first, I need your help."

Chapter 15

"Thanks for doing this, Shanice. I thought it would be fun for the kids to get out around the town for a bit. Just touch base with the real world, you know?" I called from the back of the elk train up to the front.

"It's fine! Not a big deal," Shanice called back to me. Suddenly, the elk Mary and I were riding burst into a faster gallop, racing ahead to the front to pace Shanice's mount.

She looked sideways at me and smiled. "It's easier to talk this way. I go down a couple times a week anyway to pick up the supplies that Carly orders for us at the bar. I asked for a few extra volunteers this time." She pointed back at the train behind us, this time made up of both bulls and cows.

"Well, thanks, in any case." I didn't say anything else; just looked around at anything and anywhere but at Shanice.

"Why do you do that?" Shanice asked suddenly.

"Do what?" I whipped my head around to look at her.

"You avoid me. You've been avoiding me all week. You know that a girl can smile at a boy without wanting to jump his bones, right?"

My mouth and face must have matched what my brain was doing at that point. Shanice laughed heartily.

"You should really see your face right now."

"I—I'm not trying to be rude. If anything, I'm trying *not* to be rude. I don't want you to feel like I'm staring at you, or objectifying you or anything," I backpedaled. Was I that obvious?

"Dude, you're 'dangerous-object'-ifying me. You avoid me like I'm gonna cut you or something. Am I that scary?"

"No! You're not scary. I'm not scared. I want to treat you with respect, is all." I was floundering.

"Well, your respect feels an awful lot like the opposite. You think I'm cute?" She was full-on facing me now, sitting sideways on the elk.

"Well, I—yeah, I mean—I don't... You're..." I stuttered.

"Smooth," she laughed. "Real smooth. Look; it's really easy. You like somebody, you just be cool. Don't be a creeper, don't be an ass. Just right in the middle: be cool."

"Cool, got it. Be cool. I mean not that I—It's not—" I stammered.

She looked at me, smiled, and simply said, "Cool."

I sighed. This was not what I needed right then.

Mary was watching Shanice closely. Finally, she said, "I like your ammals."

Shanice smiled at Mary, then looked at me. "What'd she say?"

"She said she likes your animals." I pointed at the elk.

"Oh, you like my animals? Thank you! You know, they aren't mine, like a pet. They're more like my friends. We look out for each other when we're on these trips. I really like your marbles."

Marbles, Mary's latest creation and passion she'd recently created from dirt. She had a zip-top plastic bag that Rachel had given her to keep her collection in. It started out as three or four and now the bag only barely kept closed around its contents. Mary beamed in pleasure and pride.

"Wanna' play wif me?" She asked, holding the bag up.

"Oh, you know I do, when we get to town. It is on, Mary! I hope you brought your marble A-game!" Shanice teased.

"I did. Look!" Mary held up the bag again. "But jus' regular marbles."

Shanice giggled. "You sure did."

"Shanice?" Elizabeth called out from a few elk back in the line. "How long until we get there?"

"We're pretty much there, Elizabeth. Right up ahead is the clearing where I picked y'all up last week. That's where Carly and I usually load the supplies. We'll stop there."

She was right. We rode for maybe thirty more seconds, and there we were, right back where we'd started.

Shanice and I helped all the kids dismount, and Shanice went inside to let Carly know we'd arrived.

"All right," I called as she let the door close behind her. "Take your time; we're just gonna' explore town!"

I checked my watch: twenty-five minutes. "Hey guys, shall we see if there's a park in town we can play at for a few minutes? I need to stretch my legs for a bit after that ride. Who wants in?" All four of them raised their hands.

The park off the main highway through town was sad, but it checked all the boxes. There was a single slide, two swings, an old-school merry-go-round, and a large grass area surrounded by trees.

"Tag, you're it!" I said, touching Jessica's shoulder lightly and then sprinting off. Within moments, "it" had traveled down the Danton line, from Jessica to Steven, to Elizabeth and finally to Mary, whose short little legs couldn't move fast enough to catch anyone.

Eventually Steven gave in and let her tag him, then immediately set after Jessica, determined to prove who was the fastest. As they both ran for all their worth, I checked my watch again: fourteen minutes.

We played for six more minutes before I clasped my knees, pretend-gasping for air, and let Mary catch me. "Oh, man! Mary, you got me. Hey, is anyone else thirsty? Let's head over to the gas station and get a drink, shall we?"

All the Danton children flocked to the edge of the park in the direction of the station. It was all I could do to keep up. I held Mary's and Elizabeth's hands as we crossed the street. The three of us skipped as we walked the two blocks to the gas station. There weren't any cars at the pumps. Like everything else in this sad, slow little town, it seemed empty. Everything was going according to plan.

"Ooh, James, can we get slushies?" Steven begged, his hands clasped under his chin.

"And some snacks?" Elizabeth wheedled, laying the charm on thick. I swore she batted her eyelashes. I laughed.

"Sure, a slushie and one snack, each of you," I agreed. With two minutes left, we were paying at the register. At one minute I turned to lead the children outside just in time to see a large grey van pull into the station and Shanice jog across the street, grinning her infectious grin.

"Crap," I muttered to myself.

"What, no slushie for me?" Shanice called.

Three women and two men got out of the van and walked toward the gas station. One of the women went directly inside, while all the rest walked up to us, smiling.

"Hey, are you guys from around here? We're looking for some good hiking trails," one of the men called.

That was the code phrase. I offered mine back as I'd been instructed. "Depends on what you're looking for. Do you prefer waterfalls or overlooks?" There was one more reply they should give.

"Oh, neither. I'm really more of a historical signifi-cance kind of guy," the man replied.

That was it. These were Safeguard. But what was I supposed to do about Shanice?

"Historical significance?" Shanice asked, puzzled. "What do you—"

One of the women jumped forward to put her hands on Shanice's head, but she batted the woman's hands away, her eyes going wide. She looked at me, her mouth hanging open.

"James, what have you done?"

I looked away. She wasn't supposed to be here.

Shanice shoved the woman away further this time, then turned and ran. One of the men pulled a tranq gun from his jacket as Elizabeth started screaming. I grabbed hold of Jessica and Mary, pulling them both close to me.

"It's all right. Hey! Look at me. Y'all don't struggle, don't fight 'em. It's gonna' be all right!"

Steven looked like he was going to start throwing punches, or worse. He dropped his slushie and had started raising both hands with a snarl on his face, when the woman (obviously a Thinker) placed a hand on his temple, and he dropped, unconscious. The man with whom I'd exchanged phrases caught him as he fell and took him to the van.

The man who'd pulled the tranq gun had taken aim at Shanice's back, but a large hawk suddenly slammed into him from the side, setting its talons into his arm and nipping with its beak. The man screamed and dropped the gun, hitting at the bird with his free hand until it released him and flew awkwardly away, obviously having been hurt by one of the man's pan-icked swings.

In the meantime, the last woman had caught hold of Elizabeth, holding her still. The Thinker woman also put a hand to Elizabeth's head, but not before a water pipe on the side of the building blew out and a stream of water started shooting toward the woman holding Elizabeth. As soon as the Thinker touched her, though, the water changed direction, shooting out in a more natural upward spray from the broken pipe.

The woman who'd gone inside was back and sprinted to my side. Laying a hand on both Jessica's and Mary's heads, her mouth dropped open when nothing happened. I remembered my wristband: it must have negated her ability to knock the girls un-conscious. I let go of both girls, and they both went immediately limp. The woman caught Jessica as she fell but couldn't do anything about Mary. Instinc-tively, I was barely able to catch her head on the top of my foot and gently lowered it down, reaching down to hold her steady without thinking. Her eyes fluttered open, and she immediately started whimpering. When her eyes focused on me, she sobbed my name.

"Dames," she cried, reaching out with one small hand. I pulled back from her like I'd been burned.

The woman next to me looked down at her in shock, and I heard her mutter, "What the hell?" She put a hand on Mary's head, and Mary's eyes rolled back in her head, then her hand went limp again.

The woman looked at me with wide eyes. "What

just happened? She shouldn't have been able to wake up like that. What's her ability?"

"She can control earth. Dirt," I said.

She looked at me, unblinking. "That doesn't have anything to do with the brain. Are you a Thinker? Did you wake her up?"

I shook my head. "No, I don't have any ability. I think it was probably my wristband. My dad made it for me. Apparently, it negates Mythics' powers. I forgot about it; I'm sorry."

The woman didn't say anything more, just picked up Mary and loaded her into the van. I didn't offer to help any more, afraid to mess something up.

I checked my watch. It had only taken a minute, but the ordeal felt like it had lasted a lifetime. I turned around to look after Shanice. She was nowhere in sight.

The man who'd originally approached me with the code phrase spoke to me again. "James, I'm Kyle McClellan. Let's get going; Pat and Clara want you at the Safeguard training facility in Kansas ASAP."

As they loaded Jessica into the van, I had a moment of doubt. Each of the kids was buckled into a seat belt in the van, each of their heads floppy in unconsciousness. I didn't know any of the faces of the adults who had essentially just helped me kidnap the children in my care. Was it kidnapping if they were in my care? I cringed at the word as I squeezed past them into a back row, but it sure was what it felt like. Strangers getting out of a van and loading four children into it against their will? All that we were missing was some offered candy, and I would have been living out a proverbial cautionary tale.

As the last woman climbed into the van and closed both swinging doors behind her, I looked around one last time for Shanice. As we pulled out of the gas station and drove past the bar, Carly came running out the door with a shotgun in her hands and a lit cigarette between her lips. She raised the shotgun and I ducked instinctively, but the shotgun lowered when she saw me, and the cigarette fell from her mouth to the dirt. Turning in my seat, I peered behind the bar and may have only imagined a flash of light brown fur among the trees. A few minutes later, the town was behind us, and we were swallowed up by the winding mountain roads through the trees.

***

Not only were the members of the Safeguard team not talkative, but they were extremely efficient. Each member took a turn driving four hours at a time, stopping only briefly for gas and for them and me to use the bathroom. The kids they kept under. A few hours into the drive, one of the women changed the kids into essentially large diapers.

I protested, already uncomfortable with how things had felt at the gas station. I'd expected something more calm and discussion-based, rather than the bag-and-tag tactics that had been used.

"Why can't they use the bathroom at the stops like the rest of us?" I asked.

"Because, it's easier this way. They stay out the whole time. Less struggle that way." She sounded like she was discussing animals, not children.

"Well, you're a Thinker, right? Can't you make them forget that they don't know you, create a story for them, or something?"

"It doesn't work that way, kid. These aren't Hollywood Jedi mind tricks. You can't wave your hand and make them think they're fine. The mind hates holes. If I were to wipe us out or try to put something piecemeal in before we give 'em the big one, they'd wake up totally mashed on the other side. Being Swept takes time, and it's gotta be thorough. There's no room for willy-nilly nonsense." She reached for another diaper for emphasis.

I told myself that they probably did this a lot, and it probably *was* easier. I reminded myself that this was for the best; this was how the Danton children were going to get a second chance at a normal life, one where they wouldn't remember any of the abuse of their father, or the nightmare of the last four weeks.

She looked up at me again. "By the way, what did you mean, that wristband negates abilities? Like being Bitted? I didn't know that was possible with a device, and you didn't even put it on her."

"No, I guess it's like a reverse Bit: instead of being designed to stop my abilities – like I said, I don't have any—I think it's designed to stop abilities from being used on me. Pat and Clara thought my dad probably made it to protect me from Mythics."

She narrowed her eyes suspiciously. "Who's your dad?"

Inwardly, the black thing roiled. *My real dad? I don't even know. They never bothered to tell me.* "Jared Strader," I said.

"No kidding? Huh. I heard the Straders had a son with no abilities. Leave it to Jared to find a way to keep him out of everything." She didn't say anything to me for the rest of the drive.

The drive took all day, all night, and past noon of the following day. The bathroom breaks and the switching of drivers broke it up, but the bulk of the time I spent scowling at the landscape outside yet seeing none of it. I dozed off and on, but every jostle brought me back to wakefulness, each time leaving my head clouded further and further in exhaustion. I hadn't slept the night before, too anxious about what I'd planned with Pat's help. The *kidnapping* I'd planned with Pat's help.

By the time the sun crept up to peek into the windshield of the van, I couldn't tell my time spent dozing from my time awake. At one point, I looked out the window and saw several wolves, impossibly running alongside the van, their hungry eyes fixed on me through the windows. I turned back to look at the woman on the seat of the row behind me, wondering whether she could see them, too. When she saw me looking, she made eye contact with me for a moment, her face expressionless, then looked back down. I turned again to the window, but the wolves were gone. I closed my eyes and rested my cheek against the cool shock of the glass, hoping for rest.

A few moments later, I startled, but couldn't open my eyes, as I heard first my mother, then my father, then Heretic, and finally a woman's voice I didn't recognize say, "James, what have you done?" I finally opened my eyes and turned to look at the woman again. Suddenly she was all jagged teeth, wild eyes and reaching paws.

I jerked awake as the van stopped, swatting away at teeth that had nearly been at my throat. I glanced back at the woman again, who didn't even look up this time. I checked in on all the kids. Elizabeth slept next to a lightly snoring Steven on the first row, while Mary sat strapped into a booster on the row in front of me, against which Jessica's head rested heavily. All four still here, all four still out.

The van pulled away from the stop sign, turning right, away from the freeway we had exited.

As far as I could see in every direction were corn fields. Some were harvested, nothing but sharp stubs poking up into the air, and some were still standing, their dry, brown stalks shivering slightly in the wind. Far off in one field, I could see a combine making slow progress, sending plumes of dust and dry, brittle debris up into the air.

Kyle was driving. He took us a mile or two down one of the sparse branching country roads that checker-boarded the landscape, before turning into a lot with several large farm machines, a massive pole barn, and about a dozen vehicles parked in a muddy parking area.

I was surprised when Kyle drove right past the parking area and pulled the van into the open pole barn doors. I was mildly disappointed when the glare from the sun slid off the windows of the van and my eyes adjusted to the interior light of the pole barn. Absolutely nothing out of the ordinary; the bins, equipment, and workers of a typical, mid-size corn operation took up most the space in the barn. No futuristic equipment lockers, no paramilitary Safeguard drilling, not even a glimpse of any out-of-the-ordinary technology. The Safeguard training facility was a standard corn farm?

One of the women from the front seat jumped out and walked to a large section of wall paneling. She pushed gently on it, and a whole section bumped out, then slid quickly and silently to one side. The woman rolled out four gurneys and shoved them in the direction of the van.

The man who'd been attacked by the hawk protecting Shanice stood to one side, nursing his arm in a sling. They'd provided him with surprisingly well-equipped First Aid from a large backpack in the van, but his face still twitched with pain when his arm jostled. I'd even watched the woman in the front give him several stitches at one point soon after we'd been on the road. Kyle said something quietly to the man as he walked past, then clapped him on the shoulder of his uninjured arm.

Together, Kyle, the three women, and I unloaded the children from the van and onto the gurneys. They each took the head of one of the gurneys and steered them after the injured man, toward the wall where the woman had retrieved the gurneys. She gave the wall section another slight shove, and it closed back up again, sealing as invisibly as it had been before. We walked a bit further along the wall and stopped at another section, this time where there was an actual door. The man in the lead used his good arm to slide back the large door, let us all file past him into the small dirt-floored, empty storage room beyond him, then pulled it closed behind us.

As he flicked on a set of lights, my doubts rang ever louder in my brain. *This was the best they could do?*

I opened my mouth to say something when the floor of the room suddenly started lowering down the walls. The entire room was an elevator! What was it with Safeguard and having their spaces underground?

Chapter 16

I stared upward as the floor continued dropping, the ceiling and walls of the original room getting further and further away.

My mind flooded with questions. Kyle must have been watching me and guessed where my head was at, because he said, "It goes down about a hundred feet. The facility, believe it or not, is built within an entirely natural cave system. They opened some things up and smoothed some edges, sure. But, for the most part, the whole thing was here way before we were."

As he finished talking, the walls on three sides of the shaft simply ended, the floor lowering down another twenty feet before settling into a recess in the stone floor, flush.

Looking up again, clear into the open shaft that led up to the surface, I sputtered, "So how... without cables..."

"Oh, the whole thing's done with magnets. Yeah, it's pretty cool, I guess." Kyle was probably somewhere in his early 40's, but he smiled like a teenage boy, shrugging excitedly. "I was part of the team that made that upgrade several years ago."

"Oh, cool," I said, not sure what else to say.

Kyle grinned, obviously proud of his achievement.

"All right, let's head down to medical, get Greyson all squared away from that hawk attack – freaking Tamers are the worst— and get these kids prepped for final transport."

"I— have you worked with a lot of Tamers?" Shanice was weighing heavily on my mind.

"Oh, yeah. Probably a dozen or so. I can't even tell you how many times I've had to have my rabies shot because of mouse bites."

"Mouse bites?"

"Well, yeah. Most of the time we're picking kids up at home; there've been a few cats I've had to deal with, one or two dogs, but the mice—they're the worst."

Kyle pushed Elizabeth's gurney off the elevator platform and across the large expanse that was the main room of the training headquarters.

It was essentially a cafeteria. Several rows of tables and benches, with a few dozen young men and women eating lunch in identical warm up clothes.

Kyle led us toward a hallway at the front end of the room, doors clearly marked, "Medical." As we went through, I followed the train of gurneys down a hall, into another set of doors where there were several partitions set up, similar to an emergency room. Two other Safeguards, a man and a woman, directed us to separate spaces with each child, then proceeded to check the children's heart rates, breathing, and other vitals.

"Okay, this is where we part ways," Kyle smiled. "Greyson's gonna' get fixed up, then we're all headed to the airport. Our flights back to California leave in a few hours."

"Wait, so what about me?" I asked. "Am I staying here? Is Pat here? Or Clara?"

"Yeah, Pat's here. He'll be down soon, I'm sure. You'll let him know the kids are here?" Kyle directed this last question to one of the medical Safeguards, who nodded. "Great. See you around, James."

Without another word, all of them except Greyson left the room and disappeared down the hallway. Not an overly warm bunch.

I took a look back at the kids; all four of them laid out identically on their gurneys, faces pale in the stark white light of the medical bay. I couldn't look at them anymore. I stepped out into the hall and sat down against the wall, closing my eyes.

Had I done the right thing, taking them from Heretic's safe house in the mountains? They had played there. Been children there. Fit in and been comfortable. Why did every choice I had made feel like going from bad to worse? I reminded myself that this was how they would forget. This was how they would live a full, happy life, and forget everything that had happened before. It was the only way for that to happen. Safeguard was these children's only chance at forgetting their past lives and living full, happy lives. The only way. Right?

I was so lost in my own dark thoughts that I didn't hear anyone approach until I heard my name. "James?"

Clara looked down at me, her hands on her hips. I stood up quickly, stumbling. "Clara. Hey, I—" She backhanded me, hard across the face.

I stepped away from the wall, so she no longer had me pinned, bringing my hands up to protect my head from further attacks. I wasn't sure which was in more pain: the right half of my face, or my pride.

"What the hell, James? We trusted you. We let you participate in the op to get the kids back, and you screwed us all over. We trusted you! And then you disappear, entirely, for weeks, assault the team we send to bring you in when we found you for a moment, and then you have the nerve to call us and ask for a pickup from the other side of the country? That's a dick move, James. Serious dick move."

"Clara? Hey, Clara, what have we already said to the kid? I thought we agreed to let me talk to him first?" Pat came running down the hallway, half yelling, half whispering to Clara.

"You were talking out your ass, Pat. I agreed to nothing," Clara's eyes burned into me. I still stood, hands up in self-defense, genuinely unsure whether she would attack me again.

"I'm sure James probably had a good reason for absconding with the kids and knocking some of our guys unconscious, didn't you James?" Pat gripped his wife's shoulders, pulling her into his side and not subtly turning to put himself between us. He turned to smile at his wife, then looked back at me, eyes going wide. I couldn't read minds, but the look plainly said, *"Explain, quickly."*

"I didn't know what to do. I was confused. Heretic was there at the house, he said something, something only my mom used to say to me. I got confused. It made sense at the time. Then we got there, and it... made less sense. Sorry." I trailed off, realizing it sounded even more stupid than when I'd thought through it.

Pat's smile faded, he blinked several times, then he sighed sharply, looking down at the ground. "No, you were right, Clara. That's a really stupid reason. Hit him again, this time for me."

Clara pushed him away and punched him playfully in the ribs a few times. "All right, Pat, you've made your point." Looking back at me, she locked eyes with me for several seconds, then put out her hand. "We good?"

I shook her hand tentatively, unsure what else to do.

"All right, so we're glossing over everything that James did and that he left us in the lurch for weeks with no firm grasp on where he or the children were without any consequence or ill feeling? Just want to make sure we're all on the same page." Pat had a habit of talking with his hands, and gestured to all three of us exaggeratedly.

Clara gave Pat a knowing, *"Really?"* sort of look from under raised eyebrows and shook her head. Pat shrugged and shook his own head slightly.

"What? I'm good with it, I just wanted to make sure I was picking up what you were putting down. Now that I'm good, what say we get Jimmy here set up with a room?"

"Wait, what about the kids?" I asked, pointing with my chin back into the medical bay. "What's gonna' happen to them?"

"We're going to do for them what we've always done for every Mythic we scoop up. They'll be Swept, Bitted, then Hosted until they're old enough to join Safeguard, and then we'll train them up. They'll be valuable assets someday. For now, they need to go deep underground." Clara glanced at me as she said this, checking for my reaction. It was just what I wanted to hear.

"And they won't remember anything about the last several weeks, right? Or their life before? With their father? You can wipe everything of Julian Danton from their memories, right? You can do that?" I looked right at Pat. As the Thinker of the two, I wanted to look him in the eyes and get this assurance from him. The black thing inside me twisted, half in agony, half in ecstasy at the idea of forgetting.

"We can do that, yeah. You already know this, James, we've talked about this before. What are you really asking?" Clara looked at me closer, her eyes wide with realization and pity.

"I want... I want you to do it to me. I want to forget the last several weeks, all the stuff with the kids. From the time that I came home to find my parents... I want it all gone."

Clara sighed sadly, and Pat just stared. "Are you serious?" he asked. "James, are you serious? I mean, I get it, your parents died, but do you honestly want to forget all about it? What story would I even put in there in its place? You gotta' take the bad with the good, man."

"No, you don't get it." I could feel the black in me, writhing and swelling with memory. "Roger Caplan told me I was adopted. That's what I need to forget."

"Oh, hell. They never told you?" Clara's mouth hung open, and shock stretched her face.

It was all I could do to shake my head. I hated my eyes for the burn and the blur of tears. My throat constricted, and I coughed to force it open.

Pat put his hand on my shoulder. "They had to have their reasons, man. You gotta' trust that they wanted what was best for you, and for them, that meant not telling you. That happens all the time, right? People not telling their kids they're adopted?"

"Have you ever once heard of a situation where it ended up a good thing?" My voice cut at Pat. "All I can think about is that I lived with them for years, and every day that I woke up, every day we spent to-gether, they looked me in the face and opted to lie to me about who I am, about who they were. Every day, they made the conscious decision to lie. I hate what this is doing to me. I think about them, and it hurts because I miss them, but at the same time, something in me wants them dead, wants them to pay for what they did. That divide is killing me. The whole time with the kids, I couldn't sleep, couldn't be alone with my thoughts. I don't want this anymore. If you can take me back, to before I knew any of that, I'd be happy. I mean, I'd be devastated that they're gone, but there wouldn't be this... ugliness inside me. The grief I can deal with. But the hate and resentment: it's too much."

"We can't do that, James. You have too much to offer to this organization. For one, there's your father's wristband. It doesn't seem to work on anyone but you, remember? And right now, that wristband is the only thing that will allow anyone to get close to Julian Danton." Clara folded her arms. "Or have you already forgotten what a thorn he is in our collective asses? Also, you know now where Heretic's hiding in the mountains with all the children he's abducted from us over the years. Don't think we've forgotten about that little detail. We've got to jump on that before he up and moves again. Maybe even before we move on Danton. The point is, like it or not, you've become a necessary part of all of this. We can't just wipe you clean and turn you back to your old life. We need what you can do, or at least what this wristband can do. At the minimum, let us study it further, see if we can replicate its effects."

I shrugged off Pat's hand from my shoulder, turned my back on the two of them. I took a moment to think. "Fine. I'm fine with sticking around, but I want the adoption eliminated from my memory. You can keep me with Safeguard, give me the memory that I've always been with you, or whatever. Keep me around, keep the wristband around, but take away the adoption."

"That's not without risks," Pat spoke up. "Anybody who knew your parents well knew about you, and about the adoption. They weren't quiet about it with people inside Safeguard. If you didn't know about the adoption, it could come up with anyone inside the organization who knew about it. That would be no bueno for you. The brain doesn't like it when it's presented with conflicting ideas under normal circumstances. You think finding out the first time was bad? Finding out a second time when your brain's been Swept is going to destroy you. Imagine putting a vacuum hose over your lips, then plugging your nose and trying to breathe through your mouth. That's a whole lotta suck to try and breathe through, brother."

I turned around and stared at Pat, Clara's expression matching my own confusion. Pat alternated between our faces. "What? You never did that? Can't relate?"

We both shook our heads mutely.

"Well, hey, that's not my fault. But the analogy holds, believe me. Your brain is gonna' be trying to plug holes that even it knows are bunk. But without a full Reversal, it's just gonna' collapse in on itself. I've seen it happen. Well, I've read about it, in old files. It is *not* something you want to happen to you."

"So, keep me away from people who were close with my parents. You're the ranking members of Safeguard, aren't you? With my parents gone? You said you were their second-in-command. Surely you can station me with people who weren't close to them, and don't bring it up with me yourselves. They didn't do it over my entire life. Surely you can manage it over a casual work relationship for the next 30 years."

Clara and Pat looked at each other. Clara shrugged, sighed, then looked back at me and shook her head. "It's your life, James. I mean, we can probably make something like that happen; your parents had pulled back from the rank and file for the last several years, anyway. I'd sign off on it, depending on what you think." This last was directed at Pat.

Pat looked from Clara to me, and back again. He chuffed a few times at each of us, then threw up his hands. He plugged his nose with one hand, mimed holding something up to his mouth with his other, and made a tight pucker, sucking loudly through his lips.

Clara folded her arms again. Pat shrugged. "Hey, whatever, man. It's your brain on the line. Don't say I didn't tell you so."

Chapter 17

I woke up before my alarm clock. Today felt like yesterday, but something was indelibly different. I looked across the room at my roommate Dougan's sleeping form in his bunk. He was probably sleeping off the effects of the graduation party hosted for the newest members of Safeguard. He'd had considerably more than I had to drink. Frankly, I was surprised he wound up back in his bunk, instead of passed out in a hallway somewhere. Probably Clara's doing; she ran a pretty tight ship. Somehow, I couldn't see her putting up with graduating cadets sleeping off hangovers anywhere but in their own beds.

I pushed off the covers and put my feet on the cold stone floor, glad for the insulation of my wool socks. I got dressed quietly, but I doubted that, even if I'd banged and stomped up and down the room, Dougan would wake up any time before noon. I wasn't sure I'd ever seen anyone put down that much alcohol and still come up breathing.

As I pulled on the liquid armor over my head, I touched the spot where I'd been shot by Julian Danton's man what felt like years ago. "Thanks, Dad," I whispered to the dark. It had been a year since that day when I'd come home to find my mother and father murdered by Roger Caplan. A year since I'd found the kids and everything unfolded. Since joining up with Safeguard, not a day had gone by where I didn't think about my parents multiple times. Weapons training was all about Dad; anytime I fired a Con-gun or tagged someone with a Sleeper, I heard Dad's voice, guiding my shot and critiquing my form.

I smiled at the memory, of our frequent Wood walks, but was surprised, like always these days, to find my heart beating a little faster and my jaw a bit tightened. I didn't know why, but I found myself a little bit mad whenever I thought about them. Pat said it was probably some sort of transference or something like that, from all the crazy emotions of rescuing the kids several times from Danton, being on the run from Safeguard, and finally leaving Heretic and joining up with Safeguard. Made sense, I guess. It was an awful lot to process.

I let myself out of the room and closed the door gently behind me. I walked the central hall from the dormitories to the mess hall, doubtful that the chow would even be available yet. My alarm hadn't even gone off by the time I'd left my room. I smiled to myself at the thought of a very-much-hungover Dougan scrambling to find the off button on my alarm clock. He wasn't a morning person even on the best of days.

As expected, the kitchen serving windows were still closed, but I could see light around the edges of the closed doors; the cooks were hard at work, but not ready for service. I sat down at a table near the rear corner of the room with my back against the wall, my legs up on the bench, and my eyes closed. I was always amazed at how quiet it was underground. Above ground, there's always something going on, something to hear, even if it's only the wind through trees or bugs in the grass. But down here, it was good and truly silent. There's so little movement beneath the ground. It made sense to me that the most common analogy for putting things to rest was always for it to be buried.

I opened my eyes at the sound of boots coming down one of the hallways. Command corridor. There was only one person it could be this time of morning.

Clara cleared the entrance and walked straight to me, without changing direction or skipping a beat in her walk. She knew I was here; she was expecting me. I smiled in spite of myself. As much as I didn't like the idea that I'd become predictable, I didn't mind that she expected me to be up early. I liked Clara. I liked her no-nonsense attitude, her blunt way of speaking.

She pushed my feet off the bench, then proceeded to walk around the table and sat down across from me. I hid my smile. Clara could be such a jerk when she wanted, which was, admittedly, most of the time.

"Director," I said, using her official title. She hated it when I did that.

"Stow it, Strader," she shot back. I only briefly glimpsed her smile as she looked down at the folder she set on the table. She slid it across to me then interlocked her fingers and rested her hands on the table in front of her.

"We're ready to move on Danton, and I want you on the team. Not point, you just graduated, for crying out loud. But I want you on the team, for obvious reasons."

"They still haven't been able to synthesize the wristband down in R&D?" I asked, genuinely surprised, but also secretly proud of my father's obvious genius.

"Nope. In fact, they've assured me, under no uncertain terms, that this stuff isn't even an element found on earth. They have no idea where it came from, how your dad made it, or, most importantly, how it does what it does. The only thing we know now is what we did clear back that first day we met; it stops all Mythics' abilities, but only when you're wearing it, and only around your immediate person or those you're touching. For all intents and purposes, you're our secret weapon magical force field."

"So, I'm not actually *on* the team, so much as I'm an *accessory* for the team?"

Clara shrugged. "What can I say, Strader? We all have our roles to play. It just so happens that you're the only one who can possibly play yours. That being said, you obviously still have the choice. Without the kids, Danton won't be supercharged like he was the first time you and I went after him, so, even without you I like our chances, but, there's no denying that it would certainly be a slam dunk if you were involved.

But again, the decision is ultimately yours. I'd understand if you wanted to sit this one out."

"No, I'm in; for sure. So, we run the op like we have the drills and training, right? Everyone on the strike team linked up via the cables, with me providing the field?"

"Right. I still can't believe those cables transfer the energy, or the field, or whatever the heck it is that's happening. I'm just glad we stumbled on it." Clara snorted in disbelief.

"Just like grabbing onto the electric fence back home. You ever do that?" I asked, remembering passing the shock through my group of friends clear back in elementary school.

"Uh, I grew up very urban. Electric fences weren't exactly a fixture in the city." Clara laughed at me.

"Anyway, shouldn't be a problem, Director. I'd be honored to be a part of the operation," I nodded.

Clara smiled, knocked on the table, and pointed at the folder as she stood up. "Good. Study up; you roll out at thirteen-hundred."

"Yes, ma'am. I'll be ready."

***

The drive back to southern Illinois gave me more time to think than I was comfortable with. Luckily, I was in a vehicle with Sammy, the same pretty Tech I'd met back on my first assault on the Danton home. We had a lot of time to talk.

"You seriously grew up in LA?" I asked. I'd been right, then, about her sounding like she was from out West.

"Yep. Right in Monterey Park. It was a crazy place to live. So many people, so much tech. What about you? You grew up pretty close to the Danton place, right? That was your house we left from the last time we were here?"

I nodded. "Yep. Grew up in that house." *Buried my parents at that house.* Looking out the window, seeing the familiar landscape of trees, rolling hills, with the occasional rocky bluff, I got lost for a few moments in memories of smoldering campfires, the silence of the forest when you first stumble into it, and the wet-earth scent of working in my mom's vegetable garden. It still hurt some to think about losing them.

"Hey, you still here?" Sammy reached out and touched my leg. I stifled the start that her touch gave me and tried to play it cool. I turned and smiled, nodding slowly.

"Sorry, just reminiscing."

"I figured," she laughed, letting her hand slide off my leg slowly.

"It probably won't be that much longer," I forced myself into distraction. "This is the Mississippi river up ahead. The other side of that is Illinois. Probably 45 minutes until we reach Danton's place?"

The driver, Jose Flores, a Thinker from Kansas City, met my eyes in the rearview mirror, and nodded in confirmation.

Sammy saw the nod and looked at me, smiling widely. Smiling gave her beautiful dimple lines in her smooth, round cheeks. "Wow. Somebody really knows his geography around here."

I shrugged and kept my smile small. "I told you; I grew up around here."

"Yeah, well, next time we're in LA, I will impress the crap out of you. I'll take you to a burger place that will blow your freaking mind." Sammy winked, she actually winked, then made a big show of looking out the other window and losing interest.

I'd forgotten how attractive Sammy was. Maybe I'd ask her out after this was all over. She certainly seemed fun. We'd been talking for hours, and I was still as comfortable talking to her as when we'd started, a genuine first for me.

The 45 minutes passed quickly; soon we were pulling over on the same stretch of road we'd staged from the first time around. The five SUVs rolled to a stop, and the full team unloaded from the convoy. All in all, we were a group of 30 this time. This wasn't a rescue op like the first time; this was a bulldozer op to completely raze Danton's operation to the ground. Every single one of Danton's lackeys Bitted, Swept, and Hosted to a new location.

I was the "Ground" for the tip of the spear. That was the new term they'd come up with for the role I was filling. With the cable connecting all of us, me being the critical component, someone had referred to me as the ground, and the term stuck. We'd tested it

extensively in training, and, so long as the cables connected us, the effect held; no Mythic with any ability
could touch or influence us with that ability. Not
directly, at least. I mean, ability or no ability, a dump-
ster dropped on top of you would still kill you, but no
directly-ability-related means could touch us.

Jose spoke up. "All right, people, let's circle up!
We're running five teams of six, just like we trained,
two sets of Tinker/Thinker teams each plus a couple
of Techs for good measure! Techs will also act as Cave-
men in case they got Techs of their own. Only Alpha
team will be connected to the Ground by conductive
cable, for obvious reasons; no reason to make an even
bigger target than we have to. Bravo, Charlie, Delta,
Echo, your role will be both suppressive fire and Bit
and Sweep. The primary objective is Julian Danton,
alive, but the secondary is to dismantle his entire
operation, every last stinking Mutt and Jeff."

Jose paused, and looked at me. "We've trained for
months for this op. We know the layout, we know the
target, and, thanks to some slick work by Sammy, we
even know their numbers." He nodded at Sammy, who
smiled shyly and nodded back.

"Let's go kick some Danton ass." Jose pulled his
helmet into place. That was all the rest of us needed.
We *had* trained for this op for months. They'd recre-
ated the environment entirely, factored in every bush
and shrub into their virtual simulators. Between the
Tinkers and the Thinkers, we'd run virtual reality
simulations that felt like real life so many times, we

had planned for nearly every contingency we could think of.

I pulled my helmet on, piled back in the SUV I came in, and collected my things. As Jose climbed into the driver's seat, I handed out the spools of cable that would connect into everyone else's adapters on their belts, that wrapped right around their bellies beneath their suits. Exactly like the old electric fence, except different.

The convoy stopped a quarter mile up the road from the Danton driveway, an additional two hundred yard drive off into the trees until it arrived at the house. I idly wondered if they'd repaired the damage done by the fire a year ago during our last raid.

The five fireteams divided up and the other four teams melted into the shadows of the trees in the late November evening, headed for their appointed positions near the house. The other five members of Alpha team connected their cables, so that we were all linked.

Jose spoke over the comms. "Comm check, team leads check in."

"Bravo Lead, check."

"Charlie Lead, check."

"Delta Lead, check."

"Echo Lead, check."

"Alpha team moving into position, hold until my signal."

The six members of Alpha team: myself, Jose, Sammy, two Tinkers named Candace and Brian, and another Thinker, Olivia, filed through the trees off the driveway.

We stopped a few yards from the edge of the trees in front of the garage, the furthest door of which had been replaced after I'd blown it off a year ago.

"Everyone hold," Jose's voice came over the comms. "Thinkers, give me a scan of the building, I need confirmation of how many Mythics we're dealing with."

"This is Bravo Thinker One, I'm getting only one Mythic. Seeking confirmation?" the voice sounded as confused as the message made everyone else.

"Delta Thinker One, I'm also getting only one Mythic."

Everyone on Alpha looked to Jose for direction; this was not at all what we had anticipated or planned for. Why was there only one Mythic in the house?

"Alpha Lead; change of plans. All other teams move in on the house and assume breach positions at all windows and doors on the front of the house. Entry on my mark."

Jose stood up at the end of our line and was shaking his head, tapping his helmet. Alpha team looked at him in confusion, the only ones who could see him in the fading light. The other teams moved in, taking up positions at the windows and doors. This was not what we'd run in drills, but everyone knew better than to question the orders of the Lead in the field.

Jose was grabbing at his helmet now, like he was trying to get it off. Over the comms, his voice continued to give commands. "Alpha team will hold our position. All other teams, prepare for breach in five, four, three..."

Jose grabbed his electro cutter off his belt and popped the blade.

"Two."

Alpha team watched in horror as Jose plunged the electro cutter blade up into his helmet.

"One."

Jose cut away the face plate of his helmet, the entire side of his face blistered and sizzling where the electro cutter had grazed him.

"Mark."

"IT'S A TRAP! ABORT! ABORT!" Jose yelled at the top of his lungs. His yell was lost in the chaos as the windows and doors of the first level blew inward from a dozen Concussive Cannons blasting simultaneously.

Delta was the first team into the doorway. They one by one dropped to the floor, some falling to their knees, others simply going limp and falling face-first to the ground.

There were four blasts from my immediate right as Sammy's rifle went off. One by one, Jose, Candace, Brian, and Olivia each stiffened, then went completely slack, dead with a hole in their helmet. I turned toward Sammy, raising my rifle, but the butt of her weapon smashed upward into my helmet, knocking me flat on my back. Her rifle pointed right at my face, her voice came over the comms. "Don't." There was no way I could bring my rifle to bear on her before she could get a shot off. I let my weapon fall to the ground and held out my empty hands.

How did she mimic Jose's voice on the comms? We were wearing the cable! Without my doing so, the catch on my helmet released, and Sammy kicked it off, then fired a round from her pistol right into my face.

Mind-numbing pain was my best friend in that moment. It let me know I wasn't dead. The last thought that crossed my mind was relief, before the sedative did its work, and I lost consciousness.

Chapter 18

Feeling and awareness came back slowly. First, there was pain in my face. My nose felt like it took up way too much room on my face; it had to be broken. Next, I was aware of my shoulders. They ached because my hands were secured together behind me. I coerced my eyes open, wishing Pat was here to give me one of his pick-me-upper brain slaps. I could use one right now.

"You're awake. Finally. I was beginning to doubt whether Samantha had actually shot you with a sedative, and not some poison."

Julian Danton sat on a tall metal stool a few feet away from me, his arms folded casually across his chest, wearing his signature slacks, dress shirt, and blazer. Did the man ever dress down? He even dressed up to interrogate and harass his prisoners.

Through significant effort, I made my eyes focus on Danton. "Where's the rest of my team?" I slurred.

"They're all dead, James. I had no use for any of them. I'm afraid that I have no use for nearly any of you. The only reason you're still alive is so that you can tell me where my children are. Samantha scoured Safeguard's accessible databases, but there seems to be no record of where they're hidden, probably for precisely this reason; so that I can't find them, even with help from the inside. But that's why we're having this little conversation. So that you can do me and my children one last favor and tell me where they are. So, I'm going to ask you just the one time, James: where are my children?"

I tried to come up with something pithy to say, but all my drug-fogged brain could come up with was, "Forget it, Danton."

The corners of his mouth lifted in a smile, but his eyes narrowed with malice. "Now, James, I think you should reconsider. I know you're probably thinking that the tables are laid just the way they were the last time we met. But that was before I knew your little secret." Danton reached into a waist pocket of his blazer and pulled out my wristband.

I groaned, and my heart and breathing both quickened in sudden fear. Without the wristband, I was entirely vulnerable to anything Danton wanted to do to me, ability-related or otherwise.

"I'm glad you understand where things lie now. Your team died remarkably quick, James. I've had well over a year now to develop and master my abilities, and, I must say, I've gotten quite good." He stood up off his stool and walked around behind me, his hands in his pants pockets as he spoke quietly. "Have you ever known anyone with cancer, James? Bone cancer, specifically? I've always heard that it's one of the most painful varieties out there." His voice dropped to barely above a whisper as he stood behind me, where I couldn't turn to see him directly. "Imagine the pain from abnormal bone growth, occurring over months and years, then imagine what it's like to have that growth occur over the course of moments. I can cause cancer, James. Not only that, but I can take it away. I can give you bone cancer, right now, cause tumors that grow in moments, then snap my fingers and reverse the process. I can do it over and over again, until you give me what I want."

"You're literally the cure to cancer, and you're using it to torture people to get what you want? You're a real class act, Danton," I spat, unable to see him behind me.

"Oh, spare me the sanctimonious preaching, James. I'm doing exactly what the world is prepared to accept from people like me. How exactly do you think I would be accepted if I walked into the Oncology ward —or any other ward, for that matter— of the nearest hospital and began healing people indiscriminately, like some wannabe Messiah? We live in cynical times, James. I would be ruined and crucified in the public eye before I even got started."

One of Danton's hands rested gently on my left arm, and the ache in my shoulders was drowned in a screaming flood of agony from my upper arm. I screamed and tried to pull away from his hand. The ropes apparently tied not only my hands together, but also to the chair itself, because I couldn't go anywhere. I threw myself against the ropes, wrenching my shoulders even more and not quite matching the pain from the cancer Danton had given me.

"I'd resist the urge to throw yourself like that. I can reverse the effects of what I do; I can't repair mechanical damage you do to yourself." Just like that, Danton took his hand away and the pain vanished. I slumped in the chair, my chest heaving, and sweat pouring from the end of my nose. I licked my slick salty lips and tasted blood. I must have bitten my tongue. I spat to the side, unable to even lift my head. My left arm trembled uncontrollably, spasming in confusion and pain.

"I'm a simple man, James. I have simple needs, simple wants. I can cure cancer, yes, but for a price. People are accustomed to paying for treatment. When I give them my placebos, and heal them one by one, the money will practically print itself. No research lab costs to recoup, hardly any production costs, except for the sugar pills. We're talking about nearly limitless profit on the biggest medical question and problem of the last several hundred years. It's a pharmaceutical salesman's fondest dream!" He laughed. "Now you, James, you grew a tumor in your arm the size of a grain of rice just now. Next time, I'll move up to a pea, then a grape, and so on." Danton moved casually back to the stool in front of me. "Are you familiar with the term vasovagal syncope? It's a general description of a condition in which the brain responds to stressful situations and intense pain by slowing the heart rate and dilating blood vessels in the legs, pulling blood away from the brain, resulting in loss of consciousness." He straightened his jacket and adjusted slightly on the stool, smiling casually at me. "I'd rather not have to wait for you to regain consciousness before we pick up this conversation again. I asked you a question, James."

I raised my head to the ceiling, sucking air and willing my body to stop shaking. "You're wasting your time, Danton. I don't know where they are. I'm a field agent, not a Host."

"My God, James, do they really use the cute little nicknames? Bunch of paramilitary wannabes." Danton stood up and walked to the door of the small room we were in. There were no windows. Must be a closet. He pulled it open and called, "Samantha, would you come in here for a moment, sweetheart?"

Sammy walked into view, still wearing her Safeguard field uniform, liquid armor and plate. She avoided looking at me. "What's up?"

"Samantha, what are the chances, do you think, that our mutual friend James here doesn't know where my children are?"

Sammy folded her arms across her chest. "We've already been through this, Julian."

Danton gestured to me, and there was an edge to his voice. "Indulge me."

Sammy sighed curtly and said, "They're not in the database, which means they've been intentionally kept off-books. There isn't an official protocol for that, but they would take precautions. They'd have redundancies in place."

Danton waited a moment, then prompted, "Meaning?"

"Meaning that multiple people would know about the arrangement, especially after what happened last year."

Danton looked at me but continued speaking to Sammy. "And who would most likely know about such an arrangement, Samantha?"

"The Director, obviously, maybe a few Lieutenants, and a good chance someone who has a close relationship with the children."

Danton leered. "Bingo." He stepped in front of me and stood easily, hands together behind him. "Any thoughts, James?"

"Go to hell, Danton."

"Wrong answer. I lost everything the last time you visited, James. My wife set my house on fire, then left me. My followers decided that without my children, and with all of Safeguard alerted to us, I was too large a target with not enough hitting power to be a horse worth backing. You took everything from me." He leaned down and placed both hands on the arms of the chair I was in. "I'd like you to take everything that happens from here on out very, very personally."

He grabbed my arm again and this time the pain in my arm was accompanied by a wave of nausea, then I blacked out.

***

I had no idea exactly how much time passed while I was in that closet. It must have been some sort of basement storage closet because there were no windows, and the walls were all unfinished concrete. It was dark except for a small opening at the bottom of the door. It took me several minutes after rousing to get loose of the rope, which was really more like thick twine, and be able to stand up, massaging my sore shoulders and wrists. I hadn't even noticed that my ankles had been tied to the chair with loose tethers.

The door was thick, metal, and unyielding when I tried to kick it in. My chances weren't good, kicking the opposite direction from which it opened, but I tried anyway. Every time the flat of my right boot connected with the door near the handle, I berated myself and shoved my shame and frustration into rage that jolted through my leg and transferred to the door.

Idiot. *Thud.*

Blind. *Thud.*

Sammy. *Thud.*

Whole team dead. *Thud.*

Eventually my rage fizzled out, or my leg went numb, I'm not sure which happened first. Then I sat down and palmed my stinging eyes. The entire team was dead. Those people I'd been training with for hours every day for the last several weeks before graduation, studying with, eating with, they were all dead. Their faces and random memories of them flickered

250 ~ JUSTIN K. NUCKLES

through my awareness. *STOP!* I shook my head and slapped my face a few times to ground myself in the moment. Survivor's guilt could come later; technically, I still had to survive. My training with Safeguard took over. Stop. Breathe.

Think. I was still alive. Danton thought I had information on where his children were being Hosted. I didn't, but he obviously thought I did, as did Sammy, apparently. Sammy worked for Danton. My mind wanted to latch onto that fact and get mad again. I had to tap on my forehead several times to bring myself back. Think.

Observe. I was in Danton's house. Probably his basement, as I'd guessed earlier. Either the basement was entirely unfinished, or only this room, but that made the most sense as to where I was. The biggest clue was the door: it was like any door that you could get from the hardware store, a security door for your house. It had all the decorative raised paneling and trim work of an exterior door, like you'd seen on the outside of a house. Metal, but not anything special. A handle on this side, locked, and a deadbolt housing. I wondered what other kind of locks were on the other side, if any. So far, the door had weathered every one of my kicks without even hinting at splintering anywhere in the frame. Observe.

The small cutout at the bottom of the door and the source of the light caught my eye. It was about three inches high, and about 18 inches wide, right at the floor. I closed my eyes and winced when it hit me. I wasn't the first person Danton had kept in this room. His children. Who knew how many hours—days he'd locked his children in this closet, not even opening the door to feed them, simply sliding a plate under the gap in the door? Revulsion at this man rolled through me, followed swiftly by regret. How many times had I had to hide or hide with those same children in dark holes in basements and holes in floors? How many times had they had to relive a lifetime's trauma?

Plan. I had to escape. There was no other alternative. I had to. It was the only acceptable outcome. What did I have? The wooden chair, which could be broken up and made into makeshift weapons, if it came to it. The rope, about six feet of it in all. My belt and pockets were all empty, unsurprisingly. Thanks to Sammy, Danton knew about every standard-issue piece of equipment on my person and where it was kept. But what about the non-standard-issue ones?

I pulled off my left boot and pulled out the insole. I put my hand back in and breathed a sigh of relief when my fingers closed around the piece of metal there. I pulled out a small knife, four inches long, essentially a single piece of thin metal with no handle scales, a short double-edged blade on one end, and a grip area with a large ring for my index finger on the other. It wasn't ideal, but it was something.

I used some of the rope to wrap around the handle of the knife, giving me a better grip, then wrapped the rest around the knuckles of my left hand. Not exactly Muay Thai wraps, but better than nothing. Now all

I had to do was wait. I pulled the chair behind the angle of the opening door, so that I could stand up and be immediately where I wanted to in order to use the door to smash into anyone coming in, as soon as I heard them undoing the locks.

Honestly, I had no idea how long it might be before they came back again. I guessed it all depended on how patient Danton was in wanting to find his children. I figured they'd be back sooner than later.

I sat there long enough, straining my ears for any movement on the other side of the door, that I had to stand several different times to stretch cramping, sore muscles in my backside from sitting. After that, I alternated standing and sitting for stretches as long as I could. My mouth was dry, and my stomach rumbled. If they wanted me to stay alive, they had to give me food and water, they knew that, right? Sooner than later? Maybe?

I bent down on my hands and knees, my cheek pressed to the cold, chalky concrete floor, and peered out the food slot. The room on the other side was finished with carpet, walls covered in drywall and painted, but entirely empty. I couldn't see the door to the room from my angle, but the dimensions of the room I could see made it clear I was in a bedroom. The light was natural light from a window, not electric ceiling lights, based on the shadows in the corners opposite my closet cell. I listened close, but there was still no sound.

I stood back up and resumed my restless dance

between sitting and standing. The light from under the door started to fade as the sun went down, leaving me in almost complete blackness.

Finally, I heard the door of the room outside open, and a quick knock on my cell door. "Knock-knock, James. Are you awake and decent? We didn't finish our conversation earlier."

I stood up and pushed the chair back as far as I could, out of the way. This was it; it was now or never. I squeezed the knife and flexed my left hand, adjusting my grip on the wrapped ropes.

Suddenly, a wave of nausea crashed down on me that drove me to my knees, my stomach convulsing with dry heaves that burned my throat and left me sputtering for breath. Danton. Of course; he wouldn't risk coming into the room with me not helpless and incapacitated. Why hadn't I thought of that? Panicking, I shoved the knife down the shaft of my boot, catching on my pant leg and jabbing my calf painfully when I shoved it through. I didn't have a chance against Danton in this condition. Best to wait and hope he slipped up. I collapsed on the floor, heaving stomach acid onto the chalky floor in the dark, beyond caring as I smeared my cheeks into the resulting runny paste. I could do nothing but listen as Danton undid what sounded like several locks on the outside, including the deadbolt and handle lock, and opened the door.

I couldn't even look up as he said, "My, my, we have been busy, haven't we? I had my doubts about the twine, which is why I picked up a little something at the hardware store while I was out."

"Now," he said, picking up the chair and moving it back slightly from where I lay, huddled and shaking, on the floor, in a pool of my own sick. "About my question earlier."

I closed my eyes, and a scream tore my acid-raw throat as pain radiated outward through my body from the explosion in my left arm.

Chapter 19

Days passed that way in the basement, some of them I spent conscious, tracking the passage of the days by the light from the window of the room outside. Others passed completely unmarked, as I recovered shakily from Danton's most recent visit.

I think he gave up, figuring that I probably didn't actually know where his children were after about the fifth or sixth day of his interrogations—I couldn't remember. Eventually, he stopped asking about his children altogether. Yet his visits persisted; I got the distinct feeling that he simply liked hearing me scream.

I never had any chance to fight back. Every visit was the same. He'd knock on the door, asking me if I was awake and decent, then the sickness would hit. After that, it was only a question of how long I'd make it before passing out that day. I really wasn't sure how many days had passed before I started counting. I'd use my knife to scratch marks in the underside of the chair, where Danton wouldn't see it and investigate what I'd used to make the marks.

I never left the room; barely enough food and water to keep me alive was slid through the slot at the bottom of the door, and there were buckets for me to go to the bathroom into that were emptied each time I was unconscious. Sammy was the only weak link in Danton's armor at this point, and so far, I hadn't seen her since that first instance.

After seven marks on the underside of the chair with no opportunity to act against my captors, I decided to be more proactive. I started using the knife to carve at the door frame around the hinges. Danton always sat in the doorway, careful not to come too far in (my buckets smelled awful after the first couple of days). He never turned on the light in the closet and certainly wouldn't ever come in and close the door. The only challenge was how far I could carve out before it impacted the swinging of the door and Danton noticed. I chipped away a little bit at a time, keeping the shavings small. I hid a few of them in my waste bucket, and crammed others into the small cracks between the floor and the walls.

I kept hoping that Sammy would open the door one day. I was confident that, if she would ever open the door without Danton around, I could overpower her. But she never did. She was probably aware of the same thing. She was only around when I was unconscious; I felt sure it wasn't Danton taking care of my waste buckets. He probably felt that was beneath him.

It had been a few days since the last time Danton had come in. I'd passed out at the end, like the others, but it was the worst so far. I felt like I had been turned inside out and set on fire with that last one. Danton hadn't even bothered telling me what he was doing.

I'd screamed until my breath ran out, then fought for breath to scream some more until I finally passed out again. I hadn't seen or heard from Danton or Sammy since then.

I was scratching away at the door frame with my knife, listening for the bedroom door outside, when I heard instead a small sharp crack, then a slight rattling and some bumps. I dropped to the floor, peering out through the slot. The door remained closed, and the room empty, as far as I could see. But there was a shadow moving on the floor outside my closet. Someone was at the window.

My heart skipped a few beats and quickened its tempo; someone was at the window. It was entirely possible that I was about to be rescued. Hopefully it was a much larger Safeguard strike team. In any case, they didn't have Sammy sabotaging it from the inside. Either way, they knew enough to be at the window outside my closet cell. I was ecstatic. I rapped lightly on the door three times, in sequences of three. Once quick, once slow, quick again. Not only Morse code for "SOS," but signals in series of three was the universal signal for help in distress. I hoped, whatever they took from it, it would be something like, "Hurry up and get me out of here."

For several seconds there was no sound, and absolutely no movement from the shadow. The pause went on long enough that I started to wonder if I'd imagined it. Were hallucinations a side effect of one of the many diseases and conditions Danton had tried out on me in the last several days? Nope. The shadow moved again, then a pair of boots hit the carpet softly below the window. I had to stifle a yell. I was almost certainly getting out of this hellhole. The boots crept silently to the door, and I stood up, stepping back to give myself space to assess the person coming in. Better safe than sorry.

I could hear a soft clicking and clatter as the locks were undone, then the handle turned slowly. The door crept open, and suddenly I was looking at a helmeted head in a dark jacket and hood. "You?! What are you doing here?" I hissed.

Heretic eased the rest of the door open, putting one hand on his hip. "Would you rather stay?" came the digitized reply.

In lieu of an answer, I pushed past him and surveyed his handiwork at the window. The entire pane of glass had been smoothly cut from the rest of the sill and lay on the ground outside. I turned to face Heretic and braced my back against the wall, putting my hands together to form a platform. Heretic held up a finger, then walked back to the closet and closed the door, reengaging all of the locks. Then he turned and took a few quick steps toward me and vaulted cleanly out the hole without even holding onto the frame for support. He somersaulted on the frost-wet grass, then turned and extended a hand back through the hole. I grasped onto it and he pulled me easily out through the window. I'd forgotten how much stronger Heretic obviously was than he looked. I raised into a crouch, puzzled as to why Heretic had chosen the middle of the day for his rescue, if that's indeed what this was.

Heretic stayed crouched at the window, and I strained to see past him to what he was doing. He was holding the pane of cut glass, with a single finger through a small hole in the center, back in position with the edges of the frame. There was a quiet click then a hissing noise, and a small, intense blue flame emitted from the tip of one of his fingers, fusing the glass back together. Flame from his finger? Was Heretic himself a Mythic?

When he finished, he signaled for us to go and led me out of the yard via the same gap that Clara had created last year in the fence. As we ran quietly through the forest, I swore I heard Heretic giggle. "Let her wonder how you escaped through a one-inch hole in the window through locked doors!" He muttered. Heretic was stronger than he looked, but he was also a weirder dude than I knew, too.

***

I didn't like motorcycles. I'd never had the desire to ride one or own one like several of my friends in high school, and even in college. That made the prospect of the next several hours west on the back of Heretic's wild-looking street bike uncomfortable on all levels.

"Are you kidding me? This is your getaway vehicle? You couldn't even opt for a car?"

"James, this motorcycle is the fastest I have, making

it the perfect vehicle for our getaway. Why do you object?"

"Why do I object? Where do I even sit? I'm supposed to perch on the back like some idiot? That isn't even a real seat! I'm like a foot taller than you; you be the monkey."

Heretic looked from the bike to me, then back to the bike. He shook his head. "No. You couldn't handle it. I'll drive."

He climbed on and pushed the starter switch. Instead of the scratching, catching, then rumble of a gasoline engine, there was a deep hum, low enough that I wasn't sure whether I was actually hearing it or more feeling it. Electric motor, then?

"Here, take this," Heretic said, shrugging out of his coat and its deep hood. His helmet glinted dully in the midday sun.

"What will you wear?" I asked. It wasn't terribly cold out right now, but I knew that would all change once we were doing the speed limit.

"I'll be fine. Hurry up."

I swallowed any pride I had remaining and arranged myself on the partial seat and high foot pegs for the passenger. "Back there you said 'her'. I assume you meant Sammy? Is Danton not there, then? Is that why you chose now to come after me?"

"Danton's gone. Grab onto me."

I put my arms around his middle, hugging without touching.

"Grab on."

"I'm fine; let's go!" I hissed, pointing with my chin.

Heretic turned his head back to me and gently goosed the throttle. The bike shot forward. I didn't. I tumbled backward off the bike and landed in an upside-down heap on the road.

Heretic looked pointedly in my direction, and said slowly, with a side-to-side tilt of his head with each word, "Grab. On."

I remounted the bike and this time wrapped my arms tightly around Heretic's waist, grabbing my elbows to lock my grip.

We shot forward, and it only got worse from there. For one, it was freezing, even with Heretic's jacket; he seemed somehow entirely unaffected by the cold. Not even a trace of a shiver, and believe me, with my arms wrapped around his waist as tightly as they were, I would have felt them.

We rode so fast that we made the other cars on the freeway seem like they were parked. I had to close my eyes and focus on simply breathing, fighting for oxygen that seemed intent on slapping my face instead of surrounding it. At several points I thought I heard police sirens behind us, but only for brief moments, and I didn't dare loosen my hold enough to turn and look.

Chapter 20

Several cramped and painful hours later, the bike slowed, and then came to a smooth stop. "How ya' doing back there?" Heretic asked.

In answer, I slid off the bike and put my numb and frozen fingers between my legs to try and warm them.

"Where are we?" I asked, looking around at the bleak, flat ground around us. I could see huge wind turbines dotting the horizon in the distance, their synchronized blinking red lights creating a surreal effect in the fading evening light.

"A few miles outside Amarillo, Texas."

"What?! How is that even possible? How fast were you going?"

Heretic shrugged. "Slow. I'm not used to having a passenger on here. Stretch your legs, get warm, then we need to get going again. Only a few more hours to our destination."

"A few more hours to California? Are you insane? There's no way."

He turned to look at me. "Not California. After you left last year, we relocated the home to land on the Navajo Reservation. Even more remote than our old location. It's not under a Brick, but we didn't have that luxury this time."

"Wonderful. That's really great for you all, but I need to head back to the Safeguard Headquarters. Clara needs to know what happened, and we need to come up with a plan to take care of Danton once and for all."

"You can't go back, James. I mean, I'll take you there if that's what you really want, but it isn't." Heretic leaned against the bike, crossing his arms.

"No, I really think it is," I snorted and turned away.

"What about your parents?"

"What do you mean, what about my parents?" I asked.

"Do you honestly think this is what they wanted?"

I turned to look at Heretic. "My parents gave their lives to protect those kids, protecting Safeguard from people working with Danton to destroy this."

"Ah. You think you're defending their legacy. So, that means you probably—yes, that makes sense. James, do you trust me?" Heretic pushed off of the bike and stood up again, walking toward me.

I stepped back, bringing my hands up in defense. "Not at all."

"That's going to make this a whole lot more painful, then." Heretic moved blindingly fast and punched me just below my rib cage, stealing my breath for a few moments. He calmly stepped up to me and put both hands on either side of my head.

Lights, sounds, and smells erupted in my head like a geyser. Oatmeal. Laughing with the kids at my house. Roger Caplan's red truck in front of my parents' house, his pain-twisted face snarling up at me, *"No way. They didn't even tell you that you were adopted? That is messed up! Boy, they screwed you as bad as they screwed the proverbial pooch!"*

It all came flooding back. The shiny bits of memories that Pat had glossed over to shield me from the truth of my adoption at my request shattered into a thousand pieces, leaving me with all the holes, the questions, the hatred, and the grief that I'd still been carrying, just without consciousness.

I fell to my knees, still struggling for breath, as Heretic backed up a step or two. "Why?" I gasped. "Why would you make me remember that? I was over it…"

"No, James, you weren't over it. True healing can't be carried out with a magical slap. Forgetting isn't the same as healing, and healing takes time, effort, and understanding. Your head may have lost the memories, but your body held onto all of your rage, all the hurt and doubt." Heretic went down on one knee and put a hand out to me, but I slapped it away.

"No. Get away from me." I pushed up from the ground and stepped back. I walked to the motorcycle and rested against it for a moment, catching my breath. "Give me the key."

"Where will you go, James? Back to Safeguard?" Heretic's electronic voice was hushed, a different tone than I'd heard from him.

"I—I don't know. Give me the key."

"James, I think it's time you knew something else." Heretic reached up to his face, grasping the goggles.

I watched as he lifted the goggles up and pulled down the covering over his face. There was a blank, slightly curved surface. Another mask. *Why bother with goggles and a face covering over another mask?*

The plate lit up in brilliant white light, and then the light dimmed, leaving an image, a face, smiling on the surface of the helmet. My mother's smiling face, her concerned smiling face, the one where her eyebrows scrunched together and upward, making those little wrinkles in her forehead.

"Jamie, we're so sorry." It was my mother's voice.

"Stop it." I whispered.

"We didn't want to hurt you. We didn't want to hide anything from you. But it was the only way. It was the only way to drive you away from Safeguard and allow you to make your own decisions." My mother's face, her talking, face, had every line, every flaw, every beautiful flaw, that I remembered.

"Knock it off." I said, my heart pounding. "This video isn't real. My parents already gave me a post-death video; this isn't it."

"This isn't a video, Jamie. I'm here; we're here."

"What?" I felt foolish responding to it.

"Your father and I, we're here, or at least digital constructs of us are here. Heretic is us; we helped make him. He's our creation."

"This isn't funny. Shut it off, or..." I trailed off, genuinely unsure that I could even threaten Heretic. So far, he'd outclassed me in every physical altercation we'd had, and I had no weapons, except...

I pulled the knife out of my boot and took a step toward Heretic. "Shut it down. I'll kill you, so help me God."

My mother's face grew stern and Heretic's hands went up on his waist, thumbs turned downward exactly like my mom's used to when she'd do that. "James Oliver Strader, don't you dare use the Lord's name in vain with me!"

I was twelve again. She'd said the exact thing to me once when I'd cursed, trying out something I'd heard at school. I'd tasted nothing but pink floral soap for the next two days.

I lowered the knife, emotions swirling in my chest like a pinwheel. I didn't know which to address first, so I stood there, staring.

Heretic—*she* took her hands off her hips and took a few steps toward me, every movement, every step, my mother's. The slight way her left foot turned outward as it always had since she'd broken her leg in a horse-riding accident as a teenager. The way she folded her arms across her chest, both hands clasping the tips of her elbows, exactly like she did when she was worried about something. And her face; her face, smiling at me, but her eyes full of worry, just like the time I'd gotten a concussion playing football with some friends and I'd woken up in the hospital to her at my side. It was my mother, standing in front of me, full of concern and worry for me.

"It really was you?" I whispered, my mouth hardly moving. "That night at Danton's, calling me Jamie, telling me to be strong? And again, in California?" I lowered the knife, but I took a step back, having to force myself to take even short breaths. "But—what? I don't understand—so, Heretic is really some sort of robot or something?"

Mom's face dimmed like a light was turned off and Heretic's hands went to his hips as his former, scrambled voice said, "I think it's a bit reductionist, to call me a robot, isn't it? I'm a complex artificial intelligence being suspended in a vehicle that represents the symbiotic marriage of a proximal replication of human tissue and transhumanist techno-physiological advancement, additionally housing not merely one but three unique and complete human personality constructs."

Heretic stood with his hands on his hips for a moment more, facing me without moving for another several moments, as if waiting for some reply from me. I shrugged slightly, raising my eyebrows. Heretic slumped, his whole body conveying defeat.

"Fine. I'm a robot."

Mom's face lit up the screen again and her voice said, "May I drive again, please? I wasn't done talking. Thank you."

I looked at my mother's face. The last time I'd seen that face, aside from on the security footage at home, was when I arranged both Mom's and Dad's bodies before I put them in the ground that terrible night. The feelings of that day, and all the accompanying pain and rage of the following weeks was threatening to boil up from its old spot in the bottom of my belly. I'd done a lot of distracting, trying to bury it in distraction and productivity, but never really done anything with it. Now, because of Heretic's Reversal—

"Stop." I wasn't sure if I was talking to Heretic, Mom, or myself at that point.

"None of this makes any sense. Mom, you aren't really here. I buried you. I buried you, I buried Dad, I buried both of you." I put the knife back in my boot, but walked away, back toward the bike again. "So, what is this? Why build a robot? Why upload a—" I looked at Heretic/Mom. *Too confusing. Just call it Heretic.*

He spoke up again, screen going dark as before. "Unique and complete human personality construct?"

"Right," I said. "A unique human personality construct."

"Unique and complete. Don't forget that part. It's important." Heretic's voice piped up.

"And yet, not really the point right now, is it?" I lashed out, getting impatient now.

Mom's voice came back. "Jamie, Heretic represents the culmination of your father's and my life's work."

"At this point, I would have thought that Safeguard would have been your life's work?" I asked.

"Oh, baby, no. Our life's work was bringing down Safeguard."

I stared, dumbfounded. I shook my head in total disbelief. "What?"

Heretic scratched at his head, just like Mom used to when she was agitated with something. "Honey, our life's work was bringing down Safeguard. You've been inside it for months now, tell me you see it. Tell me you see what they do for what it is."

"Honestly," I spoke up, "I never really thought about it, other than that you, of all people, would have a more favorable opinion of adoption." It wasn't really true; I'd gone back and forth for weeks while evading Safeguard, and still had my own reservations, truth be told. But I was mad. Plus, talking to Mom like this made me feel like a teenager again, and old habits die hard. Especially the ones we wish we could break the most. I regretted the attack as soon as I'd spoken it. I saw Mom's face wince, and she visibly tensed.

"I know, Jamie." Her voice was quiet, her tone hushed and sincere. "It kills me that you had to find out that way. Roger Caplan was abrasive even at his best. I can't even imagine how that must have felt to you." Heretic took a few steps toward me, arms reaching out like Mom used to when she'd go to hug me. I stepped back and put the motorcycle between us.

"No." was all I said.

"Sorry," Mom's voice said. "Old instincts don't simply disappear." When I didn't reply, she went on. "Jamie, it isn't just adoption. It's abduction. Safeguard takes these children from families who love them, who've taken care of them and loved them for years, and they put them with strangers, and they fill them with lies about who they are, until years later, they're forced to perpetrate the same things on other children." Her posture was angry now, short, quick movements and lots of hand-raising. "At best, it's in-humane. At worst, it's a form of abuse that we've been complicit in for way too long."

I countered. "Okay, so it's not exactly what hap-pened to me..."

"No, Jamie, it *is* exactly what happened to you."

Her words hung there like the last echoing blows of a hammer-strike, sucking the air from my lungs, and sending shakes from the base of my spine to the tips of my fingers.

"Sorry?" was all I could get out.

Even without lungs, Mom took a deep breath before saying, "Jamie, that's exactly what happened to you. You weren't placed by a mother for adoption. We took you, without permission, without consent, without caring. You had a family who loved you, and we took you away from them." Her voice was trembling and quiet now, yet I was hanging on every word. I couldn't turn away, I couldn't look away, I was transfixed by the words coming from this robot representation of my mother.

She groaned and wiped at the screen in frustration. "Ugh! Dang it Jared, why didn't you make this thing with tears?"

"Dad's in there, too?" I asked.

"Yeah, he's here," Mom said, tapping the side of the helmet to point into Heretic's head.

"I know it's a lot to take in, Jamie; can I show you? I remember everything; do you want to see it? Heretic has my Thinker abilities. We can link up and you can essentially experience my memories as me."

I had so many questions, I was no longer thinking or processing clearly. It was like orienting myself in a thick fog. Things around seemed familiar, yet simultaneously foreign and ominous. I nodded, struggling to catch my breath.

Mom reached out to me and placed hands on both sides of my head, my vision went black, and I felt myself falling.

***

It was like watching a sunrise in fast forward. Everything went from black to tints of grey and blue, and finally to recognizable colors. I was sitting in the cab of a silver pickup, parked outside what looked like a hospital.

Sounds slowly registered as incredibly muffled rumbles, then louder varying pitches, and finally into discernible speech.

"—there's no legitimate reason to suspect that this boy might be a Mythic, Jared. Staffing issues in hospitals happen all the time, and there's never been a Mythic presenting this early, not anywhere in the records." *My mother's voice was the first sound to fully register for me.*

Dad sat in the driver's seat next to me; I was essentially seeing things from Mom's perspective. "We're not talking about a staffing issue, Deb. My guy in dispatch said that someone in the hospital, a kid, called in an absolute panic, because the nurse supposedly attending this little guy disintegrated right in front of them. Turned into a shower of dust that simply disappeared, the kid said."

Mom nodded. She'd heard all this before. "Right, but when the cops showed up, they didn't find anything out of sorts. The nurse wasn't around, and they can't seem to locate her anywhere yet, but a premature, hours-old missing persons case isn't exactly in our wheelhouse." *Mom idly fussed with a piece of equipment on her belt, rubbing the leather holster to what must have been an early version of Dad's Concussive Cannon.* "Science fair prodigies? Sure. Mind-reading 14-year-olds? Yup. Ten-year-old kid whose best friend is a lizard that fetches the kid's slippers for him? Handled it. But a kid who claims that the nurse disappeared right in front of her, with no explanation or evidence? That doesn't really have precedence, Babe."

Dad screwed up his face in thought. "It's true, but this doesn't fall under 'typical humdrum' either, does it?"

Mom laughed and waved out the window at their surroundings. "Well, we're here, aren't we? I'm not entirely the wet blanket you make me out to be. Come on, let's go inside and see if we can find the room. What was the number, again?"

Dad undid his belt and slid his Concussive Cannon off it, slid open the center console and placed both it, and Mom's, which she handed him, inside, then locked the compartment. "Room 231."

Mom and Dad got out of the truck and walked into the hospital, making for the Maternity wing. There was a keypad next to the double doors leading further into the building. You needed a passcode to get in. Dad caught the eye of a nurse walking down the hall and she walked over, pocketing the large tablet she was holding.

Mom smiled at her and shook her head slightly. "Hi again, we're here for 231. We can't remember the code; would you mind letting us in?"

The nurse, a slightly older white lady probably in her 60's, peered at Mom through plastic-framed glasses and said shortly, "I'm sorry; I can't let visitors in without a passcode. You'll have to call your friend and get it from them again."

Mom put her hand briefly on the woman's arm, near the elbow. "Oh, you don't remember us? We were in yesterday, too."

The woman blinked a few times and squinted at them, as if trying to remember something, and then smiled. "Oh, yes. I'd completely forgotten!"

Mom grinned back and made a big show of remembering, herself. "Oh! I just remembered it." *She turned back to the keypad and punched in 2-0-8-7. The magnetic locks on the door audibly disengaged, and Mom pulled the door open, holding it out so Dad could grab it. He held it for her, and they both entered in, smiling amiably at the nurse, who waved cheerily back.*

"'These aren't the droids you're looking for,'" *Dad said, quoting one of his favorite movies.*

"Obliviate," *Mom said, quoting back one of her favorite books. I got the impression that this exchange was a regular thing for them. They rode the elevator to the second floor and walked the short distance down to room number 231. Mom glanced at the name on the green chart in the bin by the door then knocked a couple of times and opened the door like a doctor might.*

"Mrs. Kline?" *Mom said cheerily.*

A woman with long, dark brown hair was holding a tiny newborn baby in her arms and cooing at it. She looked up when Mom and Dad came through the door, her hair falling back away from her face as she did.

I gasped, if only in my mind. Rachel. It was Rachel. Rachel was my birth mother!

"Yes?" *she said, still smiling from her obvious pleasure with the baby.*

"Mrs. Kline, I'm Special Agent Beesley, this is Special Agent Halpert," *Mom lied with surprising smoothness. I'd never known how good she was at lying.*

"Ma'am, we understand there was a report of an incident this morning involving one of the staff here at the hospital. Is there anything you can tell us about what happened?" *Dad spoke up from behind Mom, still standing near the door.*

"I thought the police had already been here. Are you from somewhere else? Special Agent, that's an FBI position, isn't it?" *Rachel's eyes were wide in concern.*

"They have, Ma'am, we're from another Division.

We actually have an open case involving the staff member in question, and we're trying to get some insight into where she might have gone. Is there anything you can tell us?" *Again, I couldn't believe how quick Mom came up with lies.*

"Linda Benson? I think you must be mistaken; I've known Linda my whole life! She's the nurse who delivered me; she wouldn't hurt a fly!" *Rachel seemed openly aghast at the idea.*

"Respectfully, we just need to know what happened this morning, Ma'am. No one seems to be able to find Ms. Benson, and we're wondering if maybe something happened here that could help us know where to find her," *Dad spoke up again.*

"I don't know; my daughter was the one who called 911. My friend had brought her to visit for a few minutes, but then stepped over to the cafeteria to get her some food, leaving her here with Linda. I'd fallen asleep, I was exhausted. When I woke up later, my son was crying with a fever, Linda was nowhere to be found, and my daughter had called 911, saying how Linda had disappeared right into thin air." *Rachel was rocking the baby—me. She was rocking me frantically, and I was starting to cry.*

"Nothing else out of the ordinary happen between then and now, Mrs. Kline? Anything else go missing?" *Mom didn't let it drop.*

"No, not unless you count James' pacifier. I swear he had it when I laid him down, but I couldn't find it anywhere a minute later. Other than that, no, nothing out of the ordinary." *She looked seriously worried. I was bouncing up and down in her arms, and the crying was getting worse. Suddenly, without warning, the cap, blanket, and diaper covering me simply disappeared, leaving me completely naked in Rachel's arms.*

"What the hell?" *Rachel said, holding me out at arm's length in puzzlement, looking down at her waist for the missing articles of clothing.*

Mom and Dad had both gasped when it happened, and seconds after Rachel's outburst, Mom stepped forward and took me from Rachel's arms, brushing a finger up the side of Rachel's temple as she did so. Rachel fell back, unconscious, and Mom held me close to her, putting a hand on my head and closing her eyes. A brief moment later, I stopped crying and was deeply asleep.

"What the hell was that?" *Mom whispered, looking back at Dad.* "He's like no Mythic I've ever seen. Guess we kind of know what happened to the nurse. He disappeared her! Seems like it takes a lot out of him, too. He's really hot."

Dad reached out to touch me and nodded in agreement. "So, what do we do now? Regular Sweep, Bit, and Host?"

Mom was already shaking her head. "Jer, you saw what happened. He disappears things. We don't even know what he is. There's no protocol for this. Tinks, Thinks, Tanks, Tamers, and Techs. That's what we know, that's what the protocols are written for. This little guy? He's way off the edge of the map. We don't know anything about him. If we put him in the system, we have no idea how he's going to react. We don't even really know what he made happen. Is the nurse, the stuff, invisible? Is it deatomized? We don't even know. We can't let something like that simply hang out and hope for the best." *She shook her head emphatically.* "No, we don't tell anybody about this, we Sweep the hospital, leave no evidence of him behind. I'll lay a trail that he died, call in the nurse and the attending, whatever we need to do. But he comes with us, and he stays with us until we figure this out; no paperwork, no whispers."

Dad was thinking, his fist pressed to his puckered mouth just like I remembered. "You're right. So, what do we say to people? How do we explain the fact that we suddenly have a baby overnight?"

Mom thought for a moment, herself, then spoke. "We'll say we adopted. We haven't been able to have our own kids, people will buy it."

Dad put his hands on his hips and chuckled a bit. "Deb Stryder, are you going soft on me?"

Mom punched him in the arm roughly on her way to the door. "No; shut up. This is only practical. He's a complete unknown, and therefore a threat. We keep him close."

The memory around me started to dim, fading from bright colors to blues, to grays, and finally all the way to black.

Chapter 21

I became aware of my own surroundings again sitting propped against the rear wheel of the motorcycle, Heretic sitting on his heels a few feet away, facescreen blank. I tried to focus on his screen, but my mind was racing so fast along so many different points and new revelations that I couldn't even focus. My head started to feel like I was spinning, and I closed my eyes, leaning my head back against the stationary motorcycle tire and swallowing hard.

"Don't let yourself spiral," Mom's voice called out, and her image flashed back up on Heretic's screen. "Pick a thing and say it out loud. Chew on it for a while until it seems more manageable, then choose something else."

I opened my eyes. "Rachel is my birth mother."

"Yes." Mom's voice sounded sad, but I couldn't know if it was regret, shame, or something else.

"Rachel is my birth mother." I turned the words over in my mind for another few seconds, tasting and trying out the implications. I thought back over my interactions with her at the home. Her kindness, her love and respect for children. It was easy to see where I got my appreciation for kids, then. I could do worse, I suppose.

"I have a sister," I realized out loud next.

"You do," Mom replied. She sounded less sad with this one, but there was something I couldn't identify in her voice.

"Do you know where she is? Is she still alive and..." I didn't know why that was the next question I asked, nor did I know what to ask next.

"Yes, and yes. She's all right." Mom's answers kept coming. What else did she know that she'd never told me?

I was ready for a new one. "I'm a Mythic." My heartbeat raced when I said it aloud. My blood went cold, though, when I remembered how that had been uncovered.

"Did I... Did I kill that woman? Linda, the nurse? Was she ever found?"

Mom hesitated before she answered. "She was never found, no. We kept pretty close tabs on the investigation for a lot of years and even did some poking around ourselves, but no, they never found her, not even a body."

I closed my eyes again, breathing out heavily as the weight of that statement bore down on me. I'd killed a person. Somehow, as nothing more than a newborn, I'd taken a life. How was I even supposed to feel about that?

"Say it out loud, focus your thinking," Mom said.

"I killed someone. I killed someone, dammit! How am I supposed to feel about that?"

"James, you were a newborn. What you did was no

more your control than any other reflex a newborn comes hardwired with. It wasn't your fault. The best we can figure is that she did something unintentionally that hurt you, and out of pure reflex—it can't have been anything more, James, think about it—out of pure reflex, she... disappeared? I don't know. We still don't exactly know what your powers are, truth be told." Mom came closer and sat down next to me, at the other end of the bike, not touching, but close. "We figured it had something to do with you getting upset; it always does, when children start presenting. She was unfortunate in that you got a lot more upset than other newborns. All growing up, I was around to use my abilities to help calm you down, so you didn't have another outburst. When you got to be a teen— we found something different."

"My wristband."

She nodded. "Exactly. It was like a Bit, but different. Other Mythic children, it's only a mental block; we wall off that portion of their minds until they're older and can control it. With you, I didn't even know where to look, and I wouldn't have recognized it, even if I had. I still don't know exactly what you can do, James, none of us do."

I stared at my boots, intentionally noticing the seams and stitches to stay present and out of my head. "So, how did you know what to do with the wristband, then?"

"That, we had help with. I can't tell you any more than that at this point, but we had help," Mom said, fidgeting with her fingers restlessly. She was uncomfortable still keeping things from me. *Good.*

"So, what now?" I knew that the revelations of the last half hour weren't something that I was going to be able to process through in a day. They were going to take years to sort through, probably even some therapy. I laughed, thinking about how to explain and talk through making a nurse disappear as a newborn with a therapist. The poor therapist.

"What's funny?" Mom asked, seeming concerned.

"I just thought about how much therapy I'm going to need, and how little I'm going to be able to share, someday, in order to get over all this," I laughed, shaking my head.

Mom smile-frowned in empathy and reached a hand out to run through my hair like she used to when I was a kid.

I enjoyed the moment for a bit longer, then opened my eyes again.

"Wait, so you were trying to dismantle Safeguard? Why, exactly?"

Mom let her hand drop to my shoulder and looked at me for a moment, then said, "Jared, you want to take this one?"

The face screen flashed white again, then Dad's face appeared, his kind eyes full of concern and his mouth set in a determined smiling line.

"Hey, James."

"Hey, Dad." It was too much. The reality of everything, that I was having a conversation with my parents after a year without them, was too much. I rolled over and clasped him in a hug, shedding no tears, just silently squeezing. He didn't say anything, either, simply held onto me and squeezed back. Some exchanges don't require words. Only presence.

We pulled apart, and I kind of half-laughed, half-gasped, then stood up and offered him a hand up. He took it, and I pulled him up to Heretic's full height, only coming up to my shoulders. "Well, I don't like that," he laughed. I laughed back.

"Anyway, yes. We were taking down Safeguard. It was something I inherited, and we decided, your mother and I, that we didn't agree with what it's been doing for the last hundred years. We can thank you for that."

I looked up in surprise, but he was smiling, not accusing.

"What do you mean?"

"I mean, you changed everything for us. Before you came along, it was just a job, same as anything else. We didn't love it, but it was the job we had, and we thought it needed to be done, so we did it. Until you came."

"Why? What did I do?" I asked, afraid of the answer, now.

Dad laughed. "You didn't *do* anything! You just *were*. And we absolutely adored you. Both of us. I know Mom said you were just a job, but it didn't take long at all for us to fall completely head over heels in love with you, kid. You changed everything."

"We realized that, if we loved you that much, when you weren't even really ours, what right did we have in taking you, or any other Mythic child, from a family who loved you? Your mother and I were both Generationals, Mythics born into families of already established Mythics, so there was never any Sweeping, Bitting, or Hosting for us. It didn't take us long, after getting you, to have that realization."

Connecting the dots to Rachel, I said, "And so you sought out Rachel, to make it right in some way."

Dad nodded. "Right. That wasn't until we created Heretic, which wasn't until you were a teenager. Rachel had—well—she'd already had a pretty rough several years at that point." Dad's face fell. He looked truly ashamed.

"Right." I'd remembered what Rachel had told me about her years being homeless and addicted to drugs and alcohol. Then I remembered something. "Wait. If you Swept her after taking me, why doesn't she remember her daughter? You said her daughter—my sister is fine, right? Why doesn't she remember her, either?"

"I'm with your mother on this one, bud; there are certain things we still can't tell you yet, because it isn't safe. All I can tell you is that your sister is a Mythic, too."

"Are you serious?" I shook my head. "This is insane. All right, so, what's next?"

Dad shook his head and smiled. "You always were almost *too* agreeable, you know that? What happens next is up to you. You know that was the reason we didn't tell you, didn't invite you into Safeguard to work with us, right? It wasn't because we didn't think you could handle the truth or that you weren't an asset. Not because we didn't trust you to stick with us or, more importantly, to do the right thing. We didn't tell you because we saw the person you'd become, how much you cared for others, and we trusted that you would do the right thing. Not even necessarily the thing that we wanted done, but the truly right thing."

He put one hand on my shoulder. "You've seen it from both sides, now, top to bottom. You had a family who loved you, you felt the pain of betrayal and hurt when you found out you were taken from your birth family, and you've also worked with Safeguard from the inside. You are the single best-qualified person to answer this next question: what's next?"

My eyes, wide, I turned toward the red lights blinking in synchrony in the distance, and raised both my arms, lacing my fingers together over the top of my head. I took a deep breath and let it out slowly. His words sank deep beneath my skin, settled somewhere deep down in my gut, and I could almost feel the moment when they began healing that black, broken thing that had grown and permeated throughout my entire body, and began to turn it to steel. It wouldn't happen all at once, and it wouldn't be quick, but I knew that I would be okay. So, what next?

"Next, we dismantle all of Safeguard, and bring Mythics into the open. No more abductions, no more hiding. We can do things for people; we can do things for the world. It's time we stopped hiding in the shadows and fighting amongst ourselves with people like Roger Caplan and Julian Danton. Let's bring the whole thing down."

Chapter 22

The rest of the ride to the new home was shorter even than the first ride, but just as windy and difficult to breathe through. I made a mental note to myself to fly everywhere possible after that, whenever possible.

"So, that's why you sometimes sound like you're different people talking," I said to Heretic as I slid off the back of the bike. "You literally have three different —wait. Did you say you had three distinct human uploads or something? Besides Mom and Dad, who else do you have in there?"

"Did I? I don't remember making such a ridiculous claim." Almost certainly his robot persona.

"You did."

"Well, that doesn't sound like me at all. No, I'm sure you're mistaken." He turned to me and blurted, "What have you decided to do about Rachel?"

I knew he was changing the subject, but I really couldn't ignore it; I hadn't thought about the fact that Rachel would be here when we arrived. Besides that, I'd already nearly already decided that, based on the caginess of Mom, Dad, and Heretic, that the third persona inside him must be my sister, the only question was if so, why, and was there some way I could draw her out? Thinking back on my interactions with Heretic, I figured that she must have been in control during the times when Heretic had been at his most sarcastic and casual; times he didn't sound at all like the robot, Mom, or Dad. I'd have to think about that later. For now, Rachel was the more immediate concern, inside the large, partially-completed earthship set into the side of the bare red rock.

"What does she know? What does she remember, exactly? She told me that she didn't remember either of her children. Is that true? And if so, what do you think we should do?"

"She does not remember either you or her daughter, explicitly. As you witnessed during your last visit, she somehow persists in her memory of having had children, but no explicit memory to speak of. That being said, thanks to your mother—Deby, not Rachel—I have her Thinker ability, as you witnessed."

"Yeah, hey, that's a good point. How does that work, exactly? How do you have her ability?" I put my hands on my hips, trying to think through that puzzle.

Heretic turned to me, stood silently for a moment, then simply shrugged slowly and said, "I have no idea." His goggles and face covering were back in place; I could almost pretend that he had a face underneath there, this way.

I'll have to ask Dad about that later. "Okay. Back to Rachel. I think we need to tell her. Heal her. Un-Sweep her?" I dug for a moment. "Reversal! That's what it's called. I think we need to do a Reversal on her. That's

288 ~ JUSTIN K. NUCKLES

what this is all about, isn't it? Putting back everything that was messed up by Safeguard? I think it needs to start with Rachel."

"Not an altogether terrible idea. I give it a 45% chance of failure and backfiring in your face."

I glanced over at Heretic, surprised. I smiled slightly. "You made that number up."

"I did."

I laughed. "You know, I'm still trying to figure out whose sense of humor they gave you."

Without skipping a beat, Heretic replied, "Your momma."

I laughed even harder. "Okay, so Dad. But only sometimes." I cleared my throat pointedly. "Anyway, Rachel. I think you need to do a full Reversal on her."

"Can do," Heretic replied.

We were walking up the path that led to the large front door, when suddenly a passing flock of small birds dive-bombed me, pecking and twittering angrily. I barely had time to yell and cover my face with my hands before they were pecked all over. Any and all exposed skin was quickly covered in angry, red welts, some of them bleeding slightly, when the birds left as suddenly as they had appeared.

I slowly uncurled from the fetal position I'd retreated into on the ground, in time to see an angry, dark, beautiful face disappear from the second story walkway in the front of the greenhouse.

"Shanice is still here, huh?" I winced, suddenly

remembering the less-than-positive manner in which we'd parted.

"And still angry at you, it would seem," Heretic observed dryly.

"You think?" I asked sarcastically. "Yeah, a Reversal isn't really gonna' help with that, is it?"

"No." Heretic raised a finger. "But Jared suggests chocolates. And flowers."

I looked around at the barren, empty hills and gullies for miles in any direction. "A little late for that, isn't it?"

Heretic nodded. "Yes." He paused, then looked up again. "Deby says you're screwed."

"Thanks, Mom and Dad. I'll handle this." We walked into the doors. Rachel came out of one of the far rooms, followed closely by Shanice, who turned around and walked clearly in the opposite direction.

"James? It's so good to see you! I'm glad you're..." She hesitated, looking me up and down. "Alright!" She hugged me gently, respectfully, I thought. "Where are the others? Jessica? Elizabeth?"

I shook my head. "They're not with me." I paused, unable to help myself looking at her with new eyes, taking her in for a second time, knowing who she was now.

Rachel met my eyes and smiled slightly, squinting. "What is it? Why are you looking at me like that?"

"I—" I glanced back at Heretic. Having replaced the goggles and mask, his face was inscrutable, as usual.

I looked back at Rachel. "Is there somewhere we can talk? Privately?"

Slight concern flashed over her face. "I—of course. Is everything all right? Are the kids all right?" She was concerned.

I nodded. "They're fine, I think. They've been Hosted by Safeguard, but we're gonna' go get them. We're gonna' put a stop to it."

Rachel's eyebrows rose. "Really? How are you going to do that?"

I laughed and shook my head. "I'm still working on that. Can we talk, though?"

She nodded then looked me pointedly up and down. I looked down at myself. I don't even remember the last time I'd been able to shower. I hadn't looked at my reflection for at least that long, but I could imagine how I looked: filthy, covered in dried sweat and vomit.

"Why don't you clean yourself up some first?" she offered kindly. I nodded, suddenly tired.

The shower was exhilarating. When I poked my head out, wrapped in a towel, Rachel handed me a pair of jeans that were a few inches too short and a tee shirt that said, "Springfield Tee-Ball" on the front. At least they were clean.

When I was dressed, she wouldn't even let me speak before I'd eaten three bowls of some sort of chicken and broccoli in sauce over rice. When I couldn't eat any more, she finally allowed me to finish a sentence.

"Can we talk now? It's important."

She smiled, then walked down the main hallway. I followed her into the same room she'd come out of earlier. It must have been her private room. She sat down on the bed, the only real furniture, and patted a spot a few feet away. I sat down and Heretic came to awkwardly stand in front us, looking down at me.

I looked at him for a moment, then said, "You can't always be this awkward."

Rachel giggled slightly and said, "He's right, Preacher, you're acting a little strange; are you feeling all right?"

Heretic looked from me to Rachel and back again. "I'm—Sorry." Everything in his body language spoke to discomfort and puzzlement. "I'm used to having more input in situations like these. Right now I'm feeling very... alone."

Rachel made a confused face. "I don't know what that means."

Heretic went to the wall and stood awkwardly, hands pressed to his sides. He turned one way, then the other, then actually turned and faced the wall, simply standing there.

I blinked, slowly putting together what must be happening. Most of his understanding of social cues and conventions must come from Mom and Dad, who must have really pulled back to give Rachel and me some privacy for what was about to happen. The result was slightly comical.

Rachel looked at me with a face that clearly said, *"What is going on?"* and laughed, a clear, beautiful, joyful laugh.

"Rachel, I need to ask you to do something for me. I need you to trust me, okay?" I looked into her eyes, trying to convey to her how in earnest I was.

She returned my gaze, her eyes flitting all over my face, looking for who knew what. "Okay," she said slowly and quietly.

I tried to map out what I was going to say to her next, about what I was about to ask Heretic to do for her. "I—" I began.

"You're my son." The words were quiet, barely above a whisper.

My mouth fell open. "How did you—"

"I didn't. I don't. Not until right this moment, when I got this feeling. I look at you, and there's something... familiar. Not your look, something else. Something just... familiar."

I glanced at Heretic, who, looking over his shoulder, turned back to face the wall quickly when he saw me looking. "We can help you remember. Do you want that?"

She continued to look at me, and tears welled up in her hazel eyes. "Oh, yes, please. I want that very much."

I nodded at Heretic, who was staring unabashedly now. He turned the rest of the way around and walked over to stand in front of Rachel. He knelt on one knee and reached up slightly to put a hand on either side of Rachel's head, which she bowed slightly to make it easier. She closed her eyes tightly.

Heretic held his hands there for several moments, then Rachel suddenly gasped sharply, eyes still closed. She bit her bottom lip but held her head still.

When Heretic moved his hands away a moment later, Rachel stayed in the same position, head bowed, eyes closed. "I remember," she whispered.

"The woman and the man, they told me you'd died. I believed them. I was devastated by that. I went home when they discharged me, and I couldn't function for weeks. My daughter, Raven, she—" She opened her eyes. "My daughter." She raised one hand up toward my face, but drew it back at the last moment, hesitant. "My son."

I smiled encouragingly at her. "So, you know me, then?"

"Of course not, James; we're practically strangers!" She laughed. "But I'd like to if you'll let me. I'd very much like to get to know what sort of man you've become."

"I think that's a great idea," I said, putting my hand on top of hers on the bed and squeezing slightly for a moment.

Chapter 23

I spent the rest of the day holed up with Rachel and Heretic, discussing the biggest unknown for the road ahead: my abilities. Rachel had helped to raise a lot of Mythic children in the last 12 years and had helped coach most of them through figuring out and mastering their abilities.

"So, you've never used them since that day in the hospital?" She put a hand on mine that clearly said, *"I don't blame you for Linda."* I was grateful for that.

"Huh-uh," I grunted.

"Not to your knowledge," Heretic piped up.

"Well, right. Not to my knowledge," I agreed.

"Okay, well, for most of the kids I've known, they've always talked about how they access that part of themselves like you would when you get really absorbed in something, and you lose track of time; what is that called, is there a word for it?" Rachel asked.

"I believe it's called 'flow'," Heretic offered.

Rachel snapped her fingers and pointed at him, smiling. "That's it! I knew there was a word."

I smiled, then said, "Okay, that's great, but isn't flow usually a result of something else? It's not really something that you aim for in and of itself; it's more of a happy accident of doing something else that you

294

really enjoy but that's also really challenging, right?" I could remember learning about Flow in one of my Psychology classes. "But we don't really know what it is yet that I'm supposed to be focusing on."

Heretic coughed. "There is something we can try. I could attempt to access any memory of the incident that you may have. As a newborn, there won't be much, and it will almost certainly not be clear, but it may be our best chance at figuring out what happened that day."

I exchanged looks with Rachel. She seemed as surprised by the idea as I did.

"If you think you can get anything, go right ahead," I said, shrugging. "At this point, we don't have many more options." I stood up. "Where do you want me?"

Heretic pointed back onto the bed. "Lie with your head near the edge of the bed, here. This will be a much deeper dive than I've ever done on anyone before. I'm not sure how it will affect you."

I crawled into the center of the bed and lay down, my head near the foot where Rachel sat and Heretic stood.

Heretic asked, "Ready?"

I nodded and closed my eyes.

I heard Heretic kneel, and he placed a hand on either side of my head.

It was as if all my other senses suddenly quieted. I could hear almost nothing except the blood pounding through my veins. It reminded me of when you cup your hands tight over your ears or hold a seashell up to your ear: the roar of the ocean, but steady, no ebb and flow.

After several seconds, I started to feel antsy. I wanted to open my eyes but had no idea if that even impacted what Heretic was seeing. It felt to me like I shouldn't open them. It seemed like having them open would be a little like trying to have a conversation with a television blaring right in front of you. Doable, but hard to pay attention to. I kept them closed.

Heretic gasped. "She's still there."

I opened my eyes and sat up. "There? What, you mean in the hospital? What does that mean?"

Heretic shook his head. "No. Not in the hospital. There." He pointed to my hand.

I looked at my palm, good and thoroughly confused. "I don't get it."

"When she pricked you—that's what it was, a routine heel prick—you reacted as if you were in danger. For most babies, that's nothing more than a startle response and a cry. But for you, it meant both of those, but also something much bigger. You essentially—," and he cupped both his hands and fitted them together, making a rough sphere.

I stared at him. "I don't know what that means." I imitated his movement. "I clapped?"

"No, you—," he did it again.

I copied him again. "Yeah, what? I got it the first time. That's not helpful."

Heretic hesitated. "You... squished? Compacted?"

My eyes widened. "I *squished* her?!" I was horrified.

"Yes. No! Sort of! I'm trying here! It's not like you were using the Oxford dictionary at that point, ya' know?" Heretic snapped.

I had a feeling that wasn't Heretic. It didn't sound like Mom or Dad, either. Probably the mysterious third persona floating around in Heretic's programming: my sister?

"You compacted her, but to an infinite degree. But you were still aware of her. You still felt her. And you felt her right—" he pointed to the palm of my left hand, "There."

I lifted the palm to the level of my eyes and turned it this way and that, studying it. Fleshy, lined, maybe a little bit of dirt in the creases. *I could stand to wash them.* No sign of Linda. "I don't know what that means," I shook my head.

Rachel cleared her throat. "If I may?"

Heretic and I both turned to look at her.

"Most of the time, some form of meditation helps the kids start to focus enough to find their Flow," Rachel offered. "Would that be helpful for you?"

"It couldn't hurt at this point," I said.

Rachel nodded. "Okay. Go ahead and sit down."

I obeyed.

"Go ahead and close your eyes again and place your feet flat on the floor."

I tried to hide a smile.

"Hey, no making fun! I've been doing this for Mythic kids for a long time, mister. It works!" I could hear the smile in her voice.

"I'm not laughing," I smiled.

"Put your feet flat on the floor and wiggle your toes." She proceeded to guide me through a standard relaxation meditation routine, focusing my attention at times on my breathing, feet, legs, hips, spine, shoulders, and arms. Nothing remarkable or out of the ordinary happened until she reached my hands.

"Now, I want you to focus all your attention on your hands. Practice rolling your hands into fists and feeling the tendons contract and tighten as you do. Relax them and feel them loosen. Lay your fingers flat and feel the air pass over them. Focus on the feeling inside them, air around them, the space between your fingers."

As my mind followed her direction in this way, I felt something. It wasn't anything I felt as pressure on my skin; it was something I felt, simply as an awareness. I became slowly aware of a heat, and a pressure —not on my skin—but above it, right in the middle of both palms. As I prodded this awareness in my mind, it grew. There was something there. I opened my eyes slightly. My hands were empty, and there was nothing around them. Yet, when I closed them again, there it was again. A stillness, like there was something blocking the movement of the air there, and some heat. I furrowed my brows in equal concentration and confusion.

"What is it? What do you feel?" Heretic asked.

"Preacher, hush," Rachel chided him.

"I feel something in my hands. Or above my hands.

Or something." I didn't know quite how to explain it. Closing my eyes harder, I drove all my awareness into my hands, feeling anything, everything they would send to my brain. The feeling of warmth grew. Or the awareness of it, anyway. Suddenly, from out of no-where, it took a shape in my mind. Like a ball, a sphere, hovering right above the center of my palms. "It's like a ball, right above my hands." Focusing even deeper on it, as I somehow sensed its dimensions, I realized, *not a ball, a hole*. But a hole in three dimen-sions is a sphere.

"Not a ball, a hole," I said out loud. "And it leads—"

"Stop!"

I opened my eyes, shocked. Heretic's shout had been abrupt and full of panic.

Rachel and I both stared at him.

"If you brought anything through that hole, you would have killed us all, and half of the states of Ari-zona, Utah, Colorado, and New Mexico."

My eyes went as wide as saucers. "How exactly would that have happened?"

"I just... remembered something. It's been there, in the back of my mind, but I couldn't put my finger on it until now. I know what this is. What you've done is transferred Linda to a pocket dimension: a piece of space and time outside our own, accessible only to you." Heretic's voice was full of sadness.

"Why is that bad? Doesn't that mean that I can bring her back? If she's been outside time, doesn't that mean that she'll be fine? I can bring her back and she'll be like she was when she went in, right?" I liked the idea of her not being dead. "And what do you mean, 'remembered something?' You're a robot!"

"No. You didn't just put her in. Things that go into this pocket dimension, they aren't unchanged. They're completely changed. Linda most definitely no longer exists as Linda. Every molecule that made her up still exists in the pocket dimension, but it's been changed to antimatter." Heretic gave a quick sigh when he finished his sentence. He ignored my last question.

"I'm sorry, antimatter?" I asked.

"What's antimatter?" Rachel echoed.

"Antimatter. It's essentially opposite day for molecules. So, you know how molecules are essentially made up of protons, neutrons, and electrons, right?" Rachel and I both nodded. "Well, antimatter is matter that's essentially switched. Instead of positively charged protons, they're negatively charged antiprotons, instead of neutrons, antineutrons, and instead of negatively charged electrons, positively charged positrons. You follow?"

We both nodded.

"On the surface, the matter is unchanged. Same number of each respective particle in each specific molecule, right? Yeah, except that, as soon as the antimatter molecule encounters its regular matter counterpart, they annihilate each other, releasing an insane amount of energy. Realistically, if we're talking a woman who weighed somewhere in the neighborhood of 175 pounds, you're essentially talking about the energy equivalent of hundreds of thousands of atomic bombs."

I stopped breathing. I instinctively balled my fists, willing everything in me to close that hole and never let it open.

"So, I'm a doomsday device. A suicide bomb doomsday device." My voice cracked slightly.

"You? No, you'd be fine. You're literally made for this. But everything within..." Heretic seemed to be thinking. "Yeah, I don't even know how far that blast would extend. Heck of a lot farther than Hiroshima, that's for sure."

"How is that even helpful?" I asked. "In what world does that accomplish anything helpful?"

"Well, on the upside, you're going to live a long and healthy life," Heretic chimed in.

I looked at him, suspicious. "What do you mean?"

"Well, one side-effect of this particular ability is that matter held in this pocket dimension extends your life, essentially feeding into the longevity of your cells."

I retched. "So, I'm an Armageddon vampire. Great. How does this help? Am I supposed to blow up all of Safeguard? Or absorb them all?"

Heretic shook his head. "No. You're thinking too simply. Instead of absorbing people, what do people shoot?"

"Bullets? Darts?" I realized, catching on.

"Exactly. You can make yourself impervious to any kind of projectile attack. Also, dial it back from

302 ~ JUSTIN K. NUCKLES

explosions. Instead of a bomb, think a match. What do you get from a match?"

"Light and heat? I can create flashbangs and heat up weapons to disarm people with heat?" I nodded my head side-to-side. "All right, not entirely useless. Mostly."

"You'll get more creative," Heretic said. "Wait until you're more familiar with it."

"How exactly do I get more familiar with it, Heretic? Am I supposed to play with atomic bombs?"

"Put yourself into your pocket dimension."

I looked dumbly at Heretic, then at Rachel. She raised her hands. "Don't look at me; this went way beyond my pay grade a long time ago."

"I'm going to bed. Let's pick this up tomorrow," I pleaded. "Where do I sleep?"

Chapter 24

I wanted nothing more than to sleep, but it seemed like sleep wanted nothing to do with me. I was lying on a rough mattress in one of the halls. With the relocation last year, they hadn't had time to expand quite as much as they had at the last location, apparently. It seemed like every time I closed my eyes, I would remember something new that changed my life in some significant way that I'd learned that day.

I was a Mythic. Rachel was my birth mother. My adoptive parents' personalities existed inside an advanced robot. I had a sister, who I'm pretty sure for some reason was also uploaded inside of Heretic. I had pocket dimensions holding potential global nuclear annihilation at my fingertips.

That was the one I kept coming back to. All the other stuff, my complicated life's history and strange relationships, I'd heard of happening before. Well, aside from the advanced robot with human personality upgrades. That was admittedly new. But pocket dimensions filled with nukes: that was truly something I'd never heard of before. That one took the cake.

After what I was sure was several hours of restless adjusting and repositioning, I remembered Rachel's meditation. World-altering discoveries aside,

I'd become fairly relaxed over the course of her guidance. I started focusing on my breathing as I lay there, counting breaths, slowing rhythms until I'd worked through nearly all her tips that I could remember. My thoughts naturally followed her progression, eventually ending up focused on my hands again.

I recoiled momentarily, justifiably leery of initiating World War III from my bed, but then remembered that this place and this power had existed for over twenty years with (nearly) no mishap. Apparently, there was no danger of anything simply falling out. I let myself relax again and mentally probed the spheres in the palms of my hands once more.

What had Heretic said? Put myself in my pocket dimension? How did that even work? I imagined myself being sucked, cartoon-like, into a tiny hole the size of a tennis ball. Despite the inherent risk involved in the fact that this could be a distinct possibility, I smiled. I imagined myself being sucked in, going headfirst into this tiny door that only I could see. I imagined squeezing out the other side of that hole and finding... What, exactly?

It took me a moment to realize that I no longer heard the sounds of a house asleep. There was no hum of the few electrical appliances, no cadence of crickets hiding somewhere in the dark. No occasional grunts and rustle of cloth as over two dozen sleeping children adjusted in their sleep. I suddenly realized that I heard nothing. Not merely quiet, but *nothing*.

I opened my eyes. I was no longer lying down on my

makeshift mattress. I was upright in a space of nothing. There was no ground beneath my feet, no roof
over my head, no walls in sight. Everything was dim,
the sort of blue, dim light you get a few hours before
sunrise. There was no visible source of light, it seemed
to come from nowhere and everywhere at the same
time. There was hardly anything around me. I noticed
three clouds of slightly shifting substance, suspended
in the air, like I was, extending in a line away from me.
The two on the ends were significantly larger and a
different color than the third in the middle. I went to
take a few steps forward, but walking did absolutely
nothing. Instead, I simply floated over to the swirling
clouds, independent of my useless attempts at steps.

The first cloud hung near me, a rough orb of swirling blue with veins of gold light that arced and swirled
within it. I looked at it closely, careful not to touch
it. Its movements were hard to describe. *Like a water
bubble in space*, I realized, recalling videos I'd seen of
astronauts in orbit.

Staring at it, I leaned closer, putting my head slowly
to within a few inches of the sluggishly spinning,
shimmering mass. As I did, I had the strangest sensation; a wash of emotions and sensations crashed over
me. Caring, physical exhaustion, love, joy, sorrow. For
a moment, the mass stretched and thinned, becoming a cylinder, then bulging slightly toward the upper
middle, then squished more and more into the unmistakable figure of a woman. I pulled back my head
in horror, and the mass snapped back to a shifting

bubble, sloshing up and down for a moment as it set-tled back in space.

This was Linda. Or what was left of Linda.

I gazed in openmouthed revulsion at the seemingly innocuous cloud of molecules in front of me, which now gave no outward indication that it had once been a person.

Looking at the two remaining clouds in the space, my gut twisted in disgust. What or who were those? I floated tentatively to the smaller cluster. It shimmered and undulated as unassumingly as the first had, but without the gold light. I slowly leaned my head in toward it, and instead of emotions, felt sensations. Warmth, scratchy yet soft. Suction. The cluster slowly flattened and separated into three clumps, the largest cluster going flatter and flatter, the next forming a little rounded envelope, and the third the unmistakable shape of a child's pacifier. The newborn hat, blanket, and missing binky from the hospital. I pulled back my face again, and the clouds lost shape and congealed into a single mass once more.

Looking beyond to the last large cluster, I tried to think of what else, if anything, I'd seen or heard about disappearing from around me as a newborn or as a child. Had there been some later mishap as a young child where I'd disappeared a piece of furniture or something?

Now familiar with the process, I leaned in toward the cloud and waited. Emotions hit me like a panic attack. Pain, anger, embarrassment, humiliation, rage, satisfaction, greed. The intensity of the emotions took me by surprise, as did the shape the cloud quickly assumed. There were no variations in color, no clue as to the color of the clothing being depicted on the form in front of me, and yet I could almost see the khaki slacks, the white shirt, the navy blazer.

This cluster was all that remained of Julian Danton. The revulsion was back. I had to stifle the urge to vomit. As much as I'd detested Danton, I'd never intended for him to wind up a shapeless, floating puddle of molecules.

When I'd gotten my gag reflex under control and the cloud had fallen back to endless swirling, I wondered aloud, "What happened?" The last time I'd seen Danton alive, he'd been torturing me, before I'd passed out again. My best guess? Without the wristband inhibiting my abilities, and blacking out, just as it had when I'd been a newborn, a reflex had kicked in to try and protect me from further harm. Heretic hadn't been wrong when he'd said that Danton was gone earlier that morning. Danton was good and truly gone.

I stayed for another moment in that place, simply looking at the floating puddles around me, and decided it was time to go. I figured that the best way to get out was the same way I'd gotten in. I closed my eyes and imagined myself squeezing back through that little tennis ball again, sitting back on my grass-stuffed mattress. I knew I was back when I heard crickets singing their defiance throughout the house, and muffled sounds of movement and deep breathing all around. I was back, and my world had become a whole lot stranger.

***

I was helping Heretic with the construction of an additional bank of rooms on the structure the next day. My job was to move the repurposed tires into position to form the walls, then Heretic would fill them in with dirt and we'd take turns packing it in as tight as we could with a sledgehammer held head down. We were being helped in this by a couple of boys, one about 14, the other probably six or seven. It was embarrassing to watch them work. Both boys were obviously Tanks. They hefted stacks of tires as if they were empty boxes and pounded with the sledgehammer as if it weighed no more than a judge's gavel. I kept glancing at Heretic, who simply said, "They're fast. Don't beat yourself up."

"This place isn't a House of Bricks, like the last place?" I asked.

"No. There wasn't enough time to locate another; those spots are rare. It isn't as if it's anything we can create ourselves. Somehow, they're naturally occurring."

The two boys left to go collect more tires from the pile at the edge of the construction zone, and I took the chance to talk to Heretic.

"All right, so what's our next step? Now that

Danton's gone, what's the first thing we do? How do we put a stop to Safeguard? I don't suppose asking them nicely will do any good?"

I'd told Heretic about Danton first thing in the morning. He hadn't seemed surprised. He didn't say so, but I suspected that he'd known yesterday morning, and that was why he'd been bold enough to rescue me in broad daylight.

"No. The problem is that each individual who is processed by Safeguard has been Swept. None of them knows the parents that most of them grew up with weren't their own, and none of the active members have access to the full records, so they have no idea that they exist in the system themselves. The role of maintaining records was the sole responsibility of your parents, specifically through your father's line. As the Founders, their job as history keepers was to remember and ensure that others were loyal to and observed the protocols." Heretic handed me the sledgehammer as he adjusted one of the tires, then filled it with dirt from a wheelbarrow. He stood back to allow me to take up beating the dirt.

"Each member is made to feel the same way you did before any of this, James. They each have memories of an idyllic childhood with parents who love them, for whom they would do anything. When children are Hosted with new parents, the parents themselves are Swept so that the arrangement is without flaw." Heretic took the sledgehammer back from me and took another turn himself. "In most cases, no one within the family recalls anything of their life before, based in reality. They're given narratives, but they're just that: fabricated tales to ease the mind and distract from the fact that nothing happening around them is natural."

Heretic's sledgehammer strikes had grown especially aggressive and rough. I wondered which of all the personalities swirling around in his circuits was driving the frustration and anger that was so evident in his blows.

"So, what do we do? As awful as it is, it sounds pretty efficient. How do we disrupt it?" I asked.

"Clara and Pat are the weak points right now," Heretic said. "They were not intended to be the history keepers. Because they've been Swept, they'll follow along seamlessly, but there may be doubts. It's impossible to live out a life with such a tentative basis in reality, having access to so much truth. They'll start to question things, if they haven't already. Who knows? With any luck, they may have researched themselves already, and are ripe for a revolution!"

"So, we need to talk to Clara and Pat. Find out where they're at with things?" *Could it really be as simple as that*, I wondered?

Heretic nodded, then said, "We could do that. That might be the most effective place to start. It would certainly make our primary objective a whole lot easier to accomplish, with the current Director pair on board with our aims."

"Okay, so when do we leave?" I asked, eager to begin.

"We can leave after we finish this bedroom. These children need space, and these walls aren't going to build themselves," Heretic chuffed, pointing for another tire from the immense pile the two boys had made beside us. I wiped the sweat away from my eyes and reached out for another.

***

Later that night, I was back in my pocket dimension. I followed the same relaxation technique I had before to visualize myself entering into it. It worked. I recognized better when it did this time.

I wanted to practice actually using the molecules to create reactions, the way Heretic had described. I wanted to start out with a single molecule but had no idea how to even go about that. On a whim, I closed my eyes and imagined myself taking a single molecule from the smallest puddle. I couldn't bring myself to even consider touching the other two larger puddles.

To my surprise, I felt a sudden slight warmth on my palm and somehow knew that I'd successfully called a single molecule. I drew it back, confident in my hunch.

Next, according to Heretic, I needed a regular molecule to oppose this single molecule of antimatter. I closed my eyes again and stuck my left hand, palm up, into the air in front of me. I visualized it going out into the air of the natural world and called to a single loose molecule of the same type. I was shocked when

I felt the same warmth, and intuitively knew and understood that these two were perfect mirrors of each other. I closed my fist and brought both hands back into the pocket dimension where I was. I lay both palms flat and watched my hands in amazement as I simply willed it to be so, and felt the molecules leave my hand for the other, crashing into each other in the air between my hands. A huge sudden burst of golden light made me instinctively turn away, yet there was no pain from my eyes. I simply watched as the light dimmed and faded away to nothing, leaving nothing but the sensation of warmth.

I could control this. I tried the process several times, each time using only a single molecule of matter and antimatter. Each time it was the same: a huge burst of golden light, the wonderful sensation of warmth. On a whim, I called to five molecules of antimatter with my left hand and five opposing molecules with my right. I brought them back to me, fists closed, and nervously held my breath. How firmly did I believe Heretic's claim that I was impervious to the effects of this kind of blast? He'd said I was made for this. I really hoped he knew what he was talking about.

I opened both hands at the same time and the groups of molecules flew to each other, colliding in midair and annihilating each other. The resulting explosion filled the bubble of the pocket dimension, heat washing over me and light making everything brightest gold for a few seconds. Everything gradually faded away, and I knew that my life would never be the same.

Chapter 25

I didn't have a chance to try and repair things with Shanice. She staunchly avoided me; any time I so much as walked in her direction, she would either walk deliberately the opposite direction, or dive bomb me with birds, bugs, or other small animals to drive me away. I found it amazing how compelling mice could be, after one or two good sharp bites. Kyle was right.

A few days later, we finished the new rooms, and Heretic and I were free to leave for the Safeguard compound. From my months working with Safeguard, I knew that Clara and Pat were likely still holed up there. They'd been there every day of my training; it was our best chance at finding them quickly.

I said goodbye to Rachel, waved goodbye at a distance to Shanice, who pretended she didn't see, and followed Heretic to the small rough shed that acted as his garage. There was a single large old yellow school bus parked behind the shed. That was how they'd moved all the children. Our only other options for transportation were a rusted-looking old Ford Bronco, and the motorcycle I'd arrived with Heretic on.

"These are really our only options, aren't they?" I asked, sighing deeply.

Heretic nodded slowly.

"I want a chance to drive again," I said, looking at the motorcycle.

"I'll arm wrestle you for it," Heretic stated.

***

A little under two hours later, I was stiff and cold, clasping Heretic's middle as we flew up the interstate. We were a few dozen miles away from the compound; I'd begun recognizing some of the exits from training missions I'd taken part in with Safeguard. I was looking ahead to the next exit when there was a bright flash from below the horizon, and a large mushroom cloud billowed up, directly from where I guessed the compound to be.

"What—," I gasped. I was having trouble breathing, and it wasn't because of the speed of the motorcycle.

I heard Heretic curse. He gunned the throttle, redlining the motor and sending us careening well over 250 miles per hour down the freeway. Cars were pulling off the side of the road, people shading their eyes and pointing, but unable to look directly at the flash. Some used the median between the lanes to turn around and simply head back the other direction. Lucky for us, it left the road wide open. I wasn't sure that even Heretic's enhanced reaction times and reflexes would have done much good at that speed.

As we pulled off the familiar exit and flew down the country road, the mushroom cloud loomed over us, the tail having risen up to the rest of the body

316 ~ JUSTIN K. NUCKLES

of the burst, and the whole thing already beginning to flatten and spread outward as it began to disperse. Heretic slowed the bike to a crawl, then to a stop. The fence that had bordered the above-ground portion of the compound housing the vehicles and farm equipment was all that was left, and then only in patches. It was puzzling; there were huge puddles of water all around. When I looked at them more closely, I realized that the puddles formed a large ring that followed the exact blast radius of the explosion. What was that all about? Where had all the water come from?

I looked to the center of the site. Piles and puddles of twisted, melted metal sat in heaps, all that remained of the vehicles and tractors. The center of the blast was a huge gaping hole, the open shaft where the earth had collapsed in on the entire subterranean compound. My mouth hung open, calculating how many lives must have been lost, if Safeguard hadn't had any warning or chance to evacuate. What on earth had happened? A breeze had picked up, swirling around the site.

"This isn't right," Heretic said.

"Of course, it isn't right," I agreed. "When is destruction like this ever right?"

"You misunderstand," Heretic said. "We saw the explosion. It occurred mere minutes ago. Where then, are all the fires?"

I blinked. He was right. Looking around, there was clear evidence of the enormous blast we'd witnessed, and yet there wasn't a single flame flickering anything.

Not a single fire burning, only burns and scars, as if the explosion had happened weeks ago, not moments.

The breeze that had been playful and swirling a few moments before had continued to pick up, swirling and howling now. *Do tornadoes follow nuclear explosions?* Was it a nuclear explosion? I'd never seen any evidence or heard any talk of nuclear weapons while I was with Safeguard. Nuclear weapons seemed a bit overkill when you were talking about subduing and abducting individual Mythics, most of them children. Why would they have even needed nuclear weapons?

I had no idea whether tornadoes naturally followed nuclear explosions typically, or not, but one was happening right there, right then. Heretic gunned the engine and whipped the motorcycle around, accelerating away from the site. I held on as best I could. Looking back, I saw the forming tornado hover directly over the blast site. The cloud of almost-assuredly radioactive material began to slowly twist and follow the revolutions of the tornado, collecting back together and neatly collecting in the funnel of the tornado.

This is too neat, I thought. There were no fires, now a tornado... I gasped. The ring of water around the blast. No fires, a tornado cleaning up the mess. The Dantons! The Danton children were somehow here and cleaning up the mess of the blast already.

I tapped Heretic on the shoulder and shouted to get his attention. "It's the Dantons! It's the kids! They're here! Turn around! We've got to get them out of here; the radiation, it'll kill them!"

The bike stopped, far enough from the tornado that we were no longer in danger of being blown off our feet and sent skittering across the landscape or riddled with flying shrapnel. We both turned around in time to watch as the tornado funneled the entire fallout cloud down into the open hole in the ground and slowly disappeared. My mouth fell open as the earth churned in great waves from all around the blast and crashed inward on top of the hole, covering it, and dispersing like an actual wave until the entire site resembled a freshly tilled field, no visible indication of any of the structures, above or below, that had previously been Safeguard.

When everything cleared, I saw them: four small figures, each smaller than the last, unmistakable even from this distance as the Danton children. But they were not alone. A tall, looming figure wearing a long black coat took its hands from its pockets and gathered the children close together, then they all simply disappeared.

"Did you see them?" I asked, looking at Heretic.

He said nothing, simply nodded.

"Who was that with them? Did they cause this?" I stammered.

Heretic said quietly, "I thought we had more time. I had no warning."

"What?! What do you mean, 'you thought we had more time'?" I shouted. "Do you know who that was?"

Again, he did nothing but nod.

"Care to share?" I asked.

"Someone's coming," Heretic sidestepped. "We need to get out of here."

I knew there was no arguing with him when he got like this. I held on and he rocketed the bike back up the road. We were almost to the freeway when a white SUV headed the opposite direction suddenly swerved into our lane up ahead and slid to a stop, completely blocking the road. We skidded to a halt as two figures in white Safeguard armor and helmets opened the doors and immediately trained a rifle and what I assumed was a Concussive Cannon on us.

"Turn off the bike and lay down on the ground!"

I recognized Clara's amplified voice.

I stepped off the back of the bike, pulled off the helmet I was wearing, and raised my hands above my head, making sure they could see who I was.

"Clara, it's me, don't shoot!"

"James?" Clara asked, disbelief in her voice.

"What the hell, man? Where have you been? We thought you were dead, with all the rest of the Danton Team." Pat's expressive and equally amplified voice sounded ridiculous.

Pat had lowered his Con-gun, but I noticed that Clara still had her rifle raised and trained on Heretic.

"And who's your friend?" she asked. The way that she said it made it obvious that she recognized Heretic.

"Clara, he's with me. We aren't here to hurt you or anyone else." I realized what it looked like to her. Here was a soldier who'd gone MIA, presumed dead at the site of a botched operation, turned up miraculously alive, in the company of an individual they already considered a terrorist to their operation, and fleeing the site of the destruction of their entire world. This was not how I had wanted this conversation to start off.

"What did he do, James? We saw the mushroom cloud. What happened?" Clara's voice was hard, like ice. She obviously suspected the worst already.

"We didn't do anything. We were headed to the compound to meet with you and Pat and, like you, we saw the mushroom cloud." I swallowed. "There's nothing left, Clara. Heretic knows who did it." I saw Heretic shuffle out of the corner of my eye.

"That's Heretic? Are you freaking serious? What the Hell, man? Fool me once and all that!" Pat shouted at me, waving his hands exaggeratedly. Clara didn't move.

"Let's get out of here, go somewhere safe, and discuss what we need to do. Whoever did it, he has the Danton kids," I continued.

"The Danton kids? That's impossible. We had them Hosted individually and across the country. There's no way someone could have gathered them all without our having heard about it. We'd have heard something, from someone." Clara trailed off, sounding not-quite convinced of her own statements.

"Clara, let's go. It's only a matter of time before authorities show up asking questions, and I don't think we want to deal with that headache right now. Let's meet up at the cache house over in the next county. You can follow us, we'll go slow." I tried not to over-play my decidedly weak hand.

"No. You're both with me. Pat will ride the bike, you drive, Heretic rides in the passenger seat. He makes one move I don't like, and I blow his freaking head off."

I looked at Heretic. He simply nodded once. He didn't like this any more than I did.

Pat closed the door of the SUV and walked to-ward us. Heretic and I passed him halfway, our hands raised in the air. When he was past us, we heard him say, through his loudspeaker, "Sweeet. I get to ride the awesome bullet bike. How long's it been since I've been on one of these bad boys, huh?"

Clara shouted curtly, "Still on broadcast, Pat!"

"Whoop. Sorry about that!" Pat went silent, but I watched him rub his hands together as he climbed onto the bike. I couldn't help but smile at his reac-tion. It died on my face when I looked back at Clara. She'd backed out of the driver's side doorway of the SUV and walked around the front of the vehicle. She opened the passenger side door and tossed something on the seat, then backed away from the vehicle, ges-turing with the barrel to Heretic to get in. He nodded, walked slowly to the door of the SUV and put on the handcuffs she'd left on the seat. Then he climbed in and sat down, not moving anymore. Clara motioned with her helmet for me to get in, which I did. When I'd settled in and closed the door, she'd already gotten in behind Heretic and had the muzzle of the rifle pushed up against the back of the seat at belly height.

"You try anything, you move, you even breathe in a way I don't like, and I blow a hole in your chest big enough to put my hand through. You got it, you piece of crap?" she hissed at Heretic. Again, he simply nodded.

"Drive," she said sharply to me.

Several tense minutes later, we arrived at the cache house. It was a simple run-down single wide trailer with a peeling exterior. It was nothing fancy, but it kept the rain off the equipment we stored inside. There was only one real piece of furniture, if you could call it that. There was a single large folding table with a couple of chairs around it. Aside from that, the house was full of locked cabinets and gun safes. This was for when we were running training ops in the field and needed to swap out equipment. It was stocked to equip two different fireteams with three different full variations of equipment.

Clara motioned to the chairs. "Sit."

Heretic and I both sat, trying not to move. Even though she had the rifle trained firmly on Heretic, I was afraid that if I made any sudden moves, she'd shoot him anyway. I could almost feel the tension in her trigger finger.

"We start with where you've been since the op went south, *again*," she said, suspicion dripping from her voice.

I explained as quickly as possible about the failure

of the op because of Sammy's betrayal, the deaths of the whole squad, and my imprisonment at Danton's. I told them briefly about my torture at Danton's hands, but then how Heretic had rescued me. I omitted, for the time being, the fact that I had actually killed Danton by sending him to a pocket dimension that deconstructed him to his basic molecules and simultaneously converted those molecules to antimatter; I wasn't sure they were quite ready for that, yet.

I told them about going back with Heretic, and then traveling here to speak with them with a proposition. I intentionally left out my parents having been uploaded into Heretic's interface, the fact that I was a Mythic, and Rachel's existence. All of that simply invited more questions than I felt like we had time for. I ended with the description of what had happened, starting with the flash of the explosion from the freeway, and ending with the Danton children, the mysterious figure, and their disappearing into thin air.

Pat whistled low between his teeth. "Dang. That's some truly evil stuff. So, you didn't see anybody make it out of there alive?"

I shook my head. "We didn't see any survivors or bodies before they covered everything. I don't even think anyone made it to the surface. It seems like they had no idea it was coming."

Clara shook her head. "Why would they? We didn't even know there were Mythics capable of something like this. Was it the kids?"

I shook my head. "I don't think so. I spent a good

bit of time with them, figuring out with them what all they could do, and nuclear blasts wasn't within any of their wheelhouses." I made a sudden connection. Clara seemed genuinely surprised about the explosion, which meant that she had no reason to suspect it was anything originating from within the base. And if it didn't originate from within the base, that only left the unknown man.

I looked at Heretic and said, "He's like me, isn't he?"

Heretic looked at me, hesitated, then nodded weakly.

Clara spoke up in a rush. "Wait, what does that mean? Who was this guy? And like you how, exactly? What aren't you telling us?"

"I'm a Mythic," I said, jumping right to the point. "I can convert matter into antimatter. It... explodes."

"Whoa! And exactly when were you planning on sharing this little tidbit of information with us, James?" piped up Pat from the doorway.

"I'm sorry," I said. "I didn't make the connection to the man until now; I figured the explosion had originated from within the compound. But now that we know it didn't..." I looked at Heretic again. "Who is he?"

Heretic sighed. "His name is Caine."

"Friend of yours?" Clara spat.

"No!" said Heretic forcefully. "I... I exist in part because of him, but he is no friend of mine, no."

"You exist in part?" Pat asked, mocking. "The heck does that even mean?"

Heretic looked toward me, nodded, then raised his hands to his helmet.

"Ah-ah-ah," Clara said, raising the rifle menacingly.

Heretic held up his empty hands symbolically, but continued to raise them to his head. He gently lowered the hood then pulled down the cloth and pushed up the goggles, exposing the blank faceplate.

"What-," Clara started to say, before the screen flashed white. Anticipating Clara's reaction to the flash a moment before it happened, I'd already started throwing my hands up under her rifle barrel, driving it upward. As I'd expected, she squeezed off a round, right near my head, which left me cringing in pain from the sound. I held my ears and couldn't hear much of anything for several seconds. Through the ringing, I could hear my Dad's voice; it was his face on Heretic's screen. Shockingly, both Pat and Clara seemed to be listening intently, but it was difficult to gauge their reactions beneath their helmets.

"We've always been particularly proud of you two," my Dad was saying. "You've both been absolutely stellar agents within Safeguard, and it would be an honor to serve beside you in this fashion again."

Clara spoke up. "I'm going to need a little more to go on than silky words. How do I know this isn't a trick? Because I'm assuming Heretic has access to both Thinkers and Tinkers, probably a Tech or two, there's no reason he couldn't have dug up information from someone, maybe even the real Jared and Deby, and uploaded that information to himself, since Heretic is apparently a robot. How can I possibly know?"

Dad's face went thoughtful on the screen for a moment, then he said, "Deb says I should say to you, 'Fourth of July, six years ago.'"

Clara went still for a moment, then the rifle muzzle slowly lowered to the floor.

Pat whispered, "Wait, Babe, what happened on the Fourth of July, six years—"

"Tell us who he is, and what you need us to do," Clara said.

I looked at Pat, who looked at me, and we both shrugged.

Dad's face faded from the screen, and Heretic's voice resumed. "Frankly, he's the worst news we could possibly have gotten. He's the common enemy that you never even knew we had." Heretic adjusted the goggles and face-covering back into place out of habit, I assumed. "I disagree with Safeguard on matter of principle and execution. Caine doesn't abduct Mythics; he hunts them down and murders them. Honestly, I thought we had more time. He's been active in Europe for the last several years. He has a small select band of zealots by his side, all fanatic Mythics who view him as some sort of Harbinger of the Apocalypse, basically the end of the world embodied. Functionally, they're not far wrong. Today was a small sample of what he can do. And with the Danton children at his side..." Heretic trailed off as all of our minds filled in the awful blanks.

Heretic continued, "Luckily, we have an ace up our sleeve." He was looking at me.

"Me?" I asked, incredulous. "What do you expect me to do about him?"

"We expect you to save them, James Strader. I may not have agreed with their methods, but with the destruction of Safeguard, Mythics everywhere are in peril."

***

Epilogue

The girl with the bird tattoo closed the door to the bedroom where the four Danton children now slept peacefully. They'd done a lot that day; they certainly deserved an uninterrupted night's sleep.

The villa was quiet. She took a moment to look out the open door to the third-floor balcony that faced the sea. She stepped out into the chill night air and stared up at the moon for a moment.

"I'm glad you convinced me to come here."

She startled, surprised to hear The Wolf's voice on the balcony. She'd thought he had gone hunting.

"You were right. The Repository was no place for young children." He was wearing a white button-down shirt, the top button undone, and the cuffs rolled up a few times. "They'll like it here." He gestured out across the gardens, past the dunes and to the sea.

She nodded her agreement.

"I wish you could have seen them today. They were glorious." Caine shook his head, smiling and staring at nothing in the darkness as he remembered. "The power. The precision."

He slapped the marble railing of the balcony. "It's been centuries since I've been able to eliminate on such an awesome scale."

He leaned over, rested his forearms on the railing and turned his head to look at her. "I couldn't have done it without you."

She nodded, acknowledging his praise.

"With Absalom's Mind-sculpt, the children view me as the doting father they never had. All memories of Julian Danton have been expunged from them. They'll do anything I ask them to."

She said nothing.

"Best yet, with Danton gone, the Aberration effect will renew, this time with someone of our choosing. How goes the search for the replacement?"

She spoke for the first time. "We have several optimal candidates selected. There should be a viable match among them."

Caine's eyes sparkled. "Excellent. I was so disappointed when Danton turned down my offer. His ability held such..." He sighed longingly. "Potential."

"Out of curiosity, do we know yet *how* he died?"

The girl shook her head.

"Interesting. Very interesting."

Caine tapped the railing once more as he said brightly, "No matter. Get some sleep yourself, Raven. Tomorrow is going to be an exciting day."

As she watched Caine disappear back into the villa, Raven Kline turned her face back to the moon. "It certainly is."

End of Book One

*The story continues in Book Two of the Strader
Notebooks: Mythic Uprising*

Acknowledgments

Working on this book saw me through the tumultuous 2020 COVID-19 Pandemic. It was very-much needed creative outlet during a time of absolute insanity. I want to thank all those who provided me encouragement and feedback on the book during that time: Seth Turner, Kimber Worwood, Seth Mildenhall, Dan Force, Jenny Chamberlain, Whitney Mumford, Amy Specker, and Deby Telford. Of all of these, every aspiring author deserves a beta reader like Amy Specker. Amy, your gasps of horror, your squeals of excitement, and your mystery-solving questions all written out on the pages of your reader copy made me excited about my book again. Of course, it goes (nearly) without saying that I owe so much to my wife, Clarissa. Without her encouragement to just write the dang book, it almost certainly wouldn't be complete.

Justin is a nerd. As a child, he tried to read every single book at his local library that had the word "dragon" in the title.

Justin lives in southern Illinois with his wife and children. To learn more about Justin and to follow along with his upcoming projects, follow Justin on Facebook at Author Justin K. Nuckles, on TikTok at @justinknuckleswrites, or join his monthly newsletter to get exclusive behind-the scenes content and updates on upcoming projects that aren't available anywhere else.

Lightning Source UK Ltd.
Milton Keynes UK
UKHW011324080223
416610UK00017B/2410